# Immortal Dynasty

### Age of Awakening
### Book One

## Lynda Haviland

*Immortal Diva Press*

# REVIEWS

*"Hot heroes, kick ass heroines, high stakes, and ancient prophecies...Lynda Haviland's immortal world will blow you away!"*
~ Leigh Michaels
Author of The Birthday Scandal

*"A very talented writer. Consider me a fan!"*
~ Jeff Rivera
Author of Forever My Lady and
Contributing writer to The Huffington Post

*"Lynda Haviland's 'Age of Awakening' series starts with a bang and doesn't let up. With delicious heroes and deliciously creepy villains, these books will keep you up past your bedtime!"*
~ Cecily White
Author of Angel Academy (May 2012, Entangled Teen)

*"(Immortal Dynasty) had a number of twists that surprised me. It was so well written that as these twists appeared, my thoughts were that all the clues had been there, I should have seen them coming."*
~ Mia Jasper
Spanielhill Publishing

*"If you love Egyptian mythology, a fast paced adventure, a battle between good and evil, between darkness and light, and a lively clash of wills with a dash of humor...you will love Lynda Haviland..."*
~ Amazon Reviewer

# BOOKS BY LYNDA HAVILAND

## Age of Awakening Series

*Immortal Dynasty*
*Immortal Dominion*

## Hidden Coast Romances

*Borrowed & Blue*
*Mistletoe & Magic*
*Unveiled*

## The Last Ringmaster

*The Last Ringmaster: Kindred*

This book is dedicated to my family,
whose eternal patience with my writing binges
allowed me to accomplish my dream.
Thank you for putting up with dust,
dirty laundry and plenty of processed foods.

# ACKNOWLEDGMENTS

This book would not have been possible without a brilliant team of gods and goddesses. Their divine skills inspired me and gave life to this story: Ruth, my tour group goddess and mistress of symbolism; Ehab, my god of Egyptology *(aka: The Silver Fox)*; Judy, my photographic goddess and eternal rough draft reader; Cecily, my critique goddess and convention buddy; Lisa, my graphic design goddess; and Leigh, my editorial goddess and mentor.

To all of my friends and extended family, I have always been in awe of your encouragement and complete faith that someday you'd see my book in print.

Of course, my biggest thanks to my husband Joe, the culinary god that feeds my body and soul. You have my eternal love.

# CHAPTER ONE

*Egypt, 1333 B.C.*
*Deir el Bahari, Mortuary Temple of Hatshepsut*

"Do not be afraid, *nefer*." Her priest stood beside, stroking her hair soothingly. She was a goddess. Of course she was not afraid. She clenched her jaw tighter to halt the chattering of her teeth.

"I will not be buried in the sand!" Vexed and impatient, she stomped a bare foot against the cold granite pedestal underneath. Alive or dead, everything here ended up buried in the sand.

"Shaila, please, you must remain very still." His apple-scented breath whispered across her cheek. She felt his fingers trembling.

Covering his hand with her own, she reassured him. "Good life to you, my priest. You have served me with honor and loyalty."

His eyes grew moist and shone with pride. A smile added more crinkles to his wizened face. He returned to his chant, a plea to the goddess Inanna to aid and bless this ceremony.

Flickering torchlight barely penetrated the darkness of the preparation room. Mirrors bounced images of dancing flames onto dusty walls. The smell of burning coal could not mask the acrid odor of human sweat. Her skin flinched as the priest applied the first strokes of a hot, sticky substance to her flesh. She heard two preparers laboring around her. One mumbled a prayer to the gods for forgiveness.

Anger suffused her body, giving her strength. She should have been able to live through eternity. Now she would have to hide from it. She was condemned to this fate because of Lilith.

*That Underworld witch!* Lilith's dark soldiers now attacked daily, proving her determination to kill the child and anyone who guarded him. Shaila had promised to protect the babe, whom the prophecy said was destined to save her kind and human kind.

Shaila defied her priest's order to be still and turned her head. The child, wriggling within a cocoon of linen on another table, shared her fate. She could almost smell the sweet jasmine soap his mother bathed him with. The tiny babe was eerily silent. Her lips curved into a slight smile as she remembered how strong his little fingers were. Barely a moon cycle old, yet he had gripped her braid with strength. She hoped he would be strong enough to survive this.

A preparer dipped the wrapped babe into a bowl of the sticky liquid. She could barely see the twisting form in the semi-darkness, but she heard his howls of displeasure. An instinct to protect poured like hot metal through her veins and pooled within every muscle. Sweat beaded across her forehead from the effort of keeping the beast inside her at bay, but a warning growl vibrated deep and low within her throat.

The babe grew still, and Shaila shivered as the tension in her body cooled. The preparer nestled the bundle into the stiffened arms of the wetnurse, who had earlier stepped proudly into the chamber, ready to serve her goddess. The painful process of embalming the living had wiped the pride from her face quickly. Hysterical shrieks of fear still echoed in Shaila's mind.

A young scribe had diligently carved the magical

spells of resurrection onto the lid of the sarcophagus which would carry the babe and his caregiver into the future. The walls beyond were filled with the prophecy in vibrant detail: the story and the warnings. Her priest, gifted with the Sight, had said there could be no mistakes if the prophecy was to be fulfilled.

Lilith would be told that her soldiers had succeeded in killing them. Instead, they would lie undisturbed, hiding from those who sought their destruction. Shaila would be a silent, golden guardian, protecting the tomb and its occupants until fate would free them to fulfill their destiny.

"Shaila?" She felt the priest's fingers on her jaw, turning her face toward him as he brushed the last of the wet mixture across her forehead. In his final step, he took off his necklace. The golden symbols on the medallion glittered in the flickering light. Pure light energy pulsed around it in a blue glow. She felt him press the disk into the sticky layer across her chest like pressing a wax seal. "Close your eyes, *nefer*. I shall await you on the other side of time."

Through her eyelids, she could see a golden light shimmering from the damp ceiling to the floor. Her priest's plea to Inanna for aid had been answered.

A soft and familiar female voice hovered in the darkness. "I am Inanna a'k'Suen, Lady of Life, daughter of the Great Dragon Queen." Hot air pulsated around them. Blue bolts of energy fingered across the ceiling of the dark room like lightning. "Shaila a'k'Hemet, are you certain that this is the only way?"

Shaila heard the concern in the disembodied voice. Her jaw stiffened by the hot, sticky substance, she answered back mentally.

*Yes, Mother. If not this, then death will claim us before the prophecy begins. My priest has foreseen it.*

"And his vision is infallible?" Disbelief infused

her mother's honeyed voice.

*I would not otherwise trust my life to it. His visions are indeed vague, but have all come to pass nonetheless. And you know Lilith better than anyone. She will not stop until the babe has been destroyed.*

"Cannot your powers protect you, Shaila?"

*I cannot cheat death, but I can delay it. We are not blessed with the gift of leaping time, but I can hide from it. This is the only way to keep the babe safe.*

"His safety is indeed our responsibility. His destiny must be protected."

*And this will ensure that I am there to protect him…to train him.*

"Then, we must not delay. My heart goes with you on your journey, my daughter."

One swift bolt flashed across the tomb. An eerie silence hovered, followed by the hollow thumping of skulls landing on the stone floor. The human preparers had been silenced for eternity, so that none would know who hid in this special tomb. She hoped that all of their lives, and deaths, would not be for nothing.

"The water of life is removed from your veins." Cold words from a voice so warm and angelic.

Shaila sucked in a deep, ragged breath as pain seared across her skin. Her flesh prickled and tightened as she felt the blood drying in her veins. She wanted to scream as fear gripped her mind. Instead, she gripped the dagger in her fist even tighter.

"Your astral spirit is separated from your body."

Her heart pumped furiously, rebelling at the lack of blood to sustain it. Her world crushed in. Wave after wave of cold pressure pounded against her. She refused to allow fear to be the last thoughts in her mind, even as the final pulses claimed her eyes. The darkness consumed her.

The ending words of the spell were muffled as a

final pulse of energy crystallized across her entire body, squeezing her as the metallic gold shell hardened. Slowly, consciousness began to fade...and she knew she feared death.

*Oh, goddess, what have I done?*

\* \* \*

*Present Day, Boston*

Another cramp seized his thigh. Darius ached to stretch his long legs, but a few butt clenches were the best he could manage in the tiny booth. Using a napkin, he wiped the condensation off of his beer bottle and used it to attempt to remove a layer of stickiness from the tabletop.

How in the world had he let his grandfather talk him into waiting for the call in this shit hole? Like every other bar on this end of town, it was the size of a closet and packed with dusty sports memorabilia. Midnight whistled from a clock somewhere on the wall. In less than twelve hours, he was getting out of town. His first vacation in... Well, his first vacation ever. Period. *Damn, what is that smell?*

Slick graphics and overly dramatic music drew his attention to the small flat-screen television set hanging behind the bartender. A local newscast interrupted the basketball game with breaking news.

Police had made yet another gruesome discovery of a mutilated teenager's body, the seventh in a string of unsolved murders in the past two months. Serial killer? Gang war? It was all speculation, but after a long, scorching summer and a hot, sticky fall, the city simmered with fear.

"Can I getcha another beer?" The enthusiasm of the cocktail server grated against his current state of aggravation. Her musky perfume did a valiant job of trying to play with his senses, but nothing could truly overpower the awful smell that seemed to permeate this place.

"No, thanks." He shook his head. She placed the check on the table and left. *Hallelujah.*

Beyond his grandfather's shoulder, he watched her flirt with a couple of guys at the next table. Tossing her deep red curls over her shoulder, she leaned over to collect the empty bottles. As her skirt lifted, he had an unimpeded view of thighs and softly rounded skin. If he'd wanted to know what went best with a plaid mini skirt-- well, now he knew. A red thong.

Darius ignored the frown wrinkling his grandfather's face. "What?"

"Are you listening to me?" The old man looked straight into Darius' eyes. "Ah! You attempt to blank your face. You are tuning me out again."

"Sorry, but I'm getting tired of waiting for your associate to call." Darius covered a yawn with the back of his hand. "Why couldn't we just meet him in his office during regular hours? We're just picking up a few pictures. What's with all the cloak-and-dagger drama?"

Papa Shadi shifted in his seat, pulling thoughtfully on his crisp white goatee. His face wore a myriad of wrinkles and crinkles. A few age spots dotted his coffee-colored skin, but his blue eyes sparkled like an inquisitive child. He was pushing mid-seventies, but Papa Shadi was still pretty adventurous.

Even through the pungent bar smells, Darius could detect the scent of apple wood. The old man's tweed jacket seemed infused with the smoky aroma from his sheesha pipe, which he'd savored at length before they left home.

"Artie Johnson is a busy man. He is the Director of the Art Fraud unit of Customs. He refers clients to us. He is my friend, and he understands the importance of the prophecy."

Darius sighed. He was far too exhausted for another recap on Papa Shadi's prophecy theories. "Please don't. I've heard all this before."

"I repeat it because it is important that you believe it." Round, thin-wired spectacles framed the disappointment in his grandfather's eyes like an art frame.

Darius had heard the same theories for more than twenty years, since he'd come to live with the old man. Always his grandfather would show visible distress whenever Darius would reject those beliefs. He knew it was a fruitless effort, but he tried again to put logic over theory.

"There is nothing to believe. Those ancient civilizations died out thousands of years ago. Even their languages are extinct. Just because they carved stories into a wall doesn't make them any more real than the fairy tales written today."

"How can you say such a thing?" Papa Shadi's wooden cane thumped the floor. His emotions wobbled in his whispered voice. "You've seen the walls of the crypt in Denderah. You've read them as clearly as I did. The ancient knowledge was supposed to be preserved. The prophecy is real."

"I've been collecting these old relics for you and your clients for many years. I have yet to see anything magical or meet any so-called immortal beings."

"Ach. How would you know?" His grandfather's hands shook as he readjusted his patch cap. "I will not give up on you, Darius. You must learn to believe the prophecy."

"Stop it, Papa." Darius held his palm up. "This

subject makes you too excitable. Save it for your secret society buddies."

"Excitable--" Papa Shadi abruptly stopped whatever he was about to say. "You know, believing in something and being emotionally attached are not wicked things to be avoided."

Darius turned his head to the rain-blurred window next to their table. "I believe that success comes from great planning, and that emotional attachments can make you weak and vulnerable. I don't believe in magic or ancient beings."

He caught a glimpse of the redhead making her way across the bar again, checking her empty tables for tips.

There was no place in his life for women. Their kind of love sucked the soul from your body and left you in the gutter to rot from the inside out. His mother was a perfect example of that. She'd taken his love and twisted it for her own benefit. She'd taught him to steal. Then, instead of using the money to feed them, she drank it or shot it into her veins.

Papa Shadi was different. Darius would never consider his grandfather's love and sentimentality as a weakness, because he'd also taught Darius strength, loyalty, and respect. He'd taken a rebellious kid and patiently but firmly turned that boy around. Papa Shadi was the foundation of Darius' life. His anchor.

Papa sighed. "I hope this isn't another wild geese chase."

"Goose chase, and I hope it isn't, too." Darius ignored the stickiness of the table and leaned on his elbows. "Anything will be more exciting than this place."

"Yes, you will be excited when you see her." Papa was emphatic, thumping his cane on the floor again. "Artie swears that they have the statue, and he finally has the proof of it."

"You've waited all these years to see that statue. A few more minutes won't kill you."

"I am too old to wait a moment longer. I feel older than dust."

"*Dirt.*"

"Yes, of course. I just feel so tired." Papa Shadi seemed momentarily distracted, absently fingering the gold medallion he always wore.

"Now that you've found it, you're going to need something new to obsess on."

"*She* is not an obsession. The Lady of Flame is imperative to the prophecy. She is a *medjai*, a protector. She must sleep no more. The demon army grows, and while they are waiting to free the beast of the Underworld, they feed on human souls." His grandfather pointed to the television screen above the bar. Reporters were still hovering around the bloody crime scene like flies.

"That's not a demon army. That's a drug war. That's teenagers overdosing, and street gangs at war with each other. I grew up on those streets...remember? It's always been bloody." Darius massaged the headache blooming in the back of his head.

"No. That is the work of demons." Papa whispered so low it was almost too hard to hear.

"Demons of teenage angst." Darius leaned back, rubbing at the sticky residue on his shirtsleeve. "You said *they* have the statue. Who's *they*?"

"Lilith Troy has her." Papa Shadi hugged the cane, and leaned in closer to Darius. "And she's declared herself to be the Dragon Queen." He snorted, as if something about that was funny.

"You wanna run that by me again? You think a lingerie-model-turned-makeup-mogul is some demon queen? Oh, Papa. Let's not--"

"Fine. Fine." He patted Darius on the forearm. "Let's not go off on a tangle."

"*Tangent.*"

"Yes." Papa Shadi seemed to retreat into his own thoughts, a wistful smile lighting up his face. Darius knew he was thinking about the statue again. "I can't wait to finally see her for myself. It has been such a long time since--"

"I'm a thief, not an idiot." Darius pinched the bridge of his nose, reining in his discomfort. Hell would freeze over before he stepped one toe into the Troy Estate.

Rumors of demonic rituals had swirled around for decades about the old mansion and the tunnels underneath it. Many of them sounded a lot like the prophecies his grandfather loved to talk about. But they made for good stories to scare the crap out of little kids on Halloween.

It wasn't the rumors of the old house, however, that caused his stomach to lurch. Darius didn't know Lilith, but he knew her son. As an adult, Therion might be one of Boston's local military heroes, but as a teen, he'd been nothing short of a vicious bully. Back then, Darius had been a favorite target of Therion's street gang.

"No. You are not an idiot. You have the smarts to get inside every major museum around the world!" Papa Shadi poked Darius' left shoe with the tip of his cane. "And I believe the correct term is not *thief* but *retrieval specialist.*"

Darius watched a security guard enter the tiny pub and approach the bartender. "Doesn't matter how you sugar coat it, Papa. I steal things."

"Yes, but you steal from thieves. You return things to their proper owners."

"That still makes me a thief." *But a damn good one.*

"Like that English fellow, Robin."

Darius chuckled. "Okay. Maybe I am kinda like Robin Hood. I have been arrested by plenty of sheriffs."

Papa Shadi stroked his beard and shrugged. "A criminal record means nothing when you work for family."

After chugging down a draft, the security guard turned and headed straight toward them.

Darius smirked. "As my employer, I wonder if that makes you just as guilty."

"Guilt by association? Probably." Papa Shadi pointed his cane toward the approaching guard. "Looks like Artie is ready for us."

Finally escaping the sticky booth, Darius tossed a nice tip down for the perky cocktail waitress with the cute red thong under her mini kilt. Passing her on the way out, he easily read the smoky, suggestive look in her light green eyes. He did like green eyes.

* * *

"I can't wait to see her."

Darius smiled at Papa Shadi's unrestrained excitement.

Within minutes, the security guard led them across the street, through a delivery door, and up to the eighth floor in a service elevator. As the doors swooshed open, big block letters announced the field office of U.S. Customs & Border Protection, the agency sworn to protect citizens from the illegal entry of people and goods.

As he did anytime he entered a museum or federal building, Darius quickly slipped on a pair of gloves. The crack about sheriffs really hadn't been off the mark. He'd been arrested or detained so many times he'd lost count. If any art or antiquities went missing, he was top on the list of suspects.

Even though he was probably on a video camera, he still took the precaution of keeping his fingerprints to himself.

Mr. Artie Johnson, he presumed, stood just inside the first door past the receptionist's desk. This was definitely a government man: just shy of middle age, average height, slim but a slight paunch, standard issue black suit and boring tie.

What was not average about the man was the sweat trickling down his neck and the shifty way his brown eyes darted between every corner of the room. *He's spooked.*

Without any introduction, he motioned for Papa Shadi to open a brown leather satchel on the desk. Darius kept his eyes on the nervous man who made a distinct effort to stay as far away from the desk as possible.

A quick intake of breath told him that his grandfather had found the photo of the statue. "Yes. There she is. Isn't she beautiful?"

Darius dragged his eyes away from watching Mr. Artie. He had to see what his grandfather had been so obsessed with for all these years.

*Beautiful?* That word didn't give enough credit to the sculptor. She was…breathtaking. Even in a glossy photograph he could see the detail in her exotic features. She looked commanding in her pose, her knife gripped with determination. She also looked…

Heavy. She appeared to be a typical life-sized statue plated with gold. That would make her extremely heavy. Always a challenging factor in retrieval.

What was he thinking? He wasn't going

anywhere near the Troy Estate.

"Artie, you found the sword, too?" A tone of reverence hovered in the old man's voice. "Look, Darius. This sword belongs to the Lady of Flame. It was created for her."

Darius curved his lips doubtfully. "The goddess or the statue?"

Papa Shadi's eyes flickered with annoyance. "You know the ancient Egyptians believed that if you could speak aloud the true name of someone...or something...you controlled it."

"You've known my name all these years and haven't controlled *me* very well." Darius tried to chuckle at his own joke, but one stern look from Papa Shadi silenced him.

"The name of the sword is *Farvadin*," he whispered. "It means *guardian*. The Lady of Flame used it to lead her *medjai* warriors. Only she can wield the sword and invoke its full power."

A high-pitched sucking sound came from the reception area. It could easily have been the night cleaner's vacuum, but Artie Johnson darted from the room like a terrified rabbit. Darius realized he was scratching the hell out of his palm: his sixth sense telling him something was not right.

"Grab the bag, Papa. Let's go."

The lights in the reception area flickered. Television screens hung silently from the ceiling. Rows of seats in the waiting area sat empty. Artie cowered by the elevator, pounding on the buttons. As the eerie sound grew, the security guard twirled in confused circles, looking for the source.

They weren't alone. Yet, Darius couldn't say how he knew that.

His grandfather looked heartbroken. "I am sorry. There is so much more to tell you. I waited too long."

Darius followed Papa's gaze toward a darkened corner. The shadow seemed unnaturally dark and stretched from floor to ceiling. Strange, it was like he was looking into a deep, black void. Then he felt it. The void pulsated. Cold vibrations swept over him rhythmically, raising the hairs on his arms. His palms continued to itch.

Bolts of pure energy lashed out from the void, whipping through the room and fingering everything. The televisions screamed to life and exploded in a shower of sparks. Fluorescent ceiling lights fizzled out. The receptionist's handsets popped off their cradles, smacking against their charging stations.

The security guard leaped toward the elevator, but a violent bolt slashed through the man's chest. His body slumped forward. Artie screamed and continued pounding on the elevator doors. *What the hell?*

Darius stepped protectively in front of his grandfather, prepared to face whatever was coming. He felt an urgent hand on his shoulder.

"Darius," Papa Shadi whispered. "Lilith sends her demons to silence us. She must be stopped."

It disturbed him that he could not see into the blackness. Darius started to argue, but for once he held silent. Instead, he moved them both back away from the void, nearly tripping over a fallen television screen. He maneuvered them behind the desk.

Peering back into the void, he noticed a yellow glow moving toward them from deep inside the darkness.

"What's happening?" He looked toward his grandfather's face, which was surprisingly calm.

Papa Shadi nudged him in the arm with his cane. "Remember the prophecy."

The lamp from Artie's office provided meager light, but even in the semi-darkness the old man's eyes sparkled with anticipation, not fear. Darius wondered if the old coot had been expecting this. The yellow glow advanced toward them quickly now. The light divided into three distinct pairs of eyes.

Darius sat back and mentally counted to ten. This was not happening. Maybe he was hallucinating. More likely, he was having a nightmare, induced by his grandfather's prophecy theories. He felt his grandfather move closer to him.

"Darius," he felt the old man's light grip on his shoulder and the cane nudging his arm again. "Get the Lady of Flame. She will help you."

*Right!* A statue was not going to keep him out of the loony bin. "Papa, whatever happens, stay right here."

Darius didn't wait for a response. He simply expected his demand to be followed. He kept his eyes fixated on the void and the three looming forms taking shape within it.

Two thin shapes slithered into the room and took up flanking positions. They looked almost like a couple of college guys, sporting name brand jeans and Harvard polo shirts. Until their cheekbones popped and stretched outward. Shiny fangs swung down from the roofs of their mouths. Forked tongues flickered between the dripping fangs. Sniffing the air, they seemed to be studying their surroundings.

Finally, the third form stepped from the void. This one exuded an air of authority.

*Think!* Darius rubbed the back of his head. His mind screamed with questions that he dared not ask out loud. Not unless he wanted to give up their position before he made some quick plans. The black void now engulfed the hallway leading to the stairwell, the only way out of this office besides the elevator. Artie had slid to the floor, whimpering and sweating.

Darius glanced again at the security guard's body. The gun. It was still in the guard's holster. He wondered how he could get to it.

The lead demon didn't have scaly skin like the others, but he sported the same set of drippy fangs. All of them panted heavily. Darius felt the temperature in the room drop severely, yet sweat trickled down his back.

"Mr. Arthur Johnson? Come out, come out, wherever you are," the demon sang in a raspy voice. He strode forward, flicking back the tails of his leather trench coat. "It seems that you have been a very naughty boy. Snooping around her private collection. Shame on you. The Dragon Queen would like a word with you."

Darius put his fingers to his lips to signal for his grandfather to remain silent.

"She demands it!" An impatient roar reverberated through the empty room. The demon picked up a television screen and threw it. It shattered on impact with the wall. Artie responded with a toe-curling shriek and renewed efforts at prying open the elevator doors.

Darius leaped over the desk, starting toward the growling demon. "Damn, you could win a door prize at DragonCon."

A ragged, wet growling sound was his only response. It echoed off the tiled floors. The other two moved around him slowly, like snakes encircling their prey.

"Wow. What big teeth you have. How do I get a set of those?"

The demon laughed. "Well, come here, little human, and I will show you how."

Darius launched toward him, covering the ground between them so quickly he knew he caught the thing off guard. It was only a momentary advantage, but enough to get a kick into the demon's jaw. In unison, the other two sprang toward Darius. He used the back of the first one to springboard over the advancing pair. The moment his feet touched the ground, he spun to land enough kicks into their skulls to drop them too.

He started toward the frozen guard, leading the demons away from his grandfather. He just needed a moment to get that gun. Darius heard the blow from behind him even before he felt it. It came too quickly for him to avoid. Whistling past his ear, a demon's fist slammed down onto his collarbone. Darius felt cold tile under his cheek.

Two of the demons pressed him into the floor. For once, Darius wished he had a full head of hair, because hot drool oozed across his scalp. He shivered with revulsion, as he realized it smelled nasty as well.

"Whew, what have you been eating? Ever heard of breath mints?" His stomach roiled from the stench. He felt a kick coming, but he curled inward to absorb at least some of the blow. He coughed and gulped for air.

Darius froze as he felt a slimy fang rub against his cheek. A breathy voice too close to his ear whispered, "Human, you smell like a tasty one."

"Not now, you fools," the commanding demon barked. "The Dragon Queen doesn't like to be kept waiting. Mr. Johnson, it's time to go now."

Artie's body twisted and arched on the floor. His eyes nearly popped from his face.

Papa Shadi stepped out from his hiding place. "Take me. Leave them out of this. I am the one who knows Lilith's secrets."

"*No!*" Darius struggled to get up, but he was slammed against the floor again. His grandfather smiled. Again, he wondered if Papa Shadi had been expecting this. The old man popped a flat wafer into his mouth before lifting his cane and launching toward the demon in charge.

Darius watched helplessly as his grandfather managed to land one blow across the demon's shoulder. Roaring in outrage, the demon struck out at the old man, knocking him to the ground. Darius was horrified to realize that his grandfather lay unconscious.

The demon shrugged and picked up the old man, tossing the frail body over his shoulder. "Bring him, too. She'll want to handle him personally," he commanded before stepping back into the black void.

Darius managed to get his palms beneath him against the floor, and he shoved with all the strength he had left. Caught off guard, the creatures fell backwards. Darius dropped low and swung his foot out, swiping one of them off its feet. A sickening thud echoed as its head connected with the floor.

Darius doubled over as pain knifed through his shoulder. Something hit him on the back of the head, and his vision blurred. Darius waited for the next blow that would send him into darkness.

*No!* He refused to let this happen. His grandfather needed him. Darius looked around. Just on the other side of the demon's feet, Papa Shadi's cane lay on the floor.

Darius grabbed the cane and yanked it toward him, sweeping the demon off of its feet. The two picked themselves off the floor, snarling for another fight. Darius sprang toward the dead guard, whipping the gun out of the holster. He checked the chamber. *No fucking bullets?*

The demons tackled him from behind, but Darius managed to roll out from under them. He raced back to the broken television screen and ripped off a wickedly ragged piece.

As the first demon approached him from behind, he twisted and shoved the glass shank into the demon's scaly forehead. Darius watched in awe as the creature stumbled backward for a moment, and then its head disintegrated. Blown clean off of the neck. The headless body writhed on the floor. With a final twitch, the headless body burst into a blue flame. Only the makeshift weapon and a small pile of gray ash remained.

Darius caught the other creature retreating quickly toward the void. He snatched up his makeshift shank again and threw it at the demon's back. He was a bit rusty on his throw, but it still managed to lodge behind the demon's ear. It was close enough to accomplish the job.

Darius started running toward the void. "*Papa!*"

*What is this thing? What's on the other side?* He had to find out. He had to save his grandfather. If only he'd paid better attention all these years. Maybe then he would have a clue. Still, he was certain his grandfather had never mentioned anything like this.

A thought halted him. The demons came through this thing like a door. A portal. If he stepped through that doorway, he'd be stepping right into their turf. He suspected that he wouldn't like the odds.

His best move at this point would be to find another way into the demon nest. He just prayed that his grandfather was right. He was going to break into the Troy Estate, and he had to do it fast while he could still have an element of surprise.

Darius remembered the cane. Picking it up, he inspected it for scratches. He would take good care of it for Papa Shadi. He wished to God that Papa was here now, poking him in the ribs with the damned thing. He felt like that glass shank was shoved through his own heart.

Behind the desk, he found the leather satchel which contained the proof of his grandfather's life-long obsession. Draped deliberately across it was the gold necklace Papa Shadi always wore. Darius had never seen him without it.

The medallion was engraved on one side with old hieratic writing, which read *Brotherhood of Karnak*, one of the early names for the Illuminati. A pyramid was embossed on the other side, with an eye symbol centered inside it. He knew it to be a symbol of the brotherhood his grandfather belonged to.

Darius draped the necklace around his own neck and kissed the medallion. He swore to whatever god was listening that he would get his grandfather back, even if from hell itself. In a moment of pure rage, Darius picked up the wicked glass shard again, and threw it straight at the black void. Silently, it sliced into the dark oblivion.

The world around him pulsed violently. He felt vibrations thudding against his skull. Slowly, the void retreated. A rush of air nearly blew Darius into the swirling fury. He grabbed for the nearest chair and held on tight. Thankfully, it was bolted securely to the waiting room floor.

He would go to the demon's lair, but only on his own terms. Not theirs. The void swirled slowly shut, like watching a black hole disappear.

Warmth returned to the room.

Exhausted, Darius crawled over to the limp body of Artie Johnson. Fright permanently pasted across his face and sightless eyes stared upward from sunken sockets. Ironically, the elevator finally chimed.

The metal doors swooshed open to reveal an empty shaft. Darius grabbed the satchel and ran down the hallway leading to the stairwell. As he passed the spot where his grandfather had disappeared into the evil, black hole, his skin shivered from the icy air that remained.

# CHAPTER TWO

"Must beauty come with a temper?" Therion Troy leaned idly on the mantel of a fireplace almost big enough to stand in. He closed his eyes, savoring the delicious aroma of his brandy.

Her response came swiftly, shattering the snifter he cradled in his palm. He grumbled with annoyance as a wet, brown stain spread across his crisp white linen shirt. What a waste of good liquor.

One by one, glass fixtures popped and exploded around the room. The source of his annoyance, the beauty, flopped herself into the nearest chair, fury vibrating off her in near visible waves. She looked like a super model having her little diva tantrum. He chuckled.

"What's so funny?" she snapped.

"If those demons were still alive, you'd probably fry their asses on the spot yourself." Therion didn't share his mother's disappointment in losing a few demons. There were plenty more where they came from. He recalled the slick sound as a piece of glass flew out of the portal and knifed into the demon's skull. Fascinating.

"How hard is it to capture one pathetic human and bring him to me?" Her tawny eyes blazed.

"I'm wounded, Mother." He feigned a hurt expression. "I *am* one of those pathetic humans."

"Not for long, my son. We are so close to finding that amulet, I can almost feel its power reaching out to me." She flipped her long golden hair across one shoulder.

Lilith Helene Troy was absolutely one pissed off immortal, and Therion knew better than to push her buttons at the wrong time.

Even the black house cat seemed to know it was time to retreat. Therion grabbed the nervous feline just as she tried to slink past him. Ignoring the threatening growls, he cradled her firmly across his forearm. Curious, he spun the fat, studded collar around her neck. "Didn't know punk was in for cat accessories."

He tossed her roughly over the couch toward the door. She twisted, landing squarely on all fours, but paused to hiss at him before disappearing.

He should do the same...beat a hasty retreat. He should give his mother a little time to let the froth settle. But he didn't like doing what he *should*.

"They brought back the wrong man. He's not the Customs director who was sniffing around your private collection." He found a new glass and poured himself a fresh drink.

U.S. Customs usually wasn't a problem for them, but the Art Fraud Investigations department had influence with government agencies across the globe. They had the power to really disrupt their import and export operations.

"Fools," she sneered.

"I recognized him, though. He's that antiquities broker, the one who hires out his grandson to find stolen artifacts."

"Amazing. Maybe those foolish demons did something right after all. He may be the man who's responsible for Mr. Johnson's snooping in the first place. What I don't know is why. I want to know what he knows about me." Lounging across a red velvet sofa, she looked as dramatic and tragic as a painting of Cleopatra.

"Why keep him? He's just a trinket broker." Therion noticed the renewed flare of anger in his mother's eyes. He hated to drink fast. Brandy was supposed to be savored. He drained the crystal snifter in one gulp before anything could happen to it, frowning at the empty glass.

"They are not trinkets, Therion." She bolted upright, excitement sparkling in her tawny eyes. She giggled wickedly. "But we do have our own artifact to locate. His grandson will find it for us."

"I think Darius' reputation is highly overrated." Therion pictured the scrawny little street thief who couldn't throw a punch to save his life. Although that was long ago, he figured Darius would remember their last meeting in bloody detail. "And I'm certain he would never work for us."

"Oh, I don't agree." She hugged him from behind. "We have a bargaining chip. We have his grandfather."

"The old man's half dead."

"He's in a coma. Darius *will* bargain for the man's life."

"What if he goes to the police instead?"

"That would be most unwise." Lilith paced around the sofa. "I need to speak with him quickly, before he decides to talk to the authorities. We cannot afford to be investigated by Customs or any other agency right now. The gala is almost here, and I can't waste time dealing with interruptions between now and the unveiling of this year's product line. The new formula must be tested."

"So, you'll give him a choice then? Help us or your grandfather is toast?"

"I will not phrase it so callously. Good night. I need to think this through for a while, and you need to go change out of that filthy shirt." Lilith's face radiated with a glow of anticipation. She relished a good challenge.

As he left the room, his mind bristled at the injustice. He too craved a challenge, a test of wills. He strolled through the private gallery rooms, which contained an extensive collection of antiquities safely encased within glass boxes or hung on the wall like decorations.

His mind burned at the insult to such brilliantly crafted weapons. Instruments of strategy and power now relegated to uselessness.

He ran his fingertips across the leather hilt of an ancient sword. Cold, but it was still as strong as the day it was crafted for combat. He could almost smell the battlefield.

Therion was born to battle. The dark blood of his father pulsed wickedly through him even now. His destiny was denied to him on so many fronts. He savored the anger.

Jewels sparkled in glass cases everywhere. All of them were useless to him. There was one jewel out there in the world that held the key to his destiny. A black diamond. He'd been told that it contained his immortal powers. He'd felt it too. Felt it calling to him in the darkest hours.

He needed to change his shirt before picking up his date for the night. She was a luscious brunette with violet eyes, but she would be no challenge to him. He would get little satisfaction from his time with her.

As always, he was drawn to the far end of the room, where a golden statue of an Egyptian war goddess stood like a guardian over the gallery. A true masterpiece, it held an intense fascination for him. Her unique, exotic features made his blood pulse more quickly through his body. He cupped her golden breast. It fit perfectly in his palm.

"Good evening, doll," he whispered.

He cursed his fate. He should have been born in another time, in an age where kings ruled by blood or by the might of their army.

She was only a lifeless statue, but she evoked the kind of images in his mind that satisfied his lust for a challenge. Closing his eyes, he savored the fantasy.

Desert sands billowing behind a speeding chariot while his enemies lay like a bloody blanket across the valley floor. A great sword would fill the grip of his hand as he held it aloft. His fierce war cry would embolden his army and terrify the enemy. He would have been the ultimate hunter. The ultimate king. If only he'd been born when he should have been.

Reality rained across his mind. The breast against his palm was cold and hard, but tonight he'd find real satisfaction: one way or another.

\* \* \*

*Flashes of light toyed with Shaila's consciousness behind sightless eyes. Muted sounds broke into her hazy awareness. Like a babe in a womb, her life was suspended.*

*A voice spoke to her through the veil of shadows. A human voice. His words were muffled and distant. Warmth spread across her breast, but it made her mind scream in frustration. She longed to roar with rage. Despair, as always, set in, reminding her of failures of the past. Did she belong here? Trapped? Trapped in a cold, dark hell?*

*Only memories soothed her ravaged mind. Images flashed of bright sunlight and golden mountains. She could almost feel the warmth of the sand. Horses thundered across the plateau, as the wheels of the chariot squealed in protest. Shaila reined in the wild mares to slow their pace. She wanted to hear the laughter bubbling from beside her. Her best friend was shouting for them to go faster...and faster.*

*Thinking of Nefertiti brought joy and pain to her soul.*

*She prayed for Nefertiti's child to survive this awkward path to the future. He was the messiah of the prophecy, and Shaila had promised to protect him. He was destined to save them all.*

*Of late, the textures of sounds had become more vibrant and bold. She had never stopped feeling the vibrations of the world, but the rhythms of conversations and movement had changed. Their pace quickened and intensified.*

*Had they reached the age of the prophecy? Her astral spirit, her immortal spirit, had not returned to her. She reached out with her mind to the dimension where her spirit should be waiting, but she found only darkness in the plane where light once shone with brilliance. Yet, a great shift in the balance heralded a change coming.*

*Oh, Goddess. Is it time? I can't wait much longer.*

*Only deafening quiet answered her.*

\* \* \*

Seventeen hours ago, his world had seemed to derail and crash into a different dimension. Darius massaged the back of his head, trying to rub some sense into it.

For the past half hour, Darius had waited impatiently for his friend to meet him on the platform of the Green Line. The brisk October wind helped to cool his nerves. Goose bumps spread across his arms. He drew in deep breaths of air and waited for his brain to clear. It seemed like a stadium full of kids poured out of the archaeology building at Boston University.

As usual, the professor had his face buried in the front section of the *Globe*. If Marcus didn't look up soon, Darius was going to be peeling his friend off the front of the bus barreling down Comm Ave. Amazing how smart the professor was, but he didn't have enough sense not to get plowed by a bus.

"Marcus!" Darius yelled over the dull roar of rush hour traffic.

"Momma's been wondering when you're coming for dinner. She's still on her personal mission to fatten you up." Marcus inclined his head toward the white knuckled grip Darius held on a set of keys. "What's up? You look like hell."

"Thanks for noticing." Joining the mass of commuters, they herded into the closest subway car of the T.

"Anytime." A frown gathered across Marcus' face. "Hey, aren't you supposed to be on vacation? You know…sand, shades, suds."

Time was too important to waste. "I need your help."

He hated to admit that out loud. But he did need help, and Marcus was the only other person on this planet that he trusted completely besides his grandfather.

"What did you say?"

"I said…I need your help."

"Sure, you do." The frown changed to a more skeptical look. "You've never needed my help before. That's your problem, you know. You never ask for help. You're the type who always--"

"Marcus, can we please drop the psychoanalysis of my life?"

After hanging on to the poles for several stops, they were finally able to snag a couple of seats.

"Okay. What do you need?"

"Backup."

"Excuse me?" Marcus leaned in more closely.

"I need your eyes, Marcus. I need someone to cover my back." Darius looked his friend square in the eyes. "I only have about twelve more hours to finish preparing for a very important job."

"And I have a very important job that I'd like to keep. Thank you very much." Marcus held up two fingers. "Make that *two* very important jobs. If my boss at the museum knew your name, I'd be out of that job in a heartbeat. Guilt by association."

"Join the club." Darius reined in all of his energy to tamp down the surge of aggravation. He glanced at his watch. Seventeen hours and ten minutes since his grandfather had disappeared through a black hole. He slipped his hand inside his jacket and squeezed the medallion.

"So, what do you need to *acquire* this time?" Marcus emphasized by doing the finger quotes in the air.

"It's *whom* I need to acquire, not *what*." Darius knew his eyes openly showed his pain. For once, he didn't care to hide his emotions. "I have to strike quickly, before they prepare for it. It's too important and too challenging for me to do alone. I really need your help, Marcus. Please?"

Darius watched the tunnel lights flick by. He could feel Marcus studying him intently.

"Spill it, Dare. What's going on?"

The lights of the Boylston Street underground platform came into view. The subway jerked to a halt. Darius ground his teeth together. "Are you in or not?"

"You know I'm in."

"Papa Shadi. He's been kidnapped."

"What?" They dashed out of the subway car before the doors slid closed again. Marcus mouthed a few curse words. "You aren't joking, are you? Who...why would anyone want to kidnap Papa Shadi?" Marcus grabbed him by the shoulder. "What makes you think I can help?"

For a moment, Darius allowed a hesitant smile to curve his lips. Here was a topic that could take over his mind for a while and keep the emotions at bay. "Follow me."

Four city blocks and one plaza later, Darius led them through a kids' arcade. In the back of the darkened room, they passed through a door leading to a stairwell. Instead of taking the stairs up, he pulled Marcus behind the staircase, lifted up a metal grate from the ground, and motioned for Marcus to follow him.

In the pitch black, Darius unerringly found the switch and flicked it up.

As Marcus' eyes adjusted to sudden brightness, his jaw dropped to his chest. "Holy. Shit." The words were barely spoken loud enough to hear, reverently, as if they were standing in a cathedral. "You have seriously been holding out on me."

"This is my private research lab." It was a large room, taking up the same amount of space as the game room above it and the neighboring karate studio.

Marcus mimicked him, "*This is my private research lab.*" Then, he glared at Darius. "This a fuckin' state-of-the-art computer system! I haven't seen this much silicon since my summer job with Microsoft. Damn it, I am so pissed that you've never shown me this before."

Darius shifted uncomfortably. "I didn't have a need…until now."

"Sorry, Dare." Marcus skimmed his fingertips across the silver keyboard slowly. Three huge wall screens flickered to life at the slight touch. "Now I understand why you're the best repo man. Can she tap into the Navy satellites?"

Darius expelled a long breath he hadn't realized he'd been holding. He realized that he was grateful for not having to do this alone. "Let me introduce you to

ALICE. Short for Autonomous Logistics and Intelligence Collection Engine."

* * *

Darius needed to hurry. Dawn was only an hour away. Quickly, he positioned a clean license plate over the old one and clicked a magnetic sign on the van door. After smoothing a wrinkle out of the fictitious paint company logo, he tucked in behind the wheel.

He and Marcus had both spent most of the night programming ALICE to take over control of the security video feed at the Troy Estate. A second computer screen would help Marcus keep track of people moving around the estate using thermal imagery. Another continual audio and video stream would appear on a third screen from a camera mounted on Darius' cap.

Marcus was a true man of science. Darius couldn't blame the guy for not quite believing that demons had kidnapped Papa Shadi. Up until thirty hours ago, he hadn't believed any of it himself. He'd just always chalked it up to the ramblings of an old man whose head was so full of ancient prophecies and modern conspiracies that he finally believed them.

"Dare, this is sick how you've made this computer so easy to work with." Through the earpiece, Marcus' voice came through as clear as if he was sitting in the van next to Darius.

"I'll take that as a compliment."

"I can't believe I just watched you steal a van. Is that considered aiding and abetting a felon? You know, for a guy who doesn't really own much more than a Harley, you sure are good at taking things from others."

"If you don't own something, it can't be taken

away from you."

"You're a sad case, Dare. A shrink would have a field day with you."

"Shut up, Marcus."

"Okay, but you asked me to do this, so you have to put up with me. Consider me your official annoying sidekick."

Darius grinned. It helped his mood to picture his best friend squirming on the other end of the video feed.

Marcus's voice crackled through the earpiece. "I just checked the fresh satellite images. Damn, this is better than Google Earth. There are quite a few work vans lining up in the alley behind the Troy Estate already."

For a break in, this should be a cakewalk. Darius had been elated yesterday to discover through some cursory research that Lilith Troy was not only planning for her annual gala, but she was doing some major remodeling at her estate for it as well. That meant an army of carpenters, decorators, and painters coming and going. He could virtually hide in plain sight.

"Excellent. I'm ready to blend with the crowd."

"I hate to break it to you, buddy. But you never blend in. Tall. Lean. Bald. You're like a frickin' seven foot tall Vin Diesel."

Darius chuckled as he swung the van into the line up of work vans. "I'm not seven feet tall." He was, however, confident that he'd blend in today. He wore a basic white polo shirt and a pair of old faded jeans with various paint colors splotched all over them. Then, he topped it all off with dark shades and a faded Red Sox hat.

Parking the van in a spot that would be easy to get out of was challenging. He cursed the narrow, cobblestone alley. The best spot turned out to be at the end of the alley, furthest away from the entrance. Just in case he ran into any more of his demon pals, he'd worn a belt with a very useful buckle. He grabbed his worn backpack, containing a few tools he might need to break into or out of something, and then joined the parade of workers filing in through a large, warehouse-like entrance.

"That door seems to be at the opposite end of the house from where you want to be, Dare," Marcus whispered.

"You don't have to whisper," Darius whispered. "The earpiece is inside my ear. Nobody else will hear it."

"You're whispering."

Darius looked up at the sky. Too bad Marcus wouldn't be able to read the disgust on his face. The satellite zoom was good, but not that good. He could hear Marcus cursing at himself.

The flow of workers streamed into the house through a long hallway, which emptied into the main ballroom. Darius moved purposefully past the crews polishing marble flooring, hanging gauzy draperies, and carving designs into Greek columns. He noted workbenches and tools around the room. Wheeled trash bins were stationed around the room to dispose of things without ruining the newly marbled floors.

Even the porte cochere teemed with activity. Many embellishments were getting a good coating of gold paint. It seemed a Grecian theme was taking shape for the Troy Cosmetics Annual Gala.

Because of its age and history, it hadn't been too difficult to find architectural maps online for the Troy Estate. He hoped the old maps were still accurate. Brass and velvet stanchions cordoned off the workers from entering the rooms on the far side of the foyer. These off-limits rooms were likely the ones Lilith used to display her private collection of antiquities. Her collection was reputed to be one of the finest personal displays in the world.

According to the maps, there should be a staircase in the back room that would lead him down to a basement level. From the rumors about this old house, he figured that would be where they would be keeping his grandfather.

"I'm ready." He whispered into the little wire mouthpiece. "I'm in the foyer."

"Hang on. ALICE is on it." Darius could hear Marcus' fingers clicking across the keyboard on his end. "Okay. The security feed is on a loop, and you are now like a ghost."

Darius ducked under the cord and walked very slowly through the first room. Iridescent glass vessels sat on granite pedestals. Jewelry sparkled from within glass cases, and several highly erotic Roman bath tiles hung on the walls. A whistle pierced his ear and he cupped it reflexively.

"Now there's a few positions even I hadn't thought of."

"Marcus," Darius grounded out, wiggling the earpiece. "don't friggin' do that again. You're supposed to be keeping an eye on the thermal cameras."

"Sorry. There's not a soul near you. Geez, these rooms are more interesting than the galleries at the MFA. Someone on the floor above you is moving in the direction of the staircase."

"Okay, keep an eye on everyone." He fingered his belt buckle again, double-checking that the throwing knives were still in place. He was ready for any demons unfortunate enough to challenge him.

Darius finally entered the last gallery. A circular staircase stood in the far corner of the room. It led both upstairs to the residence level, and downstairs to the basement level.

"Okay. I see it. I'm--" Darius' voice trailed off. He couldn't have moved if he'd wanted to. In the semi-darkness of the room, a single spotlight shone down on a statue. A magnificent statue. *Holy. Shit.*

He'd seen so many wondrous artifacts in his lifetime, but this one he'd put at the top of his list. Here was something even he might consider keeping. His blood raced, tingling through his body.

She'd been stunning enough in the photograph, but here the lights and shadows together seemed to bring her to life. The amber spotlight magnified every glorious detail. The golden patina glowed like a flame.

"Wow. I've never seen anything so beautiful." Even through a darkened video feed she could apparently inspire awe in a seasoned professional like Marcus. "Can you get a little closer?"

"She's in perfect condition. Almost as if she'd been carved yesterday." The sculptor had captured a pure, realistic quality.

"Do you know anything about it?"

"She's the statue my grandfather has searched for his whole life. The Lady of Flame. I can understand his obsession now. She's the Egyptian goddess of war, Sekhmet. Usually, she would have a lion head on a human female body. But this one is all human. Very curious. She's in the typical style of clothing and stance, yet the quality is more lifelike." He studied the hilt of the dagger a little more closely. "This statue is too detailed to be from an earlier period. This much detail strikes me as from a later period...Ptolemaic maybe."

"That is one wicked-looking dagger." He heard the admiration through the static. "I wouldn't want to run into her in a dark alley. Unless she was there to save me, of course."

Her face captivated him. While he could not see the depths of her eyes, the detail in her face spoke volumes to him. The muscles in her jaw were clenched with determination. Her high wide cheekbones held aloft with confidence and pride. Yet, the crinkling around her eyes and forehead spoke to him of pain. That was something he was currently familiar with.

"Hey, Dare. Can you point that camera back down again? Let me get another look at the belt?"

"I didn't know you could read anything other than bones and dirt?" A sudden itch aggravated him. Darius reached under his shirt to scratch his chest.

"I hate to disappoint you, but that doesn't look like hieratic writing."

Darius bent down to get a better look, gently fingering the indentions carved thousands of years ago. Darius was stunned. "Sumarian? But that would be crazy. That would date this *before* the Egyptians."

She was a beautiful enigma. No wonder his grandfather searched for her his whole life.

"I can read the hieroglyphs on the base. That part is a warning to whomever possesses this statue to keep their distance, lest the lion within roar with fury and smote you as the enemy. Or something to that effect."

"What a find. I can't believe that this piece is in a private collection." Marcus sounded like he was clicking on the keyboard madly. "Uh, sorry. I forgot to keep an eye on things. Get out of there. There are two people coming at you from both directions. Hurry."

Darius barely had time to jump into a display of a funerary boat. He plastered himself on the floor behind it just as Therion entered the room.

* * *

*She felt it.*

Like waves rolling across the sea, pulses rippled against her with increasing speed and intensity.

Is it time to fulfill the prophecy? Have thousands of sun cycles passed?

Shaila could almost feel the weight of dust and age, but underneath it all, her soul had fully awakened. Her mind reviewed images collected from the passage of time in a prismatic display of color. With sightless eyes, she had only her memories and dreams to keep her company. Would the loneliness finally end?

Voices hummed around her, bringing her mind out of the mist. She heard tones spoken with excitement and awe.

The pulses continued. Something on her chest responded to them, vibrating as if in answer to a primal call.

Is it time? Is it finally the end of my nightmare?

# CHAPTER THREE

"There you are, Mother!" Therion strode across the tiled floor of the gallery, meeting his mother at the foot of the staircase. He kissed her cheek. "You really have those high-priced room designers ready to burst out of their skins. They are terrified to disappoint you."

"They should be. This year's season introduction must be flawless." Her fingers curled around his.

He watched a frown mar her features. "What's wrong?"

"I don't know. A vibration. Something new. Just a feeling that I can't identify yet."

"A disturbance in the Force?" Therion stepped away from his mother to avoid the pinch. She didn't always appreciate his sarcasm. He greeted the object of his fantasies. "Hello, doll." His rubbed his palm across the statue's abdomen. He felt his mother's icy glare.

"Are you so desperate that you need to molest a statue?"

"Oh, tell me you don't stroke that Marc Antony statue in the other room. Ah, but it's this particular statue, isn't it? You hate it. That's why you gave it to me."

She moved to touch the jaw of the statue, but hesitated. "It is a rather disturbing likeness of Inanna's daughter, but no, I save my hatred for Inanna. She feared your inherited power from Apophis so much that she had you stripped of your immortal spirit." His mother's voice dripped hatred, sizzling like acid.

He cupped the statue's breast, knowing that the

crude gesture would irritate his mother. He decided to bring up another sore subject. "I think it's time for me to get married."

"No." Vehemence sliced through her voice.

He fondled the statue again, trying to prick her jealousy. "I would like a wife like this one. Wild and ferocious." Some of his nighttime fantasies played across the screen of his mind.

The explosion of her temper brought a wide smile to his lips. The spotlight over the statue burst, as well as a glass case nearby containing ancient jewelry. She held her right palm up, and a small flame appeared. She looked ready to throw it at the statue. "Men are dirty, rutting pigs!" She seemed to catch on to his ruse. "I did not raise you to act like a horny teenager."

"I want a son, Mother."

"Speaking of sons, have you found the old man's grandson?"

"Not yet."

"We have no answer for why the old man is in this coma. Even I cannot seem to get inside his mind. I need to know what he knows. What his grandson knows."

* * *

*Leave the room, damn it!* Another painful cramp pierced through his back muscles, but Darius focused on his breathing until the pain subsided. His body was obviously still tired of being in cramped spaces. Not too mention the dust that hadn't been swept up from behind this antique in years. He pinched his nose to avoid a sneeze that threatened to blow his cover.

He'd trained his body to lie motionless for hours, but watching Therion from this close proximity knotted his gut. Memories engulfed Darius without mercy. He was eight years old again, protecting his little hideaway in the basement of an abandoned wharf building. Therion and his gang of prep school jerks had watched Darius pick pockets for money and watches. Greedily, they'd come for his stash. They beat him up, threw him into the harbor, and took off with the whole box.

Even then, he hadn't cared about the cash or the watches. They didn't mean anything to him. Only one item had special meaning for him. A single bead hung on the end of a thin gold chain around his neck. Hardly precious, it was a small oblong blue bead made of lapis lazuli. It was the only thing his mother had ever given him besides life itself. It was the only thing that reminded Darius of the days before his mother turned to drugs.

For five years, Therion and his crew haunted Darius, but eventually the scumbag had figured out how much that damned necklace had meant to him. The day before Therion left for the military academy, he'd cornered Darius in an alley, beat him, and left him for dead. Therion had ripped the necklace from him, claiming it as his war prize.

The beating Darius endured should have killed him, but the only scar that remained was the one in his heart for losing his only prized possession. *If you don't own something, it can't be taken away from you.*

Finally, mother and son moved away toward the staircase. He hoped they were going up to the residence and not down to the basement. Therion was groping the statue one last time before following his mother.

Darius glared at Therion's back, wishing to hell he could run over there and rip the man's throat out. He knew he could physically take him on now. But the only move he made was to scratch his chest again.

Alone now, Darius stood up and approached the staircase, watching the two retreat to the upper level. He couldn't stand the itch any longer and pulled the medallion out from under his shirt. He figured he was having a bad reaction to whatever metals were in it.

He started to descend the staircase, but stopped. He couldn't say why. He just felt a pull to remain on the gallery level. He backed up, and then moved to stand in front of the statue again. The pain on her face tugged at his heart. He wondered why the artist chose to capture her in such a vulnerable emotion. He easily pictured her strong and vibrant, racing wildly across a plateau in her chariot, fighting the enemies of Egypt.

Unconsciously, he stepped up onto the pedestal with her and placed his palm on her shoulder. He'd expected the golden sculpture to be cold, but it felt hot against his fingertips. He moved his hand across all of the same places he'd seen Therion touch her. Something in him wanted to remove for her the taint of his enemy's touch.

As his fingertips passed across the center of her chest, a blue light slowly sizzled to life. Darius started to step backward and nearly fell off of the pedestal. Grabbing her by the arms to steady himself, he realized that she was...trembling.

The blue light glowed brightly now, and he was stunned to recognize the shape it took. It formed a circle. Inside of it was an eye symbol within a pyramid. It was a reverse image of the one embossed on the medallion.

The air in the room pulsated. Unlike the deep cold he'd felt around the void, these pulses felt like warm liquid waves. The medallion buzzed with heat, shaking violently. The statue seemed ready to explode. His bones shuddered from the intense vibrations in the room. He had to do something.

Darius turned the medallion around so that the image on it and on her mirrored each other. The medallion whisked away from his chest and slapped into place on the statue like a magnet. Like a key.

A glow spread across the statue until it was engulfed in blue flame. The gold patina on the statue began to melt away slowly, revealing soft flesh. A chandelier burst, showering them both with crystal shards. The figure crumpled forward into Darius' arms.

*Okay, what the hell is this?* Surely someone had heard the glass shattering. Darius shifted back and forth on his feet, looking around nervously. He stood there, just gaping at the unconscious form leaning limply against him. *Shit. This is not in the master plan!*

He stepped off of the platform and laid her gently on the floor. He backed away from her, again looking around nervously. He rubbed the back of his head. *Think, Darius!*

"Marcus," he whispered. "Marcus." He tried more urgently. He heard nothing in his earpiece. Not even static. Something must have interrupted the audio feed. He wondered if Marcus had seen any of this.

He also wondered if this was what his grandfather had meant when he said to get the Lady of Flame. Was that why he'd been so obsessed with finding her? Damn, but he wished he could ask Papa Shadi right now.

He knelt down next to her body and felt for a pulse. He felt no fluttering of life, yet her body felt soft. A dead body would be hard with rigor after thousands of years.

Before his better judgment opposed it, Darius tilted her head, pinched her nose, and covered her mouth with his. Despite the flames he had seen and felt, her lips were ice cold. He gave two quick breaths. Nothing. He pumped her chest, and blew in her mouth again.

* * *

*Oh, goddess. Help me.*

*The first tingling of reality brought fear. Sensations prickled nerve ends, zinging across old pathways to her brain. Moisture trickled through dry veins, bringing life to gray, dormant blood cells. The first pumps of a renewed heart sounded like thunder inside her head.*

*What was happening? She wanted to scream with the sheer terror of it. Her flesh burned icy hot as cool air caressed it for the first time in millennia. An excruciating pain flared in the center of her chest. It vibrated unmercifully, demanding something.*

*Something answered. A burst of pure energy radiated from her heart. The feeling brought relief and joy at first.*

*Voices. There were voices around her, but they had stopped. Where had they gone? Are they frightened of her? Did she look hideous? She felt hideous.*

*Oh, goddess. What has become of me?*

*She drifted, floating weightless in gray shadows. As if she were drowning, her lungs burned. Like a nightmare, she could not seem to call out for help.*

*A warm breath caressed her. Every cell in her body hummed. The dark veil of despair lifted. Shaila pushed aside her fears and called upon her astral spirit to return and guide her.*

* * *

Suddenly, the woman expelled a cloud of dust from her lungs. She choked and gulped in fresh air.

Wrinkles on her skin filled, becoming taut and firm once again. She glowed with a more natural tone. Her arms and legs rippled with goose bumps.

Darius put a gentle hand on her shoulder, and a low moan escaped her lips. Her breathing fell to a more natural rhythm.

Now that she was no longer hidden under a golden glaze, he saw that she wore only a hip belt. The leather was dyed to a dark shade of green. He could envision that at one time the white linen skirt had proudly held starched creases. Now, it limply clung to her, just long enough to cover what was necessary.

Time hadn't sagged her figure. Tiny lotus petals had been tattooed on the areolas around pert nipples. A sudden image of tracing the path of the tattoos with his tongue sprang to mind. A lower part of his body wanted to spring to life too. He iced that line of thought.

Still unconscious, she rolled over and curled into a fetal position. With her naked back facing him, Darius could see two long, straight scars running diagonally across her shoulder blades. The top end of each scar came within a couple of inches of joining at the nape of her neck, almost forming an arrow. Between the scars, a dark dragon tattoo curled around a quiver with seven arrows of red flame.

Papa Shadi had said to find her. That she would help him. Would she?

He was probably down to his last few minutes alone here. He needed to act, and he needed to act right now. He mentally sent his grandfather his apologies, but promised that he'd come get him very soon.

Darius tried to look inconspicuous as he made his way back to the ballroom. Within a couple of minutes, he was back in the gallery with a large rolling bin filled with old drop cloths. He lifted her up and into it, covering her body with the drop cloths.

Praying that the security system was still disabled, he slowly pushed the bin back across the length of the house. The workers were all completely engrossed in their tasks, and they seemed to take no notice of him. The mid-morning sun spilled into the back entrance. Darius pulled his shades out of his pants pocket and put them on. He joined a line of workers pushing their trash bins out into the back alley.

Instead of heading for the dumpster, Darius wheeled quickly down the long sidewalk toward his borrowed van. His loot still seemed to be unconscious, and he silently hoped that she'd stay that way for a while longer. He stole a glance under the sheet. At least the look of pain was gone from her face. Now, she looked almost peaceful.

He opened the side door of the van, and lifted her out of the bin. Darius winced when he bumped her head on the edge of the van door. Gingerly, he laid her down. He felt a bit sorry that the van he'd picked didn't have cleaner carpets, but that couldn't be helped. Pushing the bin away, he rounded the van and climbed into the driver's seat.

Again, pain gripped his heart. He hated the idea of leaving his grandfather behind. He knew Papa was there. Lilith had confirmed it. Shouts bellowed from inside the estate. Men poured out of the entrance, spurred by some commotion.

Darius was out of time, but he took a moment to look back at the woman on the floor. She would help him, or she'd make a great bargaining chip. Either way, he vowed he would get his grandfather back.

Just before turning out of the alley, Darius took one last glance in his rearview mirror. Therion was running out of the house. A roar of rage thundered across the cobblestones. Darius smiled broadly for the first time in days. After twenty years, life came full circle. Darius had finally taken something special away from his childhood bully.

A few blocks away from the Troy Estate, his earpiece buzzed faintly. He could hear Marcus' scratchy voice. "Dare? Can you hear me?"

"Tell me you saw all of that."

"All of what? Everything went black not long after you had to hide."

Darius drove the van across the new bridge over to Cambridge. "Meet me at the house just like we planned. I have to ditch this van first."

"Did you find Papa Shadi? Did you get him?"

"Well, no." Darius gulped down a lump of regret. He glanced at the reflection in the rearview mirror. Her unconscious form jostled limply with the motion of the van. "But I have a huge surprise for you, and it's better than any of those dusty old bones you like to dig up." *Way better.*

* * *

"Who did this, Mother?" Her son's anger bellowed through the halls. "I know you can see these things. Who stole her from me?"

Lilith stepped away from the path that Therion was quickly wearing into the floor with his pacing. "Calm yourself. Your anxiety is interrupting my —"

"Oh, cut the karma mojo crap!"

Flame burst bright and hot above her palm. She would go to the Underworld before taking such condescension from him. Therion halted his disruptive pacing.

Dousing the flame, she crossed the room and

pointed to the funerary boat display. "Here. He lay here, watching us." It was a man. The trail was weak, but not too weak for her to miss the feel of masculine energy.

"Who?" Shards of crystal crunched under his boots.

"I don't know."

"Why don't you know?"

"It's not someone I've ever met. He left a trace amount of energy here in this spot." For emphasis, she toed the area behind the boat. Dust clung to the tips of her sandals. "Negative energy. Anger. Hatred, maybe."

"If you can feel him, why can you not tell who it is?"

"I have tried. I cannot read his energy trail. It's gone." She shook her head. It aggravated her that she couldn't see the owner of such a virile energy stream. Another possibility occurred to her. "Or he has masked his trail."

"I will rip his heart out and feed it to the demons." Therion reached for a vase. Lilith barely grabbed his arm in time. He was worse than a bull in a china shop. He was an enraged bull with his sac cinched…in a china shop. This was not going well.

"I can't believe that nobody saw this man. In broad daylight, he just waltzes in and out with a large statue. Incredible."

"Or brilliant." Lilith rubbed up and down his arms, trying to soothe his agitated spirit. She needed him calm so she could think. "The chaos around here provided excellent cover. Hide in a large group. Everybody is too busy to notice details."

"Why would someone steal *her*?" He sneered. "I mean, look around. You have hundreds of items of much greater value and much easier to run off with." A wave of his hand indicated the wealth around them.

She knew he was right. However, of all the pieces in her collection, that statue was unique. It was all that was left of a special tomb discovered many years ago.

The thief's energy finally faded from the room. She shuddered with the chill it left behind. The warmth she'd felt before was born of old hatred. She believed that memories served to guide one's soul. She had bitter memories too.

Being born of a mother from a weaker bloodline had relegated Lilith to the position of being a handmaiden to Inanna, her beautiful half-sister who was the pride of their kind. Her birth had another curse to it. As the daughter of the Lady of the Underworld, she'd been a highly sought-after consort for information...and for pleasure. *Rutting pigs!*

No, she would not miss that statue. Its image of Inanna's daughter had been a constant reminder of where she came from. She hated those memories. Yet, they also served to keep her focused on finding the amulet that contained Therion's immortal spirit. The key to unlocking the powers he was born with. They had ripped the spirit from Therion's soul even before she'd given birth to him. All of it...was Inanna's fault.

*Hatred?* It was a powerful ally. A sustaining force. Lilith could think of none in this time that hated her. Since she'd been freed from her immortal prison more than thirty years ago, life in this new world had been wonderful. She had earned success and money, and best of all, the humans adored her.

She didn't understand why, but she knew the statue had been of significant value to Therion. He had earned many enemies in his lifetime, but none that would be connected to the statue.

Lilith sucked in a quick breath. "The old man's grandson."

"Darius? That makes no sense. If rumors are true,

he has the skills to do it. But, if he had gone through the trouble to sneak in here, he wouldn't have run off with a statue. The little thief would have been here to find the old man. Darius would never have left without him."

She didn't agree. The anger the thief had left behind felt almost violent. Male antagonism that she was now convinced was directed at her son.

At the mere mention of Darius Alexander, her son's aura would flare hot with malice. He hated Darius. She wondered if the feeling was mutual.

"It is an odd item to try to fence. Whoever has it may try the black market."

"I will know if they do." Lilith rejoined Therion by the empty platform. "There is no provenance for that statue. There is nothing to lead back to us." Which made her think again of the old man in a coma downstairs. She knew very little about Shadiki Aria, but he'd been asking a lot of unusual questions about her collection.

"Why would I care about that?"

Lilith rubbed her temples. Men could be so obtuse sometimes. She realized that he had no clue why it was so important to avoid entanglements with the Art Fraud Investigations department. She definitely wanted to remain off their radar screen, and especially now before the gala. She had too much to think about. A dull ache bloomed behind her eyes.

"Because it would destroy your political aspirations." She put her palms on his cheeks, but he brushed them aside.

"They are already destroyed, Mother. Those political bastards changed my fate the day they forced my retirement from the army. I will make them pay for that. I should be General by now. I am too young and too powerful to be a *retired* Colonel." He sucked in a deep breath, turned on his heel, and headed for the staircase.

Lilith followed him to the library. He went straight to the liquor cart and poured a double shot of brandy. She watched his aura simmer down to a calmer shade as the liquor drained from the glass. "I wonder how much about us that old man knows."

"Your powers have been quite useful these past few days, Mother."

She ignored the sarcasm. "Whatever the old man knows...maybe he shared with Darius." She deliberately stressed the name of his rival, and put on her most wicked of smiles. His aura burned red again as he slammed down his glass and refilled it.

"You know the prophecy, Therion."

"Hocus pocus, bull shit. I leave it all to you." He wrinkled his face from the spicy burn of the liquor. "You told me that the prophecy said that I, your son, will rise up and smite our enemies, bringing death and destruction to the world of humans. I would love to smite the leaders of the government for retiring me, but just because it was painted on a wall will not make it come true."

"Don't mock my powers, Therion."

"Your powers are weak, Mother! There is nothing left of your kind. Those that are here are as weak as humans."

"I'm not weak!"

"You are alone. Your kind is scattered and leaderless. Now, there is only man. Men need power, and those beneath the powerful...pray. They pray to whoever gives them hope! I am not weak. I do not need to pray to anyone for help. I *will* rise up, Mother, and take back that which I earned with my blood. I conquered the world for those bastards. I cleared away the terrorist camps, and what did I get in return? They put me to pasture. Oh, they softened the blow with a noble position in some useless department."

"It is not useless. I will help you."

"No offense, Mother. Your witch powers are fun, a real show stopper, and great for your own stardom. But I do not need your help."

"Do not dismiss my powers so easily. They have benefited you before. You begged for me to use them just moments ago." Lilith sucked in her breath suddenly and clutched at his arm. "Therion, what if it was--"

"One of your own kind?" He finished for her the question she could not speak aloud. She'd known there were others still here on Earth, but she didn't know who was left. Only in the darkest of nightmares did she experience the terror. She feared her own kind coming after her again. She wanted to live. She loved the adoration of the world, even if it was only from humans.

"What if it was meant to be a sign to me? A warning?" She brought her hand back to cover her mouth, lines of worry deepening on her face. "That would explain why that statue was the only item taken. The image of Inanna's daughter."

"I want revenge," Therion threw his glass into the cold fireplace, "on all of them. After all, it is my destiny." A wicked gleam glittered in his eyes.

"Time is running out, then. We must find that amulet and restore your powers." She tossed a flame from her hand into the fireplace, where it roared across the dried logs.

The cell phone buzzed against his hip, startling him. "You'd better be calling with good news." His voice whipped through the room. "Excellent. Stay put, and call me if he leaves." He snapped the phone shut. "Darius is home."

"Excellent, indeed. Why don't we summon him here?" She opened a desk drawer and pulled out a legal pad, her hand swirling around the paper quickly.

"You want to invite him over?" Therion held his temper in check, but he could not control the sarcasm in his voice. "For what? Tea? Will you seduce him to get the answers you seek?"

"Mind your fool tongue when you speak to me." The cell phone in his hand cracked in two. "It's simple. Keep your friends close, and your enemies closer."

His anger disappeared instantly, and he allowed her to plant a chaste but overlong kiss on his lips. "I have no intention of seducing your rival. I just want to toy with him. Find out what he knows. Possibly make a bargain with him."

"I did like that statue very much." For a moment, her son looked like a young boy who'd had his bicycle stolen. *Pathetic.*

"Forget the stupid statue. What I promise is to find that amulet and restore your powers." She smoothed back the hair dangling over his eyes. "We do want to rule the world, don't we?"

Yes. She saw it clearly in his dark eyes. He wanted to crush them all.

\* \* \*

Shaila awoke to an aroma of something so delicious her mouth watered. She shivered from the overload to her raw senses. A smooth blanket was snuggled around her, and she lay on something soft but cool. She heard two men talking very near, and her heart sang with joy because the sound was not dulled or muted. From inside the statue, she had already attuned to the new vibrational patterns of this language.

It was torture to refrain from jumping into the air and screaming that she was finally alive again. But she convinced her limbs to remain very still, for neither voice sounded familiar. *Where is my priest?*

"Pass me those fries? Thanks." The first voice was full of energy and curiosity. "Did you find what you were looking for?"

"I did. I found Papa's notes on the statue. It's written in Arabic, so give me a minute to translate his penmanship." The second voice was much deeper, rich with strength. "There are references to the 18th Dynasty and the reign of Smenkhkare. It's hard to read, but I think it says that she was there to protect something."

"Protect what? A pharaoh's tomb?" It was the first voice again. "Does it say anything about a woman inside the statue?"

They were speaking about *her*.

"Here is the page where he wrote down the prophecy. I know this by heart. He lectured me with it so many times." The second voice now sounded hollow with sadness and regret.

"Your grandfather's a brilliant man, Dare, and interesting. It takes men like him, who believe in three thousand year old prophecies, to make the biggest discoveries." She appreciated the respect in that voice.

She heard a rustling that she couldn't identify, but still she held her eyes tightly shut.

The second man cleared his throat. "Before the *Age of Awakening*, a commander of armies will rise up and smite those who govern. This descendant of Apophis will be the face of evil, resurrecting a dark army and defiling the world. The sickness of evil will bring hopelessness and despair. But a light shines from the Heavens. We send a gift to man. A protector and a deliverer to smite the evil of chaos and restore the order of peace. Entombed to sleep through the ages and awaken when the evil conqueror sinks fangs into men. We pray to the gods to protect this tomb and deliver this gift to the world."

Moisture gathered in the corners of her eyes. She could have recited that from memory too. She knew the truth of those words. She helped write that prophecy. She had sent that gift. How long ago did the first voice say? Over three thousand sun cycles? It had felt like an eternity.

*Goddess, what smells so good?* She could not wait any longer. The evidence of her hunger drooled from her lips. She struggled to open her eyelids. Thousands of years nearly glued them together. Finally, they parted slightly. She winced as light lanced painfully into her eyes.

From underneath her lashes, she had a good view of the two men. They sat on the opposite side of a short table from her. She spotted what possibly was the source of the aroma. Little yellow sticks, which they fished out of a small red box made of...papyrus?

"Do you think she's really an ancient goddess?"

A shrill sound buzzed through the room, vibrating her bones and jarring her fully awake. Shocked, her heart nearly pounded out of her chest. Furious energy pieced through her veins with white-hot pain.

A growl began deep in her throat as fear launched her over the back of the long chair. An old familiar sensation tugged at the roof of her mouth. Like a lioness, she rumbled a threat between clenched teeth, which now included two thin, shiny fangs. Her chest pumped furiously as she tried to catch her breath. She prepared to pounce on anyone stupid enough to wander too close.

Her eyes darted back and forth between the two

men. The shorter of the two, with dark hair, had a shocked expression on his face. He was staring at her teeth. She lifted her upper lip, revealing a bit more of her sharp fangs. Power sang through her blood as he quickly retreated a few steps.

The other man, tall and shaven, seemed unaffected by her threats. In fact, the look in his eyes dared hers to look away from *him*. She bristled at the challenge. A sparkle of light caught her attention. Her eyes fixed on the medallion hung around his neck. It was her turn to be shocked. She sensed no power in his spirit. *Who is this human who carries an Eye of Ra?*

Again the high-pitched sound rang through the air. Cocking her head to one side, she decided that the noise was coming from a brown box hanging over a doorway.

The dark-haired man now stared at her body paint. He looked away sheepishly when the tall one cleared his throat. The irritating noise buzzed insistently a third time.

"I think I'd better get that. They don't appear to be going away."

"What? You're not going to leave me here with...her?" The dark one whispered. "What do I do with her?"

"Clothes would be a great start. Find something that will cover her up." The tall one gestured towards her bare chest. He looked square into her eyes. "You. Stay." He pointed to the long chair before striding out of the room.

She glared at his retreating back. No human had ever dared to talk to her in such a manner. It was she who commanded them, not the other way around.

She did not move while the men were gone. She just looked. Much time had gone by, as nothing around her looked normal. She knew not where *here* was or if she had reached the right time.

*My knife!* Suddenly, she felt around her waist. Her knife was gone. The adrenaline that had flown through her and given energy to her body now ebbed away. The fangs recoiled into their sheath. Then, her knees buckled under her own weight. She sank limply to the floor.

Shaila mentally cursed her body for its weakness. Her cheeks burned with embarrassment that she had to rely on the tall one to return and assist her. He lifted her up with muscles unfettered by the bondage of time. She hated this feeling of feebleness, as he carried her in his strong arms. Jealousy prickled her spirit.

He arranged her on the long chair next to the little table. The savory aroma tempted her again. Her eyes locked on the little sticks poking out of the red papyrus. Unconsciously, she licked her lips. Suddenly, the sticks were right in front of her face.

"French fries."

She looked up into warm gold-brown eyes. If not for the temptation so close to her mouth, she would have studied his eyes a bit more deeply. Instead, she slowly placed one stick on her tongue. She had no idea what it was, but it was divine. She could not get the rest into her mouth fast enough.

Shaila ignored the laughter. She wanted more. But the man just shook his head and had an apologetic look on his face. Leaning forward, she grabbed every piece of papyrus on the table. She growled with frustration at finding them all empty.

She was about to lick the salt off the red papyrus when the dark one came back. He carried a shiny black cloth. As he draped the long robe around her shoulders, a faint scent tickled her nose. The robe smelled like smoked apples.

The tall one held a flat papyrus in his hand, and

paced back and forth. He kept looking at her with a questioning look. She could see his energy aura was strong and cunning, but it was also restless. She detected pain as well. She already knew from his order and his stance that he was commanding as well, like a pharaoh. Shaila understood human kings, having worked with many of them.

"Are--" She coughed, a small cloud of dust came up from her lungs. She had heard and felt the rhythms of conversation for so long, she knew basically what was being said around her. But the effort of speaking felt raw on her throat. "Are you pharaoh?"

He finally stopped pacing and laughed. "Me? No. My name is Darius Alexander. And this is Marcus Damato." He point to the dark-haired man.

"Darius. Marcus." Her voice croaked. She mentally focused on healing the rawness in her throat. "Strong names."

"You speak English?" The tall one seemed pleased.

She scrunched her nose and nodded her head slightly. She stood up, tall and proud like a warrior. "I am Shaila a'k'Hemet."

The dark-haired one, Marcus, looked down at the papyrus spread across the table. "I thought you were the goddess Sekhmet?"

She smirked with distaste at the pronunciation. "Humans found that better to say."

"But you were an Egyptian goddess?" Marcus had much curiosity in him. She liked that.

She shrugged. "I am Anunnaki."

The tall one, Darius, seemed unimpressed. In fact, he went back to his pacing, reading the papyrus he held in his hands. Had this human really just dismissed her so casually?

"They also called me the *Mistress of Dread* and the

*Lady of Slaughter*." She tilted her head higher. The movement caused her robe to slip from one shoulder. He did stop his pacing to look at her, but amusement sparkled in his eyes instead of homage. Shaila seethed.

"Yes, and they also said that the hot desert winds were like your breath. Pleasant description, don't you think?"

She nearly exploded with the indignity. This human who admitted that he was not the pharaoh needed a lesson in manners. Gathering a small bundle of energy, she mentally pushed it toward the man. It was not large enough to throw him against a wall, but it was enough to knock him back on his heels.

"Do you mock me? Do you know who I am? I am descended of the Great Dragon Queen. I carry the bloodline of succession." Now they were getting somewhere. His eyes had changed to surprise and...distrust. This warranted a deeper look. "Have you lost your sense of honor to your gods?"

"Not *our* gods, honey. Humans stopped believing in your divinity a couple thousand years ago." He moved toward her until his face was inches from hers. "You've been replaced."

This time, she saw in detail the golden flecks in his brown eyes. Through their dark centers, she could see into his soul. His aura, the energy trail around him, was strong but enveloped with the pain of loss. Darius jerked the robe back over her shoulder.

"Replaced?" She wondered what exactly he meant by that. What had happened to her kind? What would that mean for her? For the prophecy? Where was her priest? More importantly...where was the child?

Shaila was filled with questions, but she could not be certain of how much should she reveal to these men. Darius wore the *Eye of Ra*, but that did not mean he would be an ally. He would not be an easy human to control, and she wished that he would step back a bit. She felt more constricted than when she stood entombed in the statue.

"Where am I?"

Darius remained too close. She knew his intention was to show his dominance.

"Boston. You're a long way from home. Egypt is almost on the other side of the Earth."

Shaila mentally called out to her astral spirit, but it would not answer her. Without it, she could not flash herself to Egypt and be about her business. She was stuck here. "Who is pharaoh of Buston? I must speak with him."

She stepped away from Darius, intent on leaving their dwelling, but the man would not let her pass.

"The pharaohs are long dead, Shaila. Leaving this house would be a very bad idea right now. And whatever you just did a moment ago..." He moved in even closer, until his nose nearly touched her own. "Don't you ever do that to me again."

She should have felt insulted with the impudent human. No man had ever dared to speak to her this way. Instead, her heart thumped a beat more quickly, and a spark of something hot flickered across her skin. She inhaled his scent. The warrior in her smelled a challenge.

She advanced on him with her full arsenal, the kind every female is born with.

"Darius." Shaila put her palm on his chest, and with a gentle pressure she felt the tensing and flexing of his muscles. Capturing his eyes, she leaned in so closely that his breath mingled with hers. For a moment, she thought about his lips. Just a kiss. What would he taste like? "No one commands me."

*Oh, Goddess.* His skin was so close. She could feel

the heat through his shirt. Blood pulsed more quickly through his heart, and she felt the lure of its hypnotic rhythm. What would his skin feel like? There was one enticing way she could show him who was in command.

Marcus cleared his throat, interrupting the intimate battle she'd intended to wage.

Darius glared at her. "Did you like being in that statue? Maybe I should just put you back where I found you. Let Lilith deal with you."

*It could not be! Could it?* Shaila stiffened. Destiny could not have brought her all this way into the future to drop her at the feet of that witch!

"What do you mean...let Lilith deal with me? Who is this Lilith?"

"Apparently, she's one of your Anunnaki friends." His words dripped with malice. "Maybe you should go back and help her command that little demon army of hers."

"Lilith is not my *friend.*" She completely understood why someone could hate Lilith. She wondered if he hated all of her kind this way. She never cared what others thought of her before...human or otherwise. With Lilith nearby, she desperately cared about finding the child and her missing knife. "She is my enemy."

He grabbed her by the shoulders and yanked her close. "Good. I left my grandfather behind because of you. You'd better be worth it."

# CHAPTER FOUR

Wind whipped across the Charles River, finally carrying the first fall crispness with it. Heavy gray clouds spewed inland, driven by a nor'easter supposedly brewing over the Grand Banks. Darius closed his eyes and inhaled deeply of the briny air, drawing strength from it.

He trusted his grandfather. But the lady of the flaming ego better live up to her reputation, because he wasn't going to endure her kind of aggravation for nothing. Thankfully, Marcus had agreed to stay and keep an eye on Shaila, while Darius responded in person to Lilith's invitation for a little chat.

Turning away from the river, he faced the front entrance of the Troy Estate. Fear and rage swirled inside him like a great ocean storm. Sneaking in was easy. Entering the massive estate invited felt like a monumental task. His heart pounded with each knock on the door.

A young blond man with unusually gray skin opened the door and pointed Darius toward the gallery. For the second time today, he stepped into Lilith Troy's private gallery.

Taking a more detailed observation of the antique collection, Darius found one room dedicated to Mark Antony. His likeness was everywhere: in portraits, on busts. A life-sized statue of the Roman general stood defiantly in the center of the room. Even on a short platform, the alabaster figure only came up to about Darius' eyes. He studied the features carved thousands of years ago. Something about the chin didn't instill a feeling of power. Opportunist, possibly. Politician, definitely.

Darius moved silently through the next room, an eerie feeling shivering down his spine. Ancient weapons hung everywhere: long spatha swords, pila, thrusting spears, and even a few items that looked like instruments of torture. Another display showcased a stunning Roman gladius. The dagger looked wickedly authentic, its hilt encrusted with gold and bone.

A plain sword hung on the wall above the dagger. It looked out of place in this room full of gilded and bejeweled weapons. The steel blade had long ago oxidized to a silver blue haze. The hilt might have been made of a precious metal, but he couldn't tell which one. It was wrapped tightly with brown leather straps which looked fairly new.

The security camera silently tracked him. He shouldn't touch anything, but he reached out anyway, feeling the cold timeworn edges. The ancient weapon felt warm and strong. A smile curved his lips. The blade was still amazingly sharp, leaving a tiny cut on the tip of his forefinger. He put pressure on the nick for a few moments until the small blood droplets stopped oozing.

Focusing again on the hilt, Darius wondered if the shape of it resembled the outline of a winged disk. A ruby could lie underneath the leather wrapping. It looked a lot like the sword in the photo Mr. Artie had given them. It seemed too modest to be a sword of power, but even Indiana Jones recognized that the power of the Grail was not in precious metals or jewels.

"Farvadin." Darius whispered the word into the quiet room. Well, what the hell did he expect? Did he think it would glow or rise up in the air or something?

Was it really that crazy? His grandfather had searched his whole life for a statue that ended up only a few miles away. *That* was crazy.

Darius hesitated to enter the next room. From the doorway, he quietly relived the moment he'd first seen Shaila. Like a fierce sentinel, she'd stood entombed in golden splendor for eternity. Now, all that remained was a dusty granite platform.

She'd said she was Anunnaki. If he hadn't already heard the legends of the alien race from his grandfather, he would have known of them through the ancient Summerian artifacts he'd studied in the past. The word literally meant *those who from the heavens came.*

His life would be a lot easier if they had just stayed out there in the heavens.

"Good afternoon, *little* Darius."

The room turned dark, as pure hatred clouded his vision. The voice echoed across the room from the shadow of the staircase. It was deeper now, but still recognizable as the one that haunted his darkest nightmares from childhood. A nightmare he could never seem to outgrow. Darius reined in his anger and tried to quell the lurching in his stomach.

"As you can see, Therion," Darius felt his teeth grind on each word, "I'm not so little anymore."

*Damn.* He was already being sucked into Therion's head games. Time to regain the upper hand. Darius hooked his thumb over his belt, the silver buckle resting coolly against his palm. His fingers ached to free the two throwing knives hidden inside it and bury them deep in Therion's dark eyes. Instead, he strode across the room straight toward his enemy.

Therion was every bit as tall and muscular as rumors had said. Darius smiled inwardly, thinking that fate had apparently evened the score in that department. He now stood eye-to-eye with his enemy. What Therion had in bulk and brawn, Darius was certain he could make up for in agility in outmaneuvering the big man.

"You're looking pretty fit for a *retired* colonel." He looked like He-Man in a Hugo Boss. "I love what you've done with your hair. All those cute golden spikes. The messy look is still in. Maybe you could go into acting, now that you have all this free time."

"Still the same snide little wimp." Therion sneered, revealing perfect teeth framed by that perfect face. "Careful, your jealousy is showing. Sorry for your loss." Therion's eyes trailed slowly across Darius' head.

When he was growing up on the streets, nobody ever told him to cut his hair. His long ponytail had turned into a perfect tool for Therion's gang to implement pain. After moving in with Papa Shadi, he'd shaved it all off as a break with his past. It never grew back.

He squashed an impulse to rub Papa Shadi's medallion for strength. Instead, he turned away from Therion dismissively, feigning interest in the solar boat display. He could feel the big man's eyes watching him.

"I want her back. Now!" Even with a deep voice, Therion sounded like a petulant child.

Darius turned to face his accuser, noting the ill-concealed disgust in those black eyes. "Her?"

"You know damn well." Therion closed the space between them in seconds. "Bring me back my statue. She's mine!"

Before Therion could get too close, Darius grabbed the big man by the throat with one hand, holding him at arm's length. He held his other palm up, ready to strike if necessary. He felt blood pulsing furiously underneath Therion's skin. Gritting his teeth with the effort, Darius nearly roared from the rush of adrenaline. "You would do well to keep your distance."

Light glittered off of something around Therion's neck. Darius reached for it, drawing it out from under the silk shirt. At the end of a gold box chain hung a blue lapis lazuli bead. His stomach lurched, sick with the sudden onslaught of memories. He could almost feel the bruises again from the beating he'd suffered from Therion's gang over twenty years ago.

Therion's throat vibrated with laughter. "I hope you like it. I wore today just for you, in honor of your visit."

Darius tightened his grip. Distracted by the necklace, he wasn't prepared when the strange gray doorman suddenly tackled him to the floor.

"What is it with these things?" He fanned the air in front of his nose. "What the hell do you feed your pets, Therion?"

"You're still on my playground, Darius."

He mentally dared Therion to come a little bit closer, but the man just smirked from a distance. *Oh the hell with it!*

Scrambling from underneath the demon, Darius flipped it into the boat display. Dusty, splintered planks collapsed around it. A second demon grunted loudly as it launched itself from the shadows across the room. Flicking a quick release button on the belt buckle, Darius slipped a small throwing knife into his palm. Spinning, he used the momentum to toss the shiny blade at this newest attacker. It hummed through the air and sliced easily into the demon's forehead.

"And I see you still let others do your dirty work for you." The demon writhed on the floor, a silent scream frozen on its lips. Bursting into a blue flame, it slowly disappeared. Darius aimed a second knife right between Therion's eyes. In his other hand, he held up the handwritten note. "Would that include your mother?"

Finally, he'd struck a nerve. Black eyes flared at him with angry defiance. Even the fancy suit couldn't conceal the flexing of muscles as Therion's body tensed. Darius lowered the knife, but kept his body loose and ready.

"You know, Therion, every bully has a weakness. What's yours?" A smile tugged at the corners of his mouth. "Hmmm. You know I'll find it. That's what I do. I find things...and I always find what I'm looking for."

\* \* \*

"Well, well, well. What a divine example of human masculinity." Lilith Troy stood at the bottom of the spiral staircase, posed as seductively as she did on every poster of her around the world.

*Innocent* did not seem to be the look she was striving for. Black silk crisscrossed over her chest to hang sleekly over her shoulders. More black silk clung to her hips and flared down to the floor. A gold leaf diadem pushed her hair back away from her face, but she'd pulled half of the blonde waves forward over her body. The ends curled around her bare midriff.

Darius suddenly felt like prey, locked by an intense tawny gaze. He'd heard that she had that effect on men. He'd discounted it...until now. She looked divine and dangerous.

He couldn't help but think of the statue of Mark Antony in the other room. Men rarely stood a chance when faced with a woman who understood the power of her own beauty. He knew instantly that Lilith Troy would be exactly that type of woman. A type he would be wise to avoid.

Feeling Therion move in his direction, Darius re-aimed his knife. He would not be caught off guard again.

"Enough!" A display case next to Therion shattered. Tiny pieces of glass skittered across the bare floor. The big man halted mid-step and turned his glare toward his mother.

That was the second time Darius watched glass explode along with Lilith's temper. "You must go through a lot of glass." Therion momentarily gave him a *you-have-no-idea look*, before moving slowly toward the golden beauty.

"Thank you for welcoming our guest." Lilith kissed her son on the cheek, but her voice dripped with sarcasm. "Leave us. You have things to do." She moved past him dismissively. Darius did not miss the contempt that momentarily passed across Therion's face before he left the room.

"It was you." Lilith nodded her head toward the empty platform. "Your energy is unmistakable to me now. Such angry, masculine energy, Darius Alexander." Closing her eyes, she drew in a deep breath as if savoring the aroma of a fine wine.

He was surprised to see his first knife floating in the air, gliding gently back to him from across the room. She was demonstrating more of her power. He slid both knives back into his belt buckle.

The sound of them coldly clicking back into place seemed to snap her out of her reverie. "Come with me."

"Why?" He wasn't going any deeper into this house until he knew what was going on.

"My dear, it was not a request." A warm pressure surrounded his throat, invisibly squeezing his airway.

There was nothing he could grab to relieve the pressure, so he waited for her to release him. "We have business to discuss."

She climbed the staircase without looking back, swaying her hips in a manner to draw maximum attention. Slowly, the pressure around his neck subsided. Rubbing his throat, Darius cautiously followed her up the staircase to the residence level.

Blood red was the prevailing color in Lilith's sitting room. Beyond that, the most notable feature was a huge fireplace, large enough for him to stand in.

"Thank you for coming. Please make yourself comfortable." She arranged herself across a crimson sofa, accented with brown and gold pillows. She patted an empty space next to hers.

"As you said, it was not a request." Darius ignored the invitation and pulled an envelope out of his back pocket. As he tossed it on the coffee table, the photo she'd sent him of his grandfather slid halfway out. Darius hoped his disgust showed plainly on his face. "Your message was quite clear."

"Sit. Sit down. Gods, but you really are delicious looking, especially when you're angry." She leisurely surveyed every inch of his body. "I would enjoy bending you to my will, but I did promise my son that I would not seduce you...today."

Darius was not in a hurry to test Lilith's resolve to keep that promise. He sat across from her, keeping the coffee table between them. The demon doorman appeared again, but this time he brought a tray of drinks. The demon's hands trembled, causing the drinks to slosh over the edge of the glasses. After dropping the tray on the table, the gray man nearly sprinted out of the room.

"Why haven't we met before, Darius? We both operate in the darker side of antiquities."

"I'm not a social butterfly. Where's my grandfather?"

"I think most collectors are afraid of you." She eyed him over the rim of her wine glass. "Of your reputation, which is quite impressive. One of Boston's finest young pickpockets grows up to become one of the best antiquities trackers in the world."

"The Egyptian government is one of our best clients. They would be highly interested in your collection."

"They love you. Yet, here in your own country, they don't trust you. The authorities still question you each time precious art or artifacts are stolen. I know what it's like to be falsely accused and imprisoned...by your own people." She tipped a healthy portion of the deep red wine into her mouth. She caught a stray drop with her tongue at the corner of her mouth.

Darius shifted uncomfortably. "Ms. Troy—"

"Please relax. Have a beer. It's your favorite."

"How do you know what I drink?" He wasn't about to taste anything in this house. He couldn't trust what might have been added.

"I Googled you." She drew her finger around the rim of her glass. "You have left a few broken hearts behind. Women blog." She smiled, as if there was a lot more to tell but wouldn't.

"You didn't bring me here to discuss my social life. Where's my grandfather, and why did you take him?"

"Fine. We will get down to business, but I will do the asking, and you will do the answering. Let's start with...why did you take that statue? What do you know of it?"

"I ran out of time looking for my grandfather. It wasn't hard to overhear your conversation or pick up on Therion's possessiveness of the statue. It's obviously a unique piece of artwork. Very valuable."

"How wicked of you. Vindictive and clever. You get a bargaining chip and revenge all wrapped in one beautiful package. But there is a flaw in your plan."

She didn't know the half of it. Talk about flaws. He didn't even have a statue at all. He had a stubborn goddess to contend with. "What would that flaw be?"

"I'm in charge here, not Therion. I don't care about that statue. So it's fairly useless as a bargaining chip. But take heart. You still have your little revenge on my son."

"Then, it seems as if we have nothing to discuss." He stood up to leave.

"On the contrary, we have much more to discuss. Sit down. You will tell me everything you and your grandfather know." A small note of desperation entered her voice.

"You'll need to be more specific."

"Then, let's just start with me. What do you know about me?"

"Up until yesterday, I knew practically nothing about you...or your kind. My grandfather believes in an old Egyptian prophecy."

"And you don't?" Her finely tweezed brows lifted in mock surprise.

He shook his head. "Not until three of your little demon friends jumped us. Now, where is my grandfather?"

"I said...*I* will do the asking. You will see your grandfather soon enough. What else did he tell you about us?"

"That you like the color red." He ignored her gestured invitation to sit beside her and moved to stand in front of the fireplace.

"Don't be coy with me." She pointed a dark fingernail in his direction.

"He told me that you desire to be some immortal queen."

The curls in her hair jiggled with her laughter. "Yes. I do desire to be queen."

"And to rule the world with your demon army."

"What do I care about an army? They are just a means to an end." She tossed her hand in the air flippantly.

"So that's what the mighty Colonel Therion Troy is for...to run your demon army, to smite your enemies. That's the prophecy, right? How long can you keep your son on a leash? He will outgrow his mother."

"Therion will not disappoint me. I've given him everything. He cherishes me." She swayed to the fireplace, swinging her wine glass around with her. He wondered if she was short for a goddess. The top of her head barely reached his chin. She looked up at him with large tawny eyes, which locked with his.

He couldn't look away, entranced as bronze-colored flecks started glowing. The air around him crackled, and it wasn't the fireplace.

"What would it feel like to be cherished by you?"

"You wouldn't want to mingle with a lowly human. You want to destroy us." Feeling trapped, he wanted to step away, but the air seemed to hold him captive. The glowing eyes commanded his gaze.

"Gods, no. I don't want to destroy humans, but you were meant to serve my kind. In the beginning, you worshipped us." She picked up his hands, inspecting them like a prized artifact. "Oh, Darius. To be worshiped by hands such as yours."

"Ms. Troy..."

"Shhh." She placed his hands on her hips and leaned into him. "Please call me Lilith. I'd love to hear my name from those divine lips."

A bead of sweat tickled down his back. He realized he was fighting something in the air. It felt like an emotional battle for mental survival. For control of his mind and body. His body was losing.

Heat from the medallion under his shirt and a sudden image of exotic green eyes broke the spell. His mind took full control.

"Ms. Troy, I want to see my grandfather now."

"Kiss me, first." Crimson lips parted, inviting him to explore, and then snapped shut in a tense line as she realized the spell had broken.

"Like hell."

"I grew up there. Not a happy place. I can arrange a visit for you, if you'd like." Sneering laughter filled the dark room.

"Where's my grandfather?"

"Darius, I wouldn't be this obstinate if I were you. Very sad that a strong man like you is so lonely. So empty. No, don't look at me like that. This isn't pity. My son tormented you as a boy, and I'm his mother. You can hate me too, but that won't help your grandfather."

"Don't bother to threaten me. I don't respond to threats."

"I don't want to threaten you. You have a particular set of skills, as you so aptly informed Therion. I need someone with your abilities on my team."

"I'm not much of a team player."

Lilith glared at him before moving towards a tall mirror leaning in the corner.

"Come. I will show you your grandfather, so you'll know that I honor my word."

She touched the mirror with a red-polished fingernail. The scene that played on the mirror showed Papa Shadi lying on a stone table. No blankets covered him. No monitors checked him. Darius felt blood rush to his face, suffusing him with outrage.

"You--"

"Did you think I was going to actually take you to him? Show you the way? I'm not going to make it that easy for you."

"Is he...?" He wanted to put his hands around her neck and shake that golden head of hers.

"He seems to be in a coma, but I am told that he is otherwise doing just fine."

"He should be in a hospital."

"I have a doctor taking care of him, but I will make him more comfortable. Now, I've kept my promise. You've *seen* your grandfather. It's your turn."

He didn't need his palm to itch to remind him that he was in a bad situation. His grandfather's exact whereabouts were still a mystery. The statue apparently held no bargaining value. There was no choice left to him but to find out what she wanted. That part worried him the most.

"What do you need me to find?"

"An amulet."

"What do you need this amulet for?" He nearly collapsed with relief. He'd feared what skills she'd been referring to.

"Does it matter...if it saves your grandfather? I bet you've never questioned your grandfather's reasons for sending you to collect certain artifacts."

"No, I didn't. But he wasn't holding a life hostage in exchange for my services. I would like to know all the stakes in this little game you are manipulating. Everything you can tell me about the amulet would help me to find it."

"It's an uncut black diamond with a gold Eye of Ra symbol inlaid. No larger than my thumb." She held out her hand as if to illustrate the size. "It belongs to me."

"When did you lose it?"

"It was taken from me." This time she glowered with bitterness, and she hissed. "Inanna took it. My conniving, backstabbing half-sister. I'd thought she'd given it to her daughter to guard. But that didn't seem to be the case."

"When was it taken from you?"

"By your calendar, it was right before the reign of Tutankamun."

His draw dropped slightly. A short burst of hysterical laughter tumbled out. One three-thousand-year-old woman was enough to deal with. Now, he had two.

"You're..." He cleared his throat and collected his thoughts. "How am I supposed to find something you lost over three thousand years ago? It could be buried in the sand. Is there any way of tracking its ownership? Give me something to start with."

"Start with your grandfather. He was looking for it too. He was asking the Customs director if I was looking for the amulet. He'd been sniffing around my private collection for years. He was curious about that statue too. When you bring me the amulet, he can study your new statue to his heart's content." She moved in close again.

Lilith's voice dropped to a husky plea. "Help me, Darius. Help me find my amulet, and I will release your grandfather to you unharmed." Her palms rubbed across his chest and up his neck. They paused over his temples, massaging them lightly.

A strange warmth infused his body. For a moment, the crimson lips pouting a few inches from his looked inviting. He licked his own dry lips.

"I just might have to break that promise to my son," she whispered.

"Stop." The warmth drained from his body, leaving him numb. He tried to disengage from her.

Too late. An arm snaked around his neck and a leg hooked around his knees. Catching him off balance, she rolled them both down to a black shag carpet. Straddling his thighs, she again rubbed her hands across his chest, moaning his name.

How could he possibly think about refusing an opportunity of sex? This wasn't just any woman. She'd been one of the most famous lingerie models. She'd been the star of millions of wet dreams. She was hot, and she wanted *him*.

But sleep with the woman holding his grandfather hostage? It wouldn't be worth the sense of betrayal that would poison his gut.

"Stop--" He tasted desperation from her lips as they crushed against his. "Stop."

He lifted her off of him, knowing that a soft rejection was needed to avoid a woman's scorn, especially this woman. He wasn't ready to find out what her other powers might be.

"Why do you not give in to me?" She seemed more confused than angry.

"Maybe another time, Ms. Troy."

"If you call me Ms. Troy again, I'll fry you on the spot." Now she sounded piqued. "I wait for no man."

His palm itched. She was undoubtedly holding back a lot of information, but he wasn't going to stick around any longer to pry it out of her. Darius quickly retreated to the staircase, but hesitated before leaving. "Is there anything else I need to know about that amulet?"

"Yes, there is." An envelope lifted off of a desk and sailed through the air.

Darius grabbed it before it sliced into his nose. "What's this?"

"Your deadline."

Ripping it open, he slid out a cream-colored card. It was an invitation to her gala event...a masquerade. "But this is in two days!"

"Precisely." A wicked gleam lit her tawny eyes. She was like a falcon, reaching out her talons to grip her prey. "And I can't wait to see you in your costume."

He nearly tripped down the staircase in his haste to leave the Troy Estate. He didn't know much more about his grandfather, but he had learned something that could work to his advantage. Neither one of the Troys had any clue that their statue had its own secret. That damned stubborn goddess could still turn out to be useful after all.

# CHAPTER FIVE

Darius stumbled through the kitchen door, relieved to be in his own house. Here he was safe from the possessive talons of that woman. Instantly, his mouth watered as the scent of fresh basil wafted past his nose.

"Hey, Dare. How'd it go with the old dragon lady?" Marcus slid a plate of garlic toast in front of Shaila. She devoured it. "I made a plate for you. It's wrapped up in the fridge."

"What's going on?" The kitchen was a mess, but it smelled fantastic. "Mmm. It smells just like your mother's kitchen in here. Where did all this food come from?"

"Oh, well, our little warrior here hasn't eaten in over three thousand years. She's starving." He looked a little sheepish. "So we went to the market."

"The market? You mean you took her out in public?" He took a good look at her. She didn't look half bad in an oversized football jersey and grey sweatpants.

"Kinda. Come on, it's no big deal. We just went to my uncle's market in the North End. Got a few things and came back. Nothing out of the ordinary happened...mostly."

"What do you mean *mostly*?"

"Shaila does *not* like the subway system. She doesn't like cold, dark places."

"No, I do not!" She ate like a warrior, heedless of manners. She sucked the tomato sauce from each finger, sighing with pure contentment. "This is delicious, Marcus. It is heavenly."

Marcus elbowed Darius. "A goddess has described my cooking as heavenly. I don't think there's a better compliment in the world. I think she likes me. I keep telling you, cooking is like making love to one's soul."

"You keep telling me a lot of things." He wanted to wipe that stupid grin off of Marcus' face.

"Sorry, gotta go. My shift at the museum starts in a few hours, and I need some sleep. Whatever your next plan is, count me in." Marcus made Shaila stand up and grip his right hand with hers. "This is how we say goodbye to our friends."

Darius rolled his eyes. Shaila grabbed Marcus by the face and planted a quick kiss on both cheeks. "That is how we say goodbye."

"I like your way much better." Marcus winked at her and left.

Darius hated that he felt uncomfortable in his own home. What the hell was he supposed to do with her now? Marcus was much more at ease with her.

A terrible rumbling sounded from her direction, followed by a pained expression across her face.

"Bathhouse?" She asked sheepishly.

"Oh, no." He dashed to the door, but Marcus was already gone.

* * *

Darius should have known she'd be trouble the moment her large green eyes lit up when she spied the huge tub in Papa Shadi's bathroom. She'd begun praising some goddess and mumbling excitedly in the most unusual language he'd ever heard. After all, what else would a woman want after being trapped in a dusty statue for three thousand years?

He hovered in the hallway, telling himself that he was just making sure that she didn't slip and crack her head on the tub. He valiantly tried to ignore the sighs and moans above the hum of the spa jets. She was apparently doing just fine.

As time passed and water kept running, he realized Shaila did not know that she was supposed to turn off the faucet. As he approached bathroom door, he felt the hallway carpet squish under his feet. *Shit.*

She didn't answer when he knocked on the door. He rubbed the back of his head and his jaw clenched with indecision. It had to be done now, before she flooded the whole house. He slowly peered around the door.

"Shaila, the faucet!" She still did not answer him. It looked like she was underwater. Darius rushed over and shut off the faucet. The spa jets continued tossing water and bubbles into frantic little whirlpools. He pulled out a large pile of towels and threw them onto the floor to soak up the wet mess. She was still oblivious to him, submerged with only her knees showing above the bubbles. "Shaila!"

Again, she wasn't coming up to answer him. The water needed to stop sloshing, before it started soaking the hallway and ruining the floorboards. He unclipped his cell phone and left it where it wouldn't get wet. Feeling around the edge of the tub for the spa jet button, his hand lightly brushed her shoulder.

He was completely unprepared for her defensive response. In one swift move, she'd grabbed and flipped him into the tub underneath her. She held him in place with her hand cupped around his throat.

He thanked god for the water in the tub, because otherwise that flip would have really hurt. Trapped underneath the ancient warrior goddess, he couldn't help but notice again that she was ripped. Golden skin, taut in all the right areas. Bubbles slowly dripped off of her breasts, revealing her lotus tattoos. With the centuries of dust scrubbed away, Shaila glowed. The scent of musky soap filled the air. Her dark hair dripped rivulets of water down her shoulders.

*Damn.* He couldn't help himself. A slight groan escaped his lips. This tough, green-eyed woman excited him.

Deep in meditation underwater, she hadn't heard Darius's approach. When he touched her so unexpectedly, her whole body reacted instinctively. She caught Darius around his midsection and flipped him into the tub. The movements sloshed a wave of water onto a group of towels strewn around the floor.

Her eyes focused on the room around her and understanding dawned. "I am so sorry, Darius." She withdrew her hand from his throat.

He did not seem to be angry. The heat sparking in his hazel eyes reminded her that here was something else she had not felt in over three thousand sun cycles. Desire. It zinged through her body, firing off nerve endings that now craved to be touched. She craved skin. She leaned into Darius, seeking the feel of flesh again. She had felt only cold metal for so long.

Shaila lowered her body against him and rubbed slowly up and down. The water swirled in gentle waves around them.

Still, the man would not release his fierce grip on the edge of the tub. His pulse beat quickly at the base of his neck, and a moan escaped his lips. His eyes even dilated with excitement. She wondered why, if he was this stirred by her touch, he held himself so rigid. Maybe he just needed a bit more encouragement.

Slowly, she lowered her lips to his, feeling the softness of them. Finally she felt his muscles relax. His hands felt strong and commanding as he pulled her in for a crushing kiss. He tasted of life, warm and sweet. Rubbing a path down her back, his hands massaged every inch he could reach. The feel of skin on skin felt divine as he pressed her hard against him. *Oh goddess!*

His tongue explored her lips and entered her mouth. She teased it with little nibbles, and then sucked the pain away. Her hands explored downward between their bodies but rough, wet clothing impeded her exploration. Shaila growled her frustration.

*Holy shit!* Desire hummed in his ears so loudly, he'd almost passed out. Every muscle trembled, and that scared him. He couldn't remember ever experiencing such an intense craving as this. His rational mind finally broke through the fuzziness in his brain. Control. He needed to get control of himself before he did something stupid. *Like, screw a hot warrior goddess?*

What a lame excuse for a man. Two gorgeous women in one day, and he was about to put the brakes on the second one. He was so damned to hell.

"Shaila." He gently slid her off of him to one side, aided by the buoyancy of the water. "We can't do this."

She looked stunned. "Oh, goddess! Is this not acceptable now too?"

Something buzzed, but this time it wasn't in his head.

"No, Shaila. That's not it. We just can't...I can't..." He didn't know what to say. What would she understand?

"What is it with you humans now? You travel like herded cattle. You live in isolated dwellings. You wear clothes tighter than a womb. You cover up almost every delectable part of your bodies. You seem to prefer to be alone. You..." She panted with obvious frustration.

"I can't do this right now...because I have to answer my phone." His cell phone buzzed and vibrated on the marble counter. He held up his cell phone as proof. "Because we live in isolated dwellings, we have to talk to each other through these." He had plenty of other reasons, but this one was easiest to go with.

Hauling his wet body out of the tub, he heard her laugh at the funny squishing sound his clothes made as a he tiptoed across the room over the soggy towels.

He'd missed the call, but the number was familiar. Mr. Majeed, his grandfather's closest friend and secret society brother. Stepping into the hallway, Darius returned the call.

But he could hardly concentrate on the conversation. The door to the bathroom was still open, and the sounds of soft splashing and moaning drifted out. He could clearly see her profile as she soaped up parts of her body that he had held in his hands moments ago.

"Thanks. We'll see you tomorrow." He snapped the phone shut before his voice began to betray his agitation.

*I'm a friggin idiot!* He was so tempted to drop the cell phone into the puddle at his feet, but sheer force of will rooted him to the spot. The sounds of her climax nearly broke him. The idea of living three thousand years ago sounded really good right now. Instead, he tucked his mental tail between his legs and squished down the hallway to change his clothes.

* * *

Finally, everything was clean and dry again. An extra large load of towels was tumbling and thumping along in the dryer downstairs. The hallway rug would take a lot longer to dry, but that couldn't be helped.

Passing by the bathroom, Darius knew he'd never be able to look at that tub in the same way again. Even now, he could feel his pulse quicken just thinking about her in it. He sucked in a deep cleansing breath.

Papa Shadi's cat leapt in from the window and landed on the soaked rug, apparently just arriving home from prowling the mean streets. She meowed her displeasure, flicking water from her paws with each step. Amused, he picked her up, letting her wipe her paws on his clean shirt.

"Sorry, girl." He scratched the sweet spot behind her neck, but frowned at the new, unusually fat, studded collar.

Papa Shadi had been wrong about one thing. Darius did believe in something. He believed that events occurred in a natural order. Logical progression. All of these things must be connected, and as illogical as it sounded to him…they were all tied into that damn prophecy. He did not believe in coincidence.

To save his grandfather, he had to find out everything Papa Shadi knew: the statue, the sword, the amulet, Lilith's private collection…all of it. How had his grandfather known about the woman inside the statue? Did he know why Lilith wanted the amulet? Instinct whispered that Lilith needed the amulet for reasons beyond just adding it to her personal collection. Somehow, the amulet was connected to the prophecy too.

He needed his grandfather to help him search for it. With Papa Shadi held hostage and in a coma, how was Darius to find out what the old man knew? That friggin' brought him around to square one again.

However, he did have Shaila. He had an ancient Egyptian goddess who might know something about the prophecy. She was from the same period of time that Lilith referenced. Hell, she could be related: if not by blood, then by species. She might be in league with Lilith. What loyalty was there among their kind?

She was warrior tough. Big turn on. She was also uninhibited, and that was the part that scared him. To him that meant unpredictable. You couldn't control someone with an unreliable personality. Hadn't his mother proved that?

It was a huge gamble. He would need to rely on Shaila, but he wasn't sure he could trust her. Hell, he was not going to wait until tomorrow to start asking questions.

He found the object of his frustrations pacing in the kitchen…half naked again.

\* \* \*

The bath was just what she needed physically, but mentally Shaila was more anxious than ever.

Where was her priest? Where was her mother? Why were they not there to awaken her? Why had she been in Lilith's possession? What else did Lilith have? Where was the sarcophagus with the babe she was supposed to protect? There were plenty of questions, and no answers.

She was a divine failure. Again.

She should have thought to question her priest more about this future world. The world had grown colder, and the dwellings she'd passed today had held a lifeless aura around them. Humans had prospered, but they smelled of fear and loneliness. They moved about like a farmer's herd. They covered their skins and closed their eyes, seemingly blind to the darkness growing around them.

Most troubling was the realization that her astral spirit had not returned to her as it should have when she awakened. Without it, she was disconnected from the deepest of her immortal powers. She still possessed many abilities, but not the strength she would need to protect the babe.

Added to that was the weakness from thousands of sun cycles of slumber. Physically, she had little more strength than a human.

One aggravating human came vividly to mind. She shoved aside the memory of his kiss, and replaced it with those of the first moments when she met him. He wore the *Eye of Ra*. Did that mean she could trust him? She thought not. With supreme pride he had said he stole her from Lilith. Did that mean he was responsible for her awakening? Could he have deliberately disrupted the return of her astral spirit?

The object of her thoughts sauntered into the room, carrying a black cat. Arching under the man's gentle stroking, the feline nuzzled deeper. Her purrs vibrated loudly, grating on Shaila's nerves.

"Who performed the awakening spell? You?" She could tell by the way he tensed that she had caught him off guard. He deserved it.

"What spell?" He placed the cat on the floor, and stood facing her. His aura colored with defensive energy.

"How did you resurrect my body?"

At the mention of her body, his eyes briefly flicked down to her bare breast. Her nipples hardened. She felt the hot thrill of control. Returning his gaze to hers, he slowly pulled the medallion from under his shirt.

"With this."

"Just that? No spell?" He was still too arrogant for her liking. "Where is my priest? He will know how to correct your mistakes."

"Mistakes?" He closed the distance between them

in two very determined strides.

"Yes. You did it wrong. You should have left such things to those who are—"

"Listen, your highness, I have a few questions of my own."

"I do not answer to you."

"You *will* answer me because my grandfather's life depends on it. He believed in an ancient prophecy. He spent his whole life searching for you. You are a part of it. So, let's just start with any easy one…why were you in that statue?"

He was so close that his scent filled her, calmed her. She thought about denying him an answer. He was not a part of this. Yet, he was the one to find her. Regardless of how it turned out, he had been the one to free her to fulfill her destiny.

"I was waiting. Waiting for the time of the prophecy to begin."

"What part do you play in it?" Turning away, he chased the cat off of the counter and back down to the floor.

"My priest foresaw everything. Thousands of sun cycles in the future, the dark army would rebuild. It would be a time when humans would be unprepared and incapable of defending themselves."

"So, you're here to defend us. Not a bad plan to send the warrior goddess."

"There was a flaw. He also foresaw my death. Although he could not see when, it was clear that it would occur before the time of the prophecy."

"He saw all of that?"

Shaila nodded.

"Well, he missed another important detail."

"Which one?"

"He didn't see me coming, did he? Or you wouldn't be standing in front of me."

"What do you mean?"

"I mean that if he saw me in the picture, he would have made better plans for your resurrection."

"There is another possibility. Maybe he did not see his own demise." Did that mean her destiny had been altered? And what of the babe's destiny? She had to find out what happened to her tomb. "I would like to know how I came to be in Lilith's possession. There were other items in my tomb. Items that are equally important to fulfilling the prophecy."

"Would one of those items happen to be a black diamond amulet?"

His eyes studied hers too intently. She realized he wasn't just waiting for her answer. He was judging her reaction to the question. A lie could be convenient, or it could produce more questions that she had no intention of answering. Shaila's answer would have to be an honest one.

"Yes. It was sealed in the tomb with me."

\* \* \*

*Stay!*

Shaila still reeled from his arrogance. He had actually ordered her to stay put like some trained animal, while he went off to some place called a lab. Then, he had commanded her to put those awful clothes back on.

He might carry himself like a pharaoh, but her palms ached to slap his face. A human with that kind of audacity could taunt the gods of the Underworld, heedless of the consequences. *Goddess, how will I control such a man?*

His kiss came to mind again, and this time she allowed the memory to linger. While Shaila was not the magnet of male attention that her mother was, she understood the power given to women. She just wondered if she knew how to wield it.

Startled by a thunderous roar, she ran to the window, and watched in fascination as Darius rode off on a strange looking machine, like a chariot with no horses. The world she'd left behind had no such self-moving devices. At least, not any that were accessible to the humans.

She also noticed a larger machine pull out after him, following a short distance behind.

*Keep walking around naked like that and you'll have more men under your control than you can count.*

She heard the words in her head, but they were not her own. Time had not faded her recognition of the voice. She spun around until she spied the cat sitting proudly on the counter again.

"Bessie?"

With only a whisper of sound, black fur smoothed into cream-colored skin. The cat's form arched and stretched to form a full-grown woman with black spiky hair, a variety of colorful body paints, and jewelry piercings in interesting places. Leathery fabric spooled from thin air and wrapped itself around her body. The final touch appeared from her mouth with a tiny pop…some sweet treat on a stick.

The woman launched from the counter. Shaila nearly fell over, but she welcomed the warm feeling of being totally enwrapped with arms and legs. Bessie was very dear to her. It hurt to realize that she had caused her sister pain by disappearing so suddenly and without saying goodbye. Shaila hugged her tight.

"Sister, I've missed you." Bessie wiped fat tears from her cheeks and popped the sweet back into her mouth.

"I have missed you too. I am so glad to see you." Shaila stumbled over to a chair, suddenly fatigued.

"My body is slow in remembering how to move."

"Can't you heal yourself?"

Shaila shook her head. "I cannot seem to connect with my astral spirit."

Bessie poured water into a small metal machine. "You have to try this stuff. It's called coffee. It might help perk you up. But it's really addicting."

"Bessie, where is our mother?"

The water burbled through the machine on the counter, the aroma filling the small kitchen. Bessie inhaled deeply. "I don't really know. It's been a couple thousand years since I last saw Inanna. She and Uncle Seth were dealing with a problem."

"What problem?"

"Lilith. Need I say more?" The machine sputtered as the stream of liquid came to an end.

"Tell me. What happened?"

"Lilith was up to her usual tricks, trying to rule the world and all that. The humans loved her though. Queen Cleopatra. She'd finally become queen of something, but she screwed it all up again. Nearly exposed us all."

"How?"

"By falling in love with a Roman named Marc Antony." Bessie's stomach growled. "She'd told her lover all about us. But of course, she told her side of it, making us sound like slave owners. In the end, good old Uncle Seth had to silence the womanizing idiot forever."

"What about Lilith?"

"Uncle Seth took care of her too. He sealed her in a rock and sank it deep into a seabed. She shouldn't have ever been found." Bessie poured herself a second cup, smiling as she inhaled the aroma. "God, I love this stuff."

"Do you know how she escaped?"

Bessie shook her head. "I guess we'll need to find out. So we don't make the same mistake twice."

Shaila poured herself a cup, eager to sample what her sister was enjoying. It smelled divine. Taking a small sip, she nearly gagged on the taste. She fanned the bitter burning sensation on her tongue.

"Bessie, how did I come to be in Lilith's possession? Where are the other items from the tomb? The child?"

"I've been trying to find out, but it's really hard avoiding that jerk son of hers."

"Therion?"

"The one and only. He's definitely the spawn of Apophis." She shivered and brushed her arms as if to remove something disgusting.

"Yes, but he is more like a human for now."

"Maybe not for long. Lilith has a plan to find the amulet." Bessie paused. "Today, she hired Darius to find it for her."

"Darius works for her?" Shaila's voice dropped just a fraction.

"No. He hates her guts." Bessie finished her coffee and dropped the cup into a washing area. "No, Darius is being forced to help Lilith. His grandfather in exchange for the amulet."

"How do you know all of this?"

"I'm a house cat." Bessie shrugged her shoulders. "I get around. I hear things."

"Can you help me get around too? I do not think I have the energy to transform, and I suspect I would not blend in around here in beast form."

Bessie giggled. "Yeah, well you wouldn't blend in the way you're dressed right now either. Darius was right. You need a new wardrobe."

"The styles in my memory are too old, and the styles I saw today were forgettable."

A devious gleam sparkled in Bessie's gold eyes. She reached up and opened a cubby door above the machine that made coffee. She withdrew a metal ring with something that looked like a key.

"I have a great idea. We're going to my apartment. With your exotic looks, I don't think you can pull off the steam punk look like I can. But even when you can flash on anything at will...like we can...you still need to dress with style. And I have a closet full of style."

Shaila barely restrained a grin. Darius had commanded her to stay. What was that phrase he'd used?

*Hell, no.*

# CHAPTER SIX

Darius was glad he'd taken his motorcycle, even though the ride to his lab was very short. The bite in the air helped clear his mind.

Papa Shadi's return was his first priority. Darius could see only two courses of action to attain that goal. One would be to sneak back into the Troy estate and try to rescue his grandfather again. Not the best choice now that Darius no longer had the element of surprise. The other option was to find the amulet and trade it for his grandfather -- a difficult task, and one with no real guarantee that Lilith would honor her end of the bargain.

Darius chose the second option, but he needed more information to make it work. He needed to research the discovery of Shaila's tomb. Then he should be able to track the movements of the items catalogued during the excavation. Since Lilith had provided nothing to go on, the next best starting point was Mr. Artie Johnson. He could go through Artie's satchel at home, but only from the lab could he tap into the government man's computer and email accounts. That was going to take some stealth work by ALICE.

Shaila was the factor that aggravated him the most. He'd taken a huge risk, leaving her at his house alone. But she was part of the reason he'd needed to get out of there. His simple life was gone. Well designed plans failed. His solitude invaded.

Darius remembered her kiss and the way she'd crawled up his body. His blood responded to the memory with an unexpected rush. He shifted his weight in the seat to control the pressure building. The sudden movement nearly sent his bike off the road. *How in hell am I going to control a stubborn, unpredictable goddess?*

Even though he needed her, he knew that he could never hold her captive. Part of him hoped she'd be gone when he returned. The other part prayed that she'd chosen to stay.

* * *

The sun hung low between the buildings. He'd been gone longer than he'd planned. With a sigh, Darius rolled the Harley into the garage.

The first thing that hit him upon entering the kitchen door was the rich smell of fresh brewed coffee. His houseguest was there, sipping from a mug of hot, black coffee. With each swallow she shook her head and grimaced.

The second thing took a bit longer to register in his brain. He smelled leather. And Shaila was covered in it: from halter-top to pants. Every inch fit like a second skin. He hadn't realized he'd been holding his breath until it came out in a whoosh.

"Where did you..." He licked his lips indecisively. "How did..."

Shaila put her coffee down and held her arms out. In seconds, the leather melted away. For the barest of moments, she wore nothing at all. Then, fabric appeared out of nowhere, sliding across her body and wrapping into place. A simple black dress, but again it hugged every curve of her body with custom-fit precision. She did the whole thing again, bringing back the leather outfit.

*Reality check!* Demons? Sure. Prophecy? Yep.

Shape-shifting goddess? "Okay, now that we got that cleared up." He carved another notch on the mental tab he was running on Shaila's unpredictability chart.

His grandfather's cat sat on the counter, flipping her tail. Her bright yellow eyes seemed to look up at him with annoyance. Darius put her down on the ground, ignoring her whines of protest.

He found a cup of coffee on the counter, still warm. Shaila moved closer, watching him add sugar and cream to it. He lifted his brows appreciatively. "That's excellent. Did Marcus show you how to work the coffee maker?"

She shrugged, and then reached for the sugar spoon. This time she didn't grimace as she swallowed her coffee. She laughed. "That's much better."

"Glad I could help."

"Do you plan to return me to Lilith?" She didn't make small talk, just went straight to the heavy stuff. He admired that.

"No. I can't do that." He studied her features intently. "Actually, Lilith doesn't seem to want you back." He smirked at her over the rim of the cup.

"Is this true?" Her shock was easy to read.

"How are you related to Lilith?" He grabbed the chair and turned it around, sitting in it backwards. "My grandfather said something about her being the Dragon Queen. What does that mean?"

Shaila burst out laughing. He liked the deep, rich sound. It took her a few moments to compose herself, wiping away tears from the corners of her eyes.

"She might have the title, but she will never have the true power that comes with it. Queenship is a birthright, and Lilith has no blood ties to it. Tia'Mat is our queen. If something has happened to her, then the power passes to my mother, Inanna. Then, it would pass on to me."

"Well, lucky for you she had no idea you were in the statue." He smiled at the irony of it. "You were right there under her nose the whole time."

"That was fortunate for me."

"I never meant to take you. I was there to rescue my grandfather." Guilt stabbed at his heart. If only he'd kept with the plan. Logically, the statue didn't step in front of his path. But she'd distracted him. He wanted to blame her for that.

"Why did Lilith take him?"

Darius held his tongue for a moment, still trying to subdue the rise of anger and guilt. "The short answer is that he was at the wrong place at the wrong time." Reaching for the medallion, he rubbed it between his thumb and finger. By now, he'd memorized every ridge and relief on it.

"And now that she has him, she is using him to manipulate you."

"You catch on quick. She wants that black diamond amulet. When I bring that to her, I get my grandfather back. It's pretty clear what I have to do."

"Marcus told me what you do. You find artifacts and bring them back to their rightful owners. If those who govern Egypt can trust you, then I should trust you."

"Yeah, well, I haven't decided if I can trust *you*." How could he trust her? She withheld things from him. Like that shape-shifting skill. What else could she do?

"I have lost something, too. It was in the tomb with me. It is imperative that I find it." She leaned in closer, the scent of musk soap still clung to her dark hair. The leather halter created a deep, dark valley between her breasts. "Will you help me find it?"

He hung his head down and sucked in a deep breath. He didn't need any more pressure. "I don't have time."

"You know the words of the prophecy. I heard you quote it to Marcus."

"I'd like to shove that prophecy up..." He cut himself off before he said something really stupid.

"The gift to man."

"Okay, I'll bite." He rubbed the back of his head. Life was getting messier by the moment. "What is this *gift* you need me to find?"

"An infant."

"A *what*?"

"An infant. He would be in a state of preservation, much like I was, but wrapped."

"You mean, a mummy? You need me to help you find a baby mummy?"

"Yes."

"And who is he?"

"He is the one destined to deliver the world from the evil power of Apophis. He is also the heir to the throne of Egypt. He is the messiah of my people, or what may be left of them in this world."

Darius rubbed the back of his head and sucked in his cheeks. "Please don't tell me that I have to resurrect this kid?"

She nodded.

"Yeah. Sure thing. What the hell." He stomped out of the kitchen, needing to put some space between them...again. "Last week, I didn't even believe in demons. Now I get to resurrect a kid who's supposed the save the world. What with...his rattle? Oh, God. That's rich."

\* \* \*

Shaila was getting tired of listening to the both of them: Darius and Bessie.

She plugged her ears to mute the sounds of

Darius' tongue-lashing. She might not understand it all, but she knew a curse when she heard one. His profanity was punctuated with a lot of door slamming.

Bessie's complaints, however, telegraphed straight into Shaila's mind. *He drank my coffee!* Much more difficult to tune out. *A beautiful man, but horrible timing. I swear my life is cursed.*

"Hush, Bessie. You are giving me an ache in the head."

Bessie hushed, but continued to thump her tail to show her displeasure.

"In case he does not agree to help me, I need a plan."

Shaila noticed a brown leather bag on the floor by the chair Darius had recently vacated. Drawing it closer, she pried it open and found a stack of unrolled papyrus. She marveled at how white it was. She leafed through many sheets covered with writing that she could not decipher. Finally, she came across a few coated with a cool, slick sheen. On them were images so lifelike she would swear that she could lift them off of the papyrus.

*They're called photographs.* Bessie's voice entered her mind again. *Look, that's you.*

There were no *photographs* of the babe, but one did catch Shaila's attention. "My sword. That would be very useful. Bessie?"

*You don't have to ask, Sister. I'll go scope out Lilith's place. It's probably in the weapons room, but I avoid that place. It's creepy.*

"Thank you."

"Don't thank me," Darius said. "We haven't found anything yet."

He had returned so quietly that Shaila nearly jumped out of her skin. She looked toward Bessie, but the cat was just slinking out the door.

"Let's go. This time you're coming with me." He grabbed her hand and pulled her with him, all the way out of the house. "I need my grandfather back, and I can't just sit in this house and wait for tomorrow morning to come."

"What is important about tomorrow morning?"

"That's when I'm going to grill my grandfather's best friend for information."

He marched silently along the cobblestone alleys, and she easily lengthened her stride to match his. He seemed moody. In her experience, powerful human men tended to be quite moody. She already knew he preferred being in control. She admired his confident attitude and the obvious affection he had for his grandfather.

He cursed a lot, but he seemed sincere. She believed him when he said he would not turn her over to Lilith. There was an aura of honor about him. Still, he was working for Lilith to find the amulet. Shaila could not afford to let down her guard. It was essential that Lilith not be allowed to recover the amulet, and she absolutely could not be trusted to keep her word. It was doubtful the witch would release his grandfather at all. He obviously knew too much.

In the fading light of the day, the moon already hung low to the earth shrouded in an orange haze. It was a late harvest moon cycle, a time of great energy for both light and dark powers. If she survived this coming moon cycle, she would search for her mother.

If Lilith had him looking for the amulet, then Darius could look for the child at the same time. After all, she had been in the same tomb with the babe for centuries. She wondered if Lilith had him. Did she discover the tomb? Her priest had ensured that no record of the tomb existed beyond its walls. *Oh, goddess, where could he be?*

"Darius, you saw where she kept me?"

"Yes."

"Was there a wrapped infant?"

"No. I didn't see any mummies. Her personal collection is large, but she's only known to actively collect jewelry and weapons." He slowed his pace, thoughtfully rubbing his chin. "If she's acquired mummies, it would've been a black market transaction. That's an illegal purchase, but one that I can still track."

His voice lowered to a mumble, as if he was talking to himself. "Collectors with illegal or stolen items tend to keep them close, especially if they hold significant emotional value. They worked so hard to get the items that they are compelled to display them, but in a way that only they can enjoy looking at them. If she has mummies, her pride would keep them close. Very close."

They reached a street that reminded her of a bazaar, but these shops were all inside buildings. As shadows overtook the streets, artificial lights popped on everywhere. Lights inside and out. It was disruptive to her newly-awakened senses.

They passed a shop selling big bound stacks of papyrus. Darius said they were called books, and he pointed out a small sign in the window that he said boasted an ability to find any out-of-print book in the world. He was skeptical, but he said the shop owner was a lovely woman.

Then they passed a row of windows through which she could see a large group of children in white outfits practicing fighting skills. Shaila smiled at the way his mouth moved when he said the word *taekwondo*.

"You love kids, I can see it in your face."

Shaila nodded. "Yes, they are more honest than

adults."

Deep laugher shook his body. "That has apparently not changed in thousands of years. Is this child you seek yours?"

"No. I have not been blessed with a child yet." She sighed wistfully. "The Anunnaki do not have many offspring. Our life span can reach tens of thousands of Earth years, virtually immortal compared to humans. Nature compensates by making us less fertile."

He looked like he was adding it up in his head, but then he clenched his jaw and moved her along to the next shop. It was dark inside, but little lights glowed throughout the place. A strange mix of sounds beeped and blasted all around. The sounds and lights came from many tall boxes, which children stood in front of.

Mesmerized, she stepped inside and approached the largest group in the room. She towered over them, but they ignored her. She could not read the writings on the box, but the square in the middle was filled with painted images that moved. It appeared to be a game, since the children were cheering for the boy nearest the box. He seemed to be controlling a man in the moving image. What astonished her most was the scene in the game.

The little figure ran through a maze of tombs and catacombs, fighting mummies, guards and other creatures. In one tomb, he fought using only a small dagger. He collected points with each mummy or creature he killed.

Overwhelmed by curiosity, she stepped around the group of boys to get to the side of the box. Putting her hands on it, she felt the vibrations and sounds coming from it. She tried sending her mind inside, but there were no signals with this object. Just a bunch of vibrations that did not seem to have a destination.

"Come on, Joey. Get 'im." The boys were getting very excited over the success of the game. Joey was trying to fight off mummies and obtain a golden spell book.

Shaila was fascinated with the variety of hieroglyphics throughout the scenes. Most were very inaccurate, but a symbol in body paint on one of the main players was quite real. How much did the humans of this age truly know about the medjai? She would barter her soul to the Underworld to have her warriors with her now.

In unison, the boys all turned to her. "Do you have any tokens?"

"Tokens?" She had no idea what they were asking for. Darius suddenly appeared, placing a bucket of tiny disks in her hands.

"Hi, Mr. Alexander."

"Hi, Joey. You still working on your black belt?"

"Yep. Almost there." Joey puffed out his chest. "I test for it in two months."

"Excellent. I'll come watch you when you test." Darius and the boy slapped their palms together in the air. "I need a favor."

The boy beamed. "Sure."

"You guys can share this bucket of tokens," Darius looked each of the boys squarely in their eyes, "but only if you guys will let my friend Shaila hang out with you for a few minutes. I need to run next door to the cell phone shop before it closes."

"Deal." Joey started to reach for the bucket.

Shaila held it higher for a moment, a gleam in her eyes. "I will share these tokens with you, if you will teach me how to play that mummy game."

"Wicked cool," Joey grinned. "I'll teach ya."

She handed him the bucket to share with the

other boys in the group.

"I'll be back in a few minutes." Darius leaned in closer to her ear. "Kick their butts."

"Why would I want to kick them?" He'd already moved too far to hear her, disappearing into the darkness at the back of the room. Joey pulled her over to the big square box, and dropped two tokens into little slits in the front.

"This is my favorite video game in here," Joey confessed. "It's based on the movie. Okay, this button makes your guy jump over things. This button makes him duck punches. These two are for kicking and hitting...or stabbing if you've found the dagger..." Joey rattled on about the workings of the video game.

After a couple of failed attempts, Shaila began to get the hang of game fighting.

\* \* \*

"She did *almost* beat me, Mr. Alexander," Joey blurted when Darius returned. "But Apophis got her!"

"He should be so lucky," Darius drawled.

He indicated with his head that it was time to go and moved to the back of the room. He quickly fished his new purchase out of the store bag: a disposable cell phone. Ripping it out of its plastic case, he programmed it to call his cell phone, and he tested it to be sure it worked. That gave him the return number.

"Here, take this." He handed the new phone to Shaila, but she looked puzzled. "You put it in your purse. Oh, yeah. You don't carry one of those."

Now he was puzzled. That damned leather outfit hugged her so tight there was no place to tuck the cell phone. Except maybe between her breasts. Deciding that wouldn't go over too well, he looked into the packaging and found a belt clip that looked like it wouldn't break off too easily.

"Here you go." He clipped it to the top of her leather pants. "That's where it will be. If for some reason we get separated, you flip it open and press the green button. Forget all of the other buttons. Just press the green one, hold it up to your ear like this, and you'll hear me on the other end. Got it?"

Shaila nodded.

Following him through a large metal door, she nearly jumped at the sound of it slamming shut behind them. The tiny gray room had a staircase, but instead of taking the stairs up, he pulled her behind it. Lifting up a metal grate from the ground, he motioned for her to descend into the inky darkness below. She nodded and gingerly placed a foot downward until she found the first step. Slowly, she descended into the shadows.

Darius followed her, bringing the grate down over them. Lights flickered on, revealing a large room filled with lots of metal and flashing buttons. Somehow, it all seemed more sophisticated than the gaming room above.

"This is my private research lab."

Shaila had no idea what she was looking at. But unlike the game room above, here she could feel the buzz of powerful signals. The signals gave off such a vivid aura, she could see their energy trails leading off through the walls. "What is it?"

"It's a computer. Basically, take all of the libraries across the planet and all of the great thinking minds in history…and they're in there."

"Oh." Curious, she poked one of the flashing buttons. One of three large screens on the wall sprang to life.

"Voice verification, please," a very hollow but sultry voice requested. Shaila looked around for the source of the voice. Darius pointed at the speaker.

"*Assalaam alaikum,*" Darius answered.

"And peace be upon you. Good afternoon, Darius. How may I help you?"

"She sounds very efficient." *And annoying.* Shaila did not like this cold, disembodied voice.

"Good afternoon, ALICE." Darius winked at Shaila. "If anyone ever found my lab, they wouldn't know to use Arabic for the voice recognition."

"I understood what you said. The language seems not too far off some of the sounds of my own tongue."

"Is there any language you can't understand?"

"I suppose I should be able to understand any spoken language on this planet."

"That's impressive."

"Not particularly impressive, Darius. It is very simple. When you speak, your voice sends vibrations in patterns. My mind knows how to interpret those patterns."

It was his turn to look confused. "Okay, well. Let's put the computer to work. ALICE, task initiation."

"Task initiation, verify command."

"Task. List generation search terms are Egyptian and mummy and black market."

"Task verified. List generation initiated."

He spun his chair back around toward her. "When I was here earlier, I was only focused on finding the amulet. Now you've given me another item to research."

"I am sorry."

"Don't be. Having two items from the same tomb to search for may actually help us in cross-referencing the data. The more factors, the greater the chance of success."

"Can you see Lilith's home with this?"

"Shit, yeah." He spun back to the controls. "ALICE, aerial map on screen two, please."

The huge screen on the wall became a live picture. Dwellings lined a river. Shaila marveled at the sight of miniscule machines moving along the streets, and tiny boats coasting in the water.

"Oh, Goddess. That is incredible."

"Yes, this is modern technology at its best. That is a live satellite image of Lilith's home. Watch this." Darius clicked something in his hand and the image scrolled down toward the earth, making everything larger.

"So, this is your preparation room. Is it not?"

"You could call it that. I don't leave home without every bit of information I can gain. Knowledge is power, honey."

She repeated him. "Knowledge is power. I think we had a similar saying, but that is far less wordy."

A loud beep preceded ALICE's cold voice. "Task complete. Data saved in file folder Prophecy Documents."

# CHAPTER SEVEN

Darius scanned the results of ALICE's Internet search. The list quickly grew to hundreds of online links to underground discussions on mummies. Darius narrowed down the list by cross-referencing with infant mummies and items discovered near Deir el-Bahari. Although there was no official record of such a tomb existing in that temple, he went on faith that his grandfather knew what he was talking about.

It took some effort on ALICE's part, but she eventually hacked into Mr. Artie Johnson's office computer. Since his suspicious death, the agency had digitally sealed all entry into the man's accounts.

After an hour of dead end links, Darius finally found an encrypted exchange of messages between Mr. Artie and someone with the screen name *TimeSleuth*. Piecing together the messages, Darius felt joy zinging through his body.

"Bingo! We've got a live one, Shaila." Darius rubbed his chin thoughtfully. "This guy definitely saw you. I would think he was a nut if he didn't describe you with complete conviction and accuracy. But no mention of mummies in the tomb."

"Does he mention anything about markings on the walls? Did he translate the prophecy?"

"No. He wrote that about thirty-five years ago he was working in the area as an intern and sneaked onto the site, which had just been discovered by a group of students. He described some incredibly well-preserved hieroglyphs, but he said they never got the chance to record them. They didn't have camera phones back then."

"What do you mean?"

"I mean there's no photographic evidence of the tomb. According to him, the site and all its documentation were quickly confiscated by a strange woman who claimed rights to the dig. He seemed to think there was a conspiracy of some kind concerning the discovery of it."

"Lilith?"

"He didn't say, just that she showed up out of nowhere." Darius halted before reading aloud the next set of messages. "Here's something I can have ALICE dig up. He mentioned a fire, but he didn't know the extent of the damage because they were all kept away from the scene. What concerned this guy is that no official records exist about the tomb, and...here's the kicker...most of the students who discovered it are now dead."

Darius sat back in his chair, rubbing his chin. Then, his fingers flew across the keyboard at a frantic pace.

"Oh, Goddess! Can we talk to this *TimeSleuth* person?"

"Possibly." Darius winked and executed another task for ALICE to run a back trace on the blogger's link. "Maybe we'll get lucky."

He could feel her restlessness as Shaila wandered to the far side of the room and peeked into a tall cabinet.

"Are these weapons?"

"Yes, some of them. Others are devices for tracking and listening. Spy stuff. Tools of the trade."

She ran her fingers across the cold metal barrel of one short weapon. "Darius, show me how these work."

"Trace complete. Origination IPS address found."

The computer's sultry voice echoed off the bare walls. Darius printed it out, and scanned the document.

"Okay. We'll try to reach this guy in about a half hour. It's not quite dawn yet where he seems to be."

Darius grabbed the gun and loaded it. Bringing Shaila into a second room, he pointed to the walls. "All of these rooms are sound proofed. In fact, the guy who owned this building before me originally refurbished this basement as a bomb shelter. He was a big believer in government conspiracies, and he wanted to be ready for the Russians to drop a bomb on us."

Darius quickly showed her how to load, fire, and absorb the recoil of the deadly weapon.

"Shaila, you don't seem interested in learning how to fire this weapon. Why?"

"Because it will be ineffective against those I will be fighting."

"Sure it will. I took out a few demons with just a simple knife to the head."

"I am not referring to simple demons, Darius." Shaila's hips swayed as she walked along the wall, running her hands along the padded insulation. Reaching the back of the room, she stood in front of the mark. "I am referring to Lilith, and others like her. Now, fire your weapon."

"What?"

"Shoot me."

"I'm not going to shoot at you. Can't I just shoot at the target?"

"No."

He aimed the Magnum at her head, but couldn't bring himself to pull the trigger. He rarely used guns, preferring to defend himself with hand-to-hand combat. A gun could be useful, but it could also raise the alarm of others more quickly than tripping a wire.

He could see her body tensing with irritation. She

wanted him to trust her, but pulling on the trigger was a hard move to make. He squared his shoulders and fired.

The blood drained from his face when he noticed Shaila's body recoil. He sprinted toward her, but slowed when he saw her lift an eyebrow. She was laughing at him.

"What did you do?" Approaching her, he finally saw it. The bullet was hovering in the air about a foot away from her nose.

"That tickled." Shaila laughed as the bullet suddenly pitched straight down into the ground, blowing a hole in the mat. He wanted to slap the cocky grin off of her face for scaring the crap out of him like that. "Darius, you look angry."

So, she could move things with her mind. How had he not thought of that? He'd seen Lilith move his knife through the air without touching it. What angered him was how deceptive Shaila could be. She knew way more than she was sharing with him, and maybe he should be pissed at himself for not asking her the right questions. But he'd rather be pissed at her. How could he work effectively with someone so unpredictable?

"Is there anything else you'd like to share with me, goddess?" He found a small measure of justice as the anger hissing through his teeth wiped the smile from her face.

"Like what?"

"Can you read minds?"

"No."

"Excellent." It was time to shut up and walk away.

\* \* \*

"Damn!"

Shaila cringed as Darius angrily tossed the small phone device on the counter.

"That's the third try. This guy just won't talk to me. He heard about Mr. Artie's death and now he's too paranoid to talk to anyone about the tomb."

"Darius, tell me how this cell phone thing works. How do you speak to someone on the other side of the planet?"

"Satellite signals." He was rubbing the medallion again, which told her that he was thinking of his grandfather and probably fearful of failing. "Invisible signals travel from my phone up to a device orbiting the Earth and back down to his phone."

"Travel?" She sat up straighter. This was something to be explored. "These signals have a path that they know how to follow?"

"It's not like they have a choice, but yes. It's a predictable, designed path."

Shaila looked over at the computer again, studying the path of energy she could still see radiating from it. "Darius, we have something similar that we call the astral plane. It is a dimensional path that we can tap into and use to travel. Since my awakening, I have not been able to tap into it. But I might be able to use the path of your cell phone signal to go speak with this man."

"You can do that?" It was a question, but there was no edge of disbelief in his voice.

"I should at least try." She pointed to the computer. "Your ALICE has much stronger signals. I can see them."

"Then we'll use the computer to make the call. Even better, because it'll show a different number. I don't think he'll answer another call from my cell."

*Oh, goddess, let this work.* "Okay. Make the call."

"Be careful, Shaila. No, don't roll your eyes at me.

This guy's scared. That means he's skittish. And that could make him dangerous. Don't do anything foolish."

She bit her tongue before she said something regrettable. It was so aggravating being treated this way, as if he was in charge of her. Pharaohs had sought out her advice. When would this man trust in her?

"Whatever you do, don't back him into a corner. If he feels threatened, he'll either run or try to hurt you. Here." Darius tucked a slim knife into her pocket.

She had to stop him now or she would hurt him. Instead, she put her hand on his chest. "Stop, Darius. I know what to do. His fears will work to my advantage. Just call him, please. You will hear everything, yes?"

He sighed heavily. "That's my problem. I will only be able to hear you. If I hear something going wrong, there'll be nothing I can do to help. India is on the other side of the world from here."

He slumped deeper into his chair and asked the computer to initiate the call to the man's cell phone.

"*Namasthe*?" After the third ring, a man's hesitant voice came through the computer speakers.

"Jack Davis?"

"Y-yes. Who is this?"

Darius nodded to her quickly. He was right. Even through the speaker this guy sounded nervous and distrustful. She needed to get over to him quickly before he hung up the phone.

While Darius deceptively introduced himself in Arabic as a professor, Shaila closed her eyes and focused on finding the right signal to follow. She honed in on the stronger vibrations of Darius' voice and the path it took.

Because she was not at full strength, the effort of transporting this way felt sluggish and loud. Electronic signals buzzed in her head and vibrated up and down her spine, leaving her disoriented as she arrived on the other end of the signals.

"Look, I just told you I can't help you. I've never been to Egypt. I'm not the guy you're looking for. Sorry, buddy."

"Why are you lying to him?"

Startled, the man spun around. The cell phone dropped from his hand, splintering against the bare floor. Wide-eyed and shaking, the man whipped a small gun out of a drawer and aimed it at her chest. She kept part of her attention on the man, but took a moment to observe her surroundings.

The room was small but held everything a human in hiding would need: a bed, a cooking device, and a computer. It was much smaller than the one in Darius' lab, but its signal was surprisingly strong. The glow of the sunrise framed the black drapes hanging over the windows. One small colorful rug lay in the middle of the dusty stone floor.

One wall was covered with pictures of the man. She recognized the pyramids looming behind him. Pinning him with a glare, she nearly laughed at him. His knees were literally wobbling beneath him.

"Please, Jack Davis. Sit down." She indicated the rumpled bed in the corner. "I need to know everything you saw in that tomb you wrote about, and I will only warn you once not to lie to me."

The man's face, wrinkled with age and fear, relaxed slightly, but he held his gun firmly pointed in her direction. He shook his head at the invitation to sit.

"Who are you?" His grey eyes were wide with fear, but they moved across her with curiosity.

"You do not remember me?"

"Of course not. I've never seen you before in my life. Who are you?"

"You know who I am." She moved into the man's

personal space. The gun in his hand shook violently. Darius would be very upset with her boldness right now. Slowly, she covered the gun barrel with her own hands and gently pointed it away from her.

Shaila mentally pushed a calming energy pulse toward the man. She felt his grip relax, and he allowed her to take the gun away from him. Emptying the gun, she frowned to find only one bullet in the chamber.

"For a paranoid little man, you are very poorly armed." Shrugging, she tossed the weapon onto the bed. "You must tell me about the tomb you found over thirty sun cycles ago."

"Why? I don't know anything about that tomb."

She sighed. Stubborn human. "I know you were there. You described me perfectly in your communication."

"You?" The man smelled of stale smoke and he hunched over with a severe fit of coughing. "That's crazy. You're crazy."

Backing up a few steps, Shaila willed away the leather clothes and replaced them with her pleated skirt and hip belt. She allowed her body to briefly transform into a stiffened image of the statue she had stood inside of for so long. Even without the gold crust, she knew she appeared exactly as she had when the students first entered the tomb.

As she transformed back to her modern attire, the man's eyes still lingered on her chest. He tried to lick his lips with a dry tongue, which nearly made her gag at the thought. She pulled out the slim knife Darius had given her and threw it past his head. It wobbled as the blade buried itself in the wooden wall. Fear returned to the grey eyes.

"I grow irritated by your continued denials. You were there at the discovery of my tomb. Everything in that room belongs to me. I need you to tell me what you saw and where it went."

"The hieroglyphics on the walls...they...they spoke of a prophecy. It was a warning about the end of the world."

"Forget the walls. Tell me about the mummies." She leaned into his personal space again.

"Um, there was only one sarcophagus in the tomb."

"Yes, and what did you see in it?"

"T-there was a woman in it."

"What about the infant?"

"I think there was one in it."

"You think?" This horrid smelling man was insufferable. "I need to know exactly what you saw."

"I saw a female mummy." He demonstrated by holding his palms a short distance out in front of his own chest. "I noticed the large breasts, indicating a wet-nurse. I think she may have been cradling a small mummy, but I don't remember exactly."

Shaila smiled, allowing her sharp fangs to unfold and hover menacingly close to his cheek. She felt his fear in shivering waves. "What happened to my tomb?"

A nervous laugh escaped his lips. "Um, wow. You're just as scary as the other one."

"What other one?" She pierced into his eyes and buzzed him with another energy pulse, this one not so calming. He jerked his body as if it had just been burned.

"The woman who showed up. Some official who took control of the tomb. She was just as dark and scary as you are."

"What did this woman do?"

"I didn't see her do anything."

"But you suspect her of something, do you not?" She kept her fangs within his sight.

"Y-yes. I've wondered how the tomb caught fire. It was a clean site. There were no torches. They had flashlights, and their electrical equipment was brand new. Nothing frayed or exposed."

"Do you think this woman set the fire?"

"Yes." He tried licking his lips again. "We weren't allowed to see the site ever again. I've always wondered if it even caught fire at all."

Shaila nodded in agreement. After all, she was proof that something did survive from that room. And if she survived, maybe the mummies did too.

This was going to take more energy, but she had to know for sure. Pointing to a cracked mirror above a dirty bowl, she willed an image of Lilith to appear on it. "Is this the woman?"

He looked at the image a long time, but ended up shaking his head. Remembering something he had said, she changed Lilith's blond hair to black. "How about this woman?"

He nodded enthusiastically. "Yes. Yes, that's her. It's been a long time, but I can picture her now. Those dark eyes had a scary way of seeing into you." His body shook with nervous tremors. "I've been scared for over three decades that she'd find me. Most of the students who made that discovery are dead now."

"My friend's computer found that *all* of the students are dead, except you."

He laughed nervously and spit on the floor. "Wow. Just me now. Probably because I wasn't a student. I wasn't on the list."

"How did you come to be there?"

"I was invited by one of the students." He cleared his throat. "One of the female students. I met her in Cairo when she'd arrived fresh out of the university. I was there that day as her guest, so I wasn't on any lists."

"Yet you still live in fear of being discovered."

"Yes, because I couldn't stop digging around for information on the tomb. It was as if the discovery had never happened. No trace of it exists. Then I started finding out that the students were mysteriously dying. One by one, they disappeared like victims of some Egyptian curse." He pointed to the fading image in the mirror. "She's the curse, isn't she?"

He paced the room like a caged beast, chewing on dirty fingernails.

"For my sake, I am thankful that you wrote about your experience, but it might not have been such a wise thing for you to do." She pitied the little man.

"Yeah, stupid thing to do, but I'd covered my tracks. Encrypted everything. How did you find me?"

"Does it matter?"

"Not any more. I'm a sitting duck here. Time to move again." He grabbed a box from under his bed and started throwing things in it. He hesitated for a moment, taking a long look at her. She could see in his eyes that he was adding it all up. "Does this mean the prophecy is real?"

She approached him slowly, and put her palm over his watch, infusing it with a warm glow.

"I am Shaila a'k'Hemet, and I have come to your time because of the prophecy. I must prevent the *Age of Awakening*, the event you saw inscribed upon the tomb walls."

"I believe you."

She smiled at his earnestness. "I know you do."

"What can I do?"

"You can keep living your life. Keep seeking the knowledge." She lifted her palm to reveal a strange green stone encased inside the watch. "The stone contains a protective spell."

"Protection from what exactly?" He stood taller.

Along with the spell, she had infused his aura with a spark of confidence that would hopefully grow over time.

A crazy vibration buzzed next to her hip. She found the irritating item hooked to her pants. It was the cell phone Darius had given her earlier. After a moment of silence, it jumped around her palm. She remembered Darius pulling it apart in some manner.

Opening the little device, she could hear Darius yelling her name. She cradled it next to her face like Darius had instructed, but he sounded muffled.

Jack Davis stepped forward. Reaching for the phone, he turned it around.

Now Darius's voice sounded crisp and clear...and furious.

Leaning in, she kissed him on both cheeks. "Thank you, Jack Davis. You have been most helpful. I wish you long life." She was pleased to see him blush right before she disappeared, following the cell phone's signal back to the other side of the world.

\* \* \*

All that mattered to Darius was that the signal had been strong enough to bring Shaila back. So why were feelings of anxiety still snapping through his system? He didn't have time to analyze that now. They needed to get back home.

As they stepped out into the darkened streets, Darius felt a malicious presence. He couldn't see anything, but he felt it in his gut and in his itchy palm. Someone watched them.

"Shaila. We need to get back to the house. I think we're going to have to run the whole way. It's about eight blocks. Don't ask why, because I'm not sure I have an answer."

"Just a feeling?"

He nodded, grabbed her hand, and ran. Shaila stumbled at first, but they couldn't afford to stop. He relaxed a bit when she fell into a steady pace beside him. Those long legs of hers. He shoved aside a mental image of those long legs wrapped around his waist.

Now was not the time. They had to get home. Something in the descending darkness of the night felt evil. He felt it in his soul. His mind flashed with images of demon fangs and scaly skin. The smell of their putrid breath hung in the air.

Feeling like the snakes of hell were slithering behind, he sprinted for the front door and jammed the key into the lock. Throwing the door open, he yanked her inside and slammed the door shut. In the silence of the empty foyer, they both gasped for air.

The sudden sound of talons scraping across the door had them both jumping deeper into the house. Laughter cackled outside, and then faded into the night.

"What are those things, Shaila?"

"They smelled like demons...the undead." He was amazed at how matter-of-factly she said it.

"The undead. They sound like vampires."

She shook her head again. "I am not sure what you mean by vampires."

"Vampires. They're like human bats. They use their fangs to bite you and drink your blood. Blood gives them immortality. The dead person can't go to heaven, so they're stuck here. Dead, but not dead." He took a moment to catch his breath.

"Hmm." She gave it some more thought. "I have never heard of them. Demons use their fangs to inject venom, not to drink blood. Their immortality comes from absorbing souls. The Egyptians called them the *devourer of souls*."

Darius stumbled to the sitting room. He poured two drinks and handed one to her.

"It's whiskey. Just something to take the edge off." He took a large gulp of it himself. "Tell me more about these demons. So I know what I'll be up against next time."

She nodded.

"In my time, they were humans who pledged their souls to the cult of Apophis. It was a forbidden cult, but that does not stop them. Some humans are easily tempted to the bargain in exchange for money or power."

Shaila took a sip of the whiskey and choked on unexpected burning sensation. She opened her mouth and fanned fresh air down her throat. Shaking her head to clear her senses, she looked into the glass and tried a second sip. This one slid down much more easily. "Oh, goddess, that is a powerful drink."

"What happens to these people?"

"When demon venom enters and mixes with a human's blood, it causes them to become stiff, like a statue, for a while. During that time, a human's soul can be detached from its host body and absorbed to gain life-giving energy."

"That's sick."

"Some of my kind can heal that soul and return it to its host body. We are not all evil, Darius. We share this planet with you. Well, most of us want to share it. There are others who want to go back to the time when humans served our kind as slaves."

"Like Apophis?"

"Yes. Lilith, too." Shaila drained the last of the liquid from the glass.

"Why am I not surprised?" Darius brought a rectangular device over and placed it on top of the table. It made funny beeping sounds and lit up. He spread out many sheets of papyrus next to it. "What about Therion? What is he?"

"He was born among my kind, but his astral spirit...his immortal powers...were sealed away from him, leaving him with little more capability than a human."

"Thanks," he said sarcastically. "I didn't think you held us humans in such low esteem. Now, you lump that asshole right in there with us."

"I am sorry. I did not mean to offend. I was just pointing out that he is not the threat right now. Lilith is."

"Well, now I know what makes Therion such a wonderful person. He has a god complex."

"If the cult of Apophis exists now, even with Apophis in exile, then only one of my kind could wield the power needed to command an army of dark souls. She must have grown quite strong through these years."

Darius yawned and dragged a hand across his face. She could tell he was exhausted, but he was fighting it.

He went back to the bar, poured another drink and downed it in one gulp. Reaching in a low cabinet, he slid out a black bag and tossed it across the room toward her.

Instinctively, she caught it. It fell open in her hands, revealing a beautiful gold dagger with her name carved in hieroglyphs at the handle.

"My knife." Relief swept over her so quickly she nearly screamed. She examined the hilt carefully. Everything was as it should be. All was not lost, and she could at least protect herself.

Shaila would have thanked him, but he'd collapsed on the long chair with papyrus strewn across his lap.

If he kept this up, he would be no good to her. She had just enough energy herself to assist him in getting some rest. Very gently, she waved a mental pulse of energy toward Darius. It drifted towards him like a leaf floating on the water. Invisibly, it surrounded his aura and infused it with a calm sedative.

Steady deep breaths rose and fell from his chest. She found a blanket folded by the fireplace and covered him with it.

The effort had weakened her, but there was no time for sleep. She had spent over three thousand sun cycles in the darkness. She headed for the staircase. Time to find out more about Darius' grandfather. How did he know so much about the prophecy? Why would he tangle with someone like Lilith? And did he know the true nature of the gift mentioned in the prophecy?

# CHAPTER EIGHT

Julia McNair couldn't afford to be recognized. Actually, her father couldn't afford for her to be recognized. It would ruin his perfect campaign bid for the city mayor's seat. As a recent widower, he had the sympathies of the community and a break from character attacks from his opponents.

Julia honestly didn't miss her stepmother, who'd only been about five years older than her. *Yuck!* That was gross just thinking about it. But she adored her father. He really was a great Dad. Well, he used to be, before his best friend convinced him to enter politics. She liked remembering the old days when he was just a high school economics teacher.

"Oh, shit." She ducked behind the brick wall surrounding the firehouse so she wouldn't be spotted. She peeked around the edge in time to see a short fireman stretching and yawning. They must have all been fast asleep. No wonder it took five attempts at ringing the doorbell for someone to answer it.

A part of her died inside, just watching the man lean down and pick up the bundle she'd left there. Even though she'd wrapped him tightly, the little one wriggled and squirmed in the man's arms. The infant squealed in frustration. In response, her breasts leaked and her stomach tightened painfully. She panted heavily through the pain. He was probably hungry. She hoped the man would see the formula she'd left in the basket.

Julia loved the baby, but she loved her father

more. She couldn't afford to disappoint him, to see the light die in his eyes when he realized that she wasn't his little angel anymore.

Nobody knew of her pregnancy. She'd been lucky that she hadn't gained any more weight than she could easily hide under loose clothing, or easily attribute to stress. Her father's campaign. College classes. Hiding a pregnancy. It had all been too much to bear.

Her water had broken late this afternoon after her father had left for an evening campaign party. She choked on the irony. He kissed babies while his own daughter gave birth to one on her bathroom floor.

"Bye, Ethan," she whispered into the darkness after the fireman closed the door. She'd fallen in love with the tiny infant the moment he opened his eyes. Those beautiful, deep blue McNair eyes. She'd given him a family name. Reality bites. She couldn't keep him. Life just wouldn't work that way for her.

She wiped the tears from her cheeks, and walked away from Ethan...forever. A brisk wind whipped through the alleys between the buildings, raising goose bumps across her arms. The nights were getting cooler now that fall was here. She pulled her cardigan tighter across her chest, covering the two large wet spots darkening her cotton dress.

It had been risky dropping off the baby at a fire station so close to her home in Beacon Hill, but her body was just too weak. Her muscles still ached and spasmed. Plus, her father was due home in only fifteen minutes. And there was a serial killer on the loose. She pulled the ball cap lower over her face and turned quickly down a dark path. The service alley was a great shortcut to her house, which was only a couple of blocks up the hill.

"Look, see this one? She is a perfect gift for the

Dragon Queen."

Julia halted under a dim streetlight. Instinct told her she was in trouble. She couldn't see who was nearby in the shadows, but she could hear them. The voices slithered maliciously across her spine, making her shiver uncontrollably.

"You'd better be right. I don't wish to be fried like shish kabob for failing to bring her what she wanted."

*Are they talking about me?* She stood rooted to a spot under a lamp. Her legs frozen with fear, Julia refused to leave the safety of the light. At least, it felt safer there.

"I am right. She is fresh and young. Can't you smell it? The blood of birth is inside her."

They were talking about her! She could hear them inhaling like they were savoring a delicious aroma.

"The Dragon Queen will indeed be pleased. The power she will gain from this one. Oh, she will reward us." The sound of low whistles and clapping echoed across the cobblestone alley.

She finally found her voice. "W-What d-do you want from me?" She tried to peek into the darkness to see them. "I have no money. I-I'm just going home. My father is waiting for me."

"My pretty little soul, your father will be waiting for a very long time." The light bulb above her burst, casting her into the shadows with them. When her eyes finally adjusted to the moonlit darkness, she screamed. She screamed with all of the fear in her soul.

Two pairs of wicked yellow eyes gleamed toward her. *Oh my god!* Her father had been right. *When you sin, demons from hell do come to get you.*

"Can you taste the fear in this one's soul?" The smaller one licked his lips, a forked tongue whipping in the air.

The larger one smacked the other in the back of the head. "You know better than to take from her. We need this juicy one as a peace offering for the queen, who will be very displeased at our missing the other one."

Finally, her legs moved. They tried to carry her away from the alley. But these demons from hell were much faster. Big, scaly arms encircled her, preventing her from fighting back. Peering over her shoulder, she saw two glistening fangs. As they plunged painfully into her neck, she tried to scream for help. A scaly hand covered her mouth. She almost gagged on the putrid smell of it.

She felt icy flames spread inside her body from her neck as every muscle tightened and froze. Horror and fear bubbled inside her. Silent screams ricocheted across only her mind.

The alley lay eerily silent, as the two demons carried their prize into the ebony shadows of the night.

* * *

Light flickered on the other side of her eyelids. Slowly, Julia's eyes opened and adjusted to the dim light. As she curled and winced through another spasm in her stomach, she realized that she could move again.

But hope remained buried under fear as she felt cold metal wrapped around her wrists. As she shifted her weight up on an elbow, chains rattled against stone, bringing her attention to the blood stained altar she lay across.

Torchlight shifted eerily across the room, but there were too many shadows to see clearly. Things moved in the darkness: shuffling, gurgling, breathing.

Goosebumps spread quickly across her skin.

"What do you want with me?" She flinched at the sound of her own voice as terror lifted it into a higher octave. "P-please?" *Let me go.*

Almost leisurely, a woman in a long red dress stepped into the light and approached the altar.

Relief swelled through Julia's body that it wasn't one of those disgusting demons. Had she really seen them? Or only dreamed them?

The woman who approached had friendly eyes, pale skin and tons of blonde hair. She looked and moved like a model. "What's your name, doll?"

"Julia. Julia McNair."

The beautiful woman stroked Julia's hair and down her arms, but instead of helping her off of the table, the woman pushed her gently back down.

"No, please?" Julia struggled to get back up again. "I want to go home. Please, help me?"

Fresh tears spilled from the corners of her eyes. They felt cold sliding across her cheeks and ears. Her whole body trembled, igniting another round of spasms in her belly.

As the torch light flicked across the woman's red dress, the effect was a visual wave of blood. In sharp contrast, pale arms moved away from Julia's line of sight. But across her slightly rounded belly, she felt the woman's hands swirl in circles and then pull the cotton hem upward.

"No, no, no." Julia tried to cover herself, but the woman would not allow it.

"Lie still. Do you know who I am?"

Julia shook her head, afraid to speak.

"This is my domain, and I rule here."

A demon stepped forward carrying a glass of dark liquid that looked disgustingly like blood. Julia instinctively leaned away from the demon.

The movement seemed to amuse the woman, who waved away the offered glass.

"But this is the blood from Apophis, my queen. You must use this."

The demon queen did not seem to take the impudence well. Taking the glass, she smashed it against a wall. "This she-demon will bear *my* blood, not his."

With terrifying speed, the woman's body changed. Her hair slid back into her head and her skin turned grey and thin, so thin that Julia could see the skull underneath it. Black ears slanted backward, pulling the skin away from the mouth. Deep breaths whistled through sharp teeth and four deadly fangs.

With every fiber of her body, Julia strained to pull the chains from the altar. Her voice cracked as her high-pitched scream shifted into gurgling sobs. "NO! Get away from me."

Red eyes glowed from deep sockets. The demon queen cackled with enthusiasm. "Yes, dear Julia. It's time to join my demon army. But first your human body must die."

The demon queen jerked Julia's arm up and sank glistening upper fangs deep into her skin. She thought she would feel life draining from away from her. Instead, she felt a frigid acid seep into her. For the second time tonight, paralysis overtook her body, and yet her mind remained vividly aware of each moment.

Each agonizing moment brought more pain, as if each cell in her body dried up. One by one, she felt her organs shrivel. Muscles burned with a sharp feeling of decay. Her lungs tightened and breath would only come in short bursts.

Her body suddenly arched as muscles tightened and strained. Something moved inside her. Memories of sick teenage movies...of demon-spawned babies…burned in her mind. She shrieked her denial through another contraction.

The demon queen would not release Julia's arm, continuing to inject the poison. Blood rushed past her ears in a torrent, and then slowed to a quiet thump. Then, all was quiet.

As exhaustion set in, she relaxed. She just wanted to sleep. Darkness closed in, and the last sound she heard was a child's first cry.

\* \* \*

Julia awoke to an annoying buzz. Her body felt heavier and a sense of great strength spread through every muscle. Pressure grew within her eyes, and as she blinked her vision narrowed and colored with a yellow tint.

Amazed, she sat up and smoothed her palms along her arms, feeling the dry, scaly texture. Seeing her hands, she marveled at the nails, now hardened and sharpened into black talons.

Pain ripped across the roof of her mouth, but the feeling didn't scare her. She gagged as fangs popped from their sheaths for the first time, descending past her lower lip.

A large beast stood above her. Memory dawned. It was the demon queen, and she held a newborn baby girl. Wet and bloody, she yowled angrily.

"My, my, Julia. It looks like you had another child inside of you. A shame she came out second, for she will never get to grow up like the first one." The demon queen placed the child on the altar and turned back to Julia. "Now that your human body is dead, your soul belongs to me."

Tilting Julia's face upward, the demon opened her mouth and inhaled. Julia's mouth instinctively opened and air moved in a great whoosh from inside her chest.

Memories crowded across her mind like an old-fashioned filmstrip. Images of people shifted and blended before fading to gray. Her life was disappearing. It didn't feel right. *Where am I? Who am I?*

A cloudy white orb rose up from her mouth and hovered halfway between her and the demon queen. A final image formed clearly in her mind of a wet, bloody infant. *Who is she? Is she mine? …She needs me!*

Just as the demon queen sucked the orb into her mouth with a smile laced with victory, Julia heard the cries of the child. She felt her body wriggling next to her leg. She was fighting to live. *I want to live too.*

# CHAPTER NINE

Darius woke up slowly. He couldn't remember the last time he'd slept so deeply. He actually felt refreshed, except for a heated vibration on his stomach. Looking down, he found a pair of big yellow eyes smugly staring back. "Good morning, Bessie."

He rolled off the couch, forcing the cat to make a fussy retreat.

The aroma of fresh coffee filled the air. He would have to remember to thank Marcus for showing Shaila how to do that.

The kitchen was empty, but the pot was full. He filled a large mug near to the rim and decided to go black today. He found Shaila flipping through a book on Egyptian mummies, pausing at each photograph. She was back to her half-naked outfit again.

"Time to go."

She followed him down to the garage, but he caught himself just before he hit the garage door button.

"Shaila, you might consider choosing another outfit. We can't go out in public with you exposing yourself to the world." He could feel his blood pulsing rapidly through his neck. He pulled on his shirt collar, hoping to loosen the feeling.

"You are embarrassed by me."

"Hell, no!" He nearly choked out the answer.

She gave him a look that clearly said *fuck you* in any language, past or present. But she complied.

*Damn, she looks good in leather.* With her breasts

covered with the halter, she wouldn't get arrested for indecent exposure, although the cleavage showing was arresting enough. She had the longest legs he'd ever seen. The black leather pants slid on so perfectly they sculpted every muscle along her legs. Like a new accessory, the dagger nestled inside a leather sheath strapped to her thigh.

He strapped a helmet on her head none too gently. It shouldn't matter to him how she dressed. She was a grown woman. But he felt responsible for her.

When she climbed on behind him and he felt her thighs hugging his hips, he knew it would be a long ride to Cohasset. He was counting on the cool October air to help him stay sane and focused.

\* \* \*

Wind slashed across her skin, yet she enjoyed every moment of the sensations. Exhilarating. The subway had been smelly and crowded, but this machine was pure freedom. Bess had called it a motorcycle. Shaila had not felt such thrilling speed since riding the chariots on the plateau with her best friend.

A pang of sorrow stabbed at her heart. Nefertiti would have loved riding one of these machines. The human queen had been so daring and adventurous. A kindred spirit. A brilliant life cut too short. She had made a promise to Nefertiti to keep the babe safe. Shaila would die in honoring that vow...if it came to that.

However, this moment was for savoring life, not despairing death. She wrapped her arms around Darius' waist, leaning with the curves in the manner he had instructed. The ride was more than exhilarating, it was very intimate. Her breasts warmed with the constant jostling against his back. Straddling a vibrating machine sent little sensations of heat from the spot between her legs.

By the time they reached their destination, Shaila was panting almost as much from lust as she was from the exhaustion of hanging on.

"Are you okay?" Darius caught her, as her wobbly legs would barely hold her up.

"Oh, goddess! That was exciting."

Darius grinned at the childlike enthusiasm shining in her emerald eyes. For a moment, he felt a bit goofy, proud that he'd just impressed a girl. Maybe there was something to admire in her totally uninhibited spirit, so unlike his. He was the epitome of *in*hibited. He made no moves or decisions in life without total control.

Something about this woman pulled at a deep place in his soul. A place where a bullied boy resided. One who finally wanted to be free, live life, and let go.

He shook himself. No need to go there. Marcus was probably right. He did need a shrink.

"Where are we?"

"We're at the home of Dr. Bakari Majeed, a very old friend of my grandfather's. Papa Shadi talks about him quite a lot, but I've never met him. I try to avoid these kind of doomsayers. I'm sure he knows just as much on the topic of the ancient prophecy."

They were escorted through a large home overlooking the ocean. Sunlight streamed in through huge, floor-to-ceiling walls of glass. It was bright and very contemporary. Not what Darius was expecting from his grandfather's secret society buddy.

Darius paused in front of a beautiful sword mounted above a fireplace. It was plain for an ancient weapon. Clean lines and polished steel. The hilt looked to be plated with gold and shaped into rounded but simple wings. The very tip held a rounded yellow jasper stone with brown swirls. If the hilt had been wrapped in leather strapping, he would have thought this was the same sword he'd seen at Lilith's.

"Hello, Darius." The man smiling warmly was surprisingly younger than expected. Much younger. Darius didn't even try to hide the shock that must show on his face. With an impeccable suit, dark contemporary hair, and a well-trimmed goatee, the man looked more like a corporate executive than a renowned Egyptologist. "Do you like my sword? It was forged by some very gifted monks in a hidden temple in the Sinai Mountains."

"Good morning, Dr. Majeed." Darius shook his hand. "Yes, I do like it very much. It looks almost identical to another I've seen recently."

"It's one of a set. Seven of them, to be exact." The man indicated the sofa with a stunning view of the Atlantic Ocean. "Please, call me Bakari. How is your grandfather? I haven't heard from him since last week. He was very excited about some pictures he was finally going to see of the statue."

Darius appreciated Bakari's polished manner, but he didn't like how the man kept his eyes on Shaila. There was an odd calmness in his brown eyes that belied a very controlled demeanor as he walked slowly around Shaila.

Darius shifted, uncomfortable with how deeply the two looked at each other.

"Gods be praised. He found you!" Bakari dropped to the floor on both knees, bowing low before her.

"Please, stand up."

"You are Shaila a'k'Hemet, Lady of Flame, daughter of Inanna a'k'Suen, Lady of Life."

"Time has changed things." Shaila gripped the

man's shoulders. "Please, stop."

Bakari stood up and held out his hand. "I am Bakari Majeed. I was a priest in your mother's temple in Deir el Bahri. And I have been waiting for this day for an enormously long time. How could I have forgotten those beautiful green eyes so like your mother's?"

Darius cleared his throat. He couldn't decide what was more uncomfortable: watching Bakari kneel in front of Shaila or hearing that he's as old as she is.

"I'm sorry. I just kept feeling something from this woman that I hadn't felt in a long time…"

Darius moved a few inches closer toward Shaila protectively.

"No, Darius. Not that kind of feeling," he chuckled. "It's a feeling we get in our minds that tells us one of our kind is near. It's like a sixth sense."

Bakari indicated for them to follow him to his private study. The room was two stories high with a balcony surrounding the second level. Two walls were covered from top to bottom with bookshelves holding hundreds of ancient tomes in various languages. The back wall was covered in floor-to-ceiling windows framed by heavy red drapes.

"We're here for answers, Bakari."

"I'm certain I will have some. Your grandfather may have left out many things because of your…" Bakari paused in a search though a very old mahogany desk when his eyes focused on the medallion hanging around Darius' neck.

"You can say it. Because of my closed mind. Because I long ago stopped listening."

"Where is your grandfather? Why is he not here with you and why are you wearing his medallion?"

"Fifty-six hours ago, Papa Shadi and I were attacked by Lilith's demons. They took him. And they are holding him for ransom."

Pain crossed Bakari's features. He closed his eyes, and for a moment he just stood there as if in meditation. "Your grandfather kept pointing out the signs. I encouraged him, and did not think about the consequences. I'm sorry."

"It's not your fault." Darius noted Bakari's questioning glance toward Shaila. "I tried to sneak in and rescue Papa Shadi. I discovered her by accident. The medallion triggered her resurrection."

"You mentioned a ransom." Bakari leaned back heavily into a high-backed chair. "Considering the prophecy, I'm betting Lilith wants the amulet."

"Jackpot."

Bakari gave Shaila a stern look. "Has he been told why it is so important that the amulet be kept away from Lilith?"

"Yes, but will somebody please tell me why she wants it? And while you're at it, tell me why my grandfather should be sacrificed in order to keep it from her." A rage built within Darius so fast, he started to choke.

Leaning across the desk, Bakari placed a hand over Darius' clenched fist. "There is much that you need to hear. Your grandfather has known the risks involved. You must listen."

Darius felt a strange calm flowing into him from Bakari's hand. Following the man's lead, Darius lifted his gaze toward Shaila, ready to listen to information that had not been shared with him previously. Another friggin' notch on the negative side of her *unpredictability* chart.

"I was entrusted by my mother to guard the amulet. It contains the astral spirit of the child spawned by Lilith and Apophis. Should Therion ever be reunited with this amulet, he will regain all of his dark Anunnaki powers. All of them."

A myriad of emotions passed through him. Some, even he did not understand. *Deceived* was one he recognized instantly. She'd held this back from him, when she'd known he needed it to save his grandfather. *She knows where it is.*

"What power do you fear the most?"

"We fear his ability to release Apophis from his imprisonment. An evil triad, such as Lilith, Therion, and Apophis..." Shaila sounded breathless from the very thought of such a disaster. "It would mean the end for this planet, and all that is on it. If Apophis were to be freed, it would begin the *Age of Awakening*, when all of the dead are resurrected to annihilate the living, and when darkness would prevail over light. He will not leave this planet until every soul has been beaten down into submission."

"Is that all?" He tried to sound sarcastic, but he couldn't quite get there. As angry as he was, he knew his grandfather believed every word of the prophecy. He could easily see his grandfather doing everything he could to save the world.

Bakari returned to his search of his desk, pulling open drawers and rummaging through cubbyholes. Finally, he sighed with relief. "May I show you something?"

In his hand rested a small gold box with a simple painted cartouche of Sekhmet and another symbol that Darius was not familiar with.

"May I?" Darius accepted the box, cradling it in one hand. It was lighter than he would have guessed. The gold exterior made it look heavier.

"The symbol is referred to as the *seven arrows of Sekhmet*. But the real treasure is inside the box, of course."

As he opened the box, Darius whistled

appreciatively as he viewed the beautiful ring resting on coal black silk cloth. A red ruby nestled in the center of a round sun disk, with thin wings stretching out from either side to wrap around a king's finger.

Shaila's voice shook with sadness when she spoke. "It was the ring of the pharaoh Akhenaten. Queen Nefertiti wore it briefly after his death, when she assumed the throne. She wore it until the day she was murdered." A single tear slid down her cheek before she could wipe it away. "The ring now belongs to the son of Nefertiti. He would be the rightful heir to the throne of Egypt."

"If there was a throne." He kept the sarcasm to a minimum. "That's the child you seek, isn't it?"

"Yes." Shaila rubbed her eyes, searching for the memories locked away in her mind for thousands of sun cycles. "It is time to find the child. Time to raise and train him as Shadiki foresaw."

"Time?" Darius looked skeptical. "I think we're out of time for that."

She ignored his tone. "I need time as well to find others of my kind. We will need their strength. Bakari, who is left here?"

Bakari shook his head. "There are a few, but they are scattered across the world. They have made new lives for themselves."

"What of Seth?" Shaila held her breath, knowing how important her uncle, the Lord of Command, would be to their success. As the true father of Nefertiti's son, he would move the heavens and the earth to find his child.

"He has not been seen in many decades. Papa Shadi has a crazy notion that Seth's been hibernating inside the Sphinx." Bakari twirled his forefinger around his ear.

"Well, if this child is supposed to be a messiah to

your own kind, wouldn't they come running to help out?" Darius returned the ring to the box.

"Some might. I have slept through too many ages to know how the Anunnaki feel at this time. Most were not interested in the plight of the weaker species that shared this planet, and many used your kind as slaves and consorts."

"What about you? How did you treat our kind?"

Dark shadows hid his eyes from her, but she sensed the accusation bubbling just under the surface. She had to bury a quick burst of her own ire that this man could think of her as abusive. "I have always believed that the humans deserved to exist without interference from us."

"That's easy for you to say now, when you're weak and not in control anymore." Darius moved into her personal space.

"Do you doubt my sincerity?" She refused to cower. Instead, she stood to her full height, putting her eyes just barely below his.

"No. I don't doubt that you wish to help, but I do question your true beliefs."

"Which ones, exactly?"

"The ones which say your kind are better than our kind. I have heard you several times refer to us as the *weaker species*. Tell me how you really feel, sweetheart."

There was absolutely no mistaking the sarcasm in his voice. He was judging her again. When had she ever been so judged by a human? *Never.*

"I am sorry to have offended you, Darius, but if anyone has a right to be angry, I do. I cannot deny that in many respects I do view humans as being weaker than my kind, but not in the manner you are thinking. It is not an air of superiority."

"Enlighten me."

"That is exactly what I mean. I spent many sun cycles teaching human warriors and kings to reach their full power, to free themselves and nurture all that this good earth provides for you. Do you not understand? Our species are so similar. You have much of the same capacities to use your energies as we do. But time and again, you let the judgment of others interfere in your belief of the sacred skills we taught you."

"Now you sound like Papa Shadi."

"Shadiki understood the power you have, but he despaired that greed would prevent humans from passing on that knowledge. Indeed, the human kings often kept the knowledge to themselves, wanting to be seen as gods on earth. My kind is no more god-like than yours, but your ancestors were easily led astray."

"So, humans are like lambs," his voice held a bitter edge, "easily led."

"Yes, Darius. Humans are so easy to convince that they are unworthy. But it was not the Anunnaki who imposed those ideas. You can thank your own kind for that. It was humans who began to squash the teachings and who nurtured the false energies of greed and judgment."

"Then, why help us? Why help such a faulty species?"

"Because I have always been in awe of the human spirit. Even in the darkest of circumstances, humans cling to an emotion we have little understanding of…hope. And even when I believe it is misdirected, the very existence of that emotion makes your kind strong." Instinctively, she placed her palm over his heart.

"Men like your grandfather taught me what hope meant. That it is something worth fighting for. It is exactly what inspired me to leap through time frozen in a statue, trusting in an old man's visions. I trust that destiny brought me here for a reason, and I will not fail. I cannot fail."

Nearly choking on the intensity of her own emotions, she felt his hands on her shoulders pulling her into his chest. His muscles tensed and flexed under her cheek with his own conflicting emotions. She closed her eyes, absorbing strength from him.

"Darius, it will take more than physical strength to defeat Lilith." Bakari spoke with the deep conviction of experience.

"Well, nature seems to have selected *my* species to have survived all this time." A twinkle returned to his dark eyes. "Maybe our mental strength is pretty tough after all. We don't need to be stronger. We need to be smarter."

\* \* \*

Darius winced as lightning slashed in the distance. The thunder boomed over a sea as turbulent as his heart. The northeastern storm had been gathering its forces off shore for days, waiting for its moment to besiege the coastline. Not unlike the forces gathered around his life.

They needed to return to the city very soon, before the winds would be too strong to ride in. Darius stood at the wall encircling Bakari's property, watching the waves lap up the sand along the shore below.

Bakari brought him a drink. He wished the spicy burn of the liquor could numb his pain along with his throat.

"What have I stumbled into?"

"An ancient secret, my friend."

"Why have we not known that you exist?"

"Because mankind would destroy us. I know it

sounds like a cliché to you, but humans would fear us, lock us up, and study us."

"Yet, I am supposed to believe that you're here to help us? To save us?"

"There is so much to tell you about the past, Darius."

"Well, I'm a little busy at the moment for a history lesson."

"Papa Shadi has been waiting for the right time."

"I know now that he's a part of this, but how much? Just exactly how long have you known Papa Shadi?" Darius feared he already knew the answer. He had felt it his whole life that his grandfather was different.

Shaila appeared. "Actually, Shadiki and Bakari are more different from me…than from you. They were both born human. I gave Shadiki, my priest, the gift of life. You carry it with you now." She pointed toward the medallion. "Over four thousand sun cycles ago, I used the *Eye of Ra* medallion to gift Shadiki a'Mahg with an energy force that would extend his life indefinitely."

Darius looked at Bakari, who shrugged. "I am half Anunnaki, which is why I do not wear a medallion."

Darius walked slowly back toward the door leading into the study, shivering from the bite of the ocean winds.

"What of my mother? She was human, right?" He dropped onto the end of the couch.

Bakari chuckled. "The energy from the medallion does not pass on. Your grandfather, cranky old mage that he is, has fathered many children in his long lifetime. Yes, Darius. You have a few relatives out there."

"Why didn't he tell me?"

"He isn't the fathering type, and I'm sure you know that. His fondness for you is unique. He couldn't let you suffer the same fate as your mother. She let drugs and booze claim her life, but you were different."

"I was a grimy little street punk."

"You survived. Adapted. He respected that. So, he took a step he never had before. He accepted the role of raising you. He polished up your clothes, taught you to speak properly, and channeled your talents in a better direction."

Indeed. Where would he be today if Papa Shadi hadn't taken him in? Jail, most likely. Darius wasn't a dirty street thief anymore. He spoke four languages, and he'd honed his skills to be the best antiquities retrieval specialist in the world.

"So my grandfather is over four thousand years old? That's one helluva gene pool." He massaged the back of his head and neck. The damned knot was back again. "Why did you give him this gift, Shaila?"

"Because he saved my life." Shaila joined him on the leather couch. "I was in a battle against Apophis. His powers are older and darker, which gave him a significant advantage over me. Hundreds of human soldiers already lay dead on the battlefield. I had arrived too late to fight with them. A bold priest brought us both beer, trying to appeal to us to end the battle. He had laced Apophis' drink with an herb to make him sleep."

"Couldn't you have flashed out of there?"

"A warrior does not abandon the battle." Shaila pounded the air to emphasize her opinion. "I wanted to defeat Apophis, but I had lost too much blood to heal myself. I was dying. My energy was fading. Shadiki carried me to my temple and cared for me."

Darius felt a strange pressure in his chest. He

shifted, trying to ease the tightness. "My choice is clear. I have to get Papa Shadi back, and he needs this." He fisted the medallion and kissed it.

Bakari drew a hand across his goatee. "Do you have a plan?"

"More like a sketchy idea."

"When are you going to put this sketchy idea into action?"

"Tomorrow night." Darius smiled at Shaila. "We've been invited to Lilith's party."

Bakari laughed. "Reckless boy. When you need me, count me in. Now go. Get home before the storm hits. It is a dark storm. The darkness brings many souls above ground."

"Do I need to keep garlic by my doors and windows?"

Bakari avoided the sarcasm. "They aren't vampires, but you still wouldn't want to invite them in."

"Papa Shadi must have known they were around. What did he do to protect himself? I've noticed that they will not enter my house. We were chased last night, but they didn't even try to break through the door."

"I helped him carve a protective spell into a wall in his private study. As long as it remains intact, the house is sacred ground." Bakari nodded toward Shaila. "The spell might also be protecting your spirit from being felt by Lilith."

"That's okay, Bakari. Since my awakening was," Shaila looked hesitantly in Darius' direction, "accidental, I have not connected with my astral spirit. I am weak without that connection."

Darius heard what she was not saying. She was admitting to being weak, but she was refusing to say that she was vulnerable. How could he think of taking her into a place filled with demons when she wasn't at her best? That was a risk he would need to consider.

"I have something that will help you with that." Bakari shifted a small painting on the wall behind the desk, revealing an old-fashioned safe. The dial began to spin even without being touched. It spun back and forth several times before a slight click sounded from within. Reaching inside the safe, he withdrew a small leather bag. He poured a few round wafers into Shaila's hand. "Remember the *mannah* that we would give to the pharaohs for energy and enlightenment? This is a modern version. Take them sparingly, for they are more potent."

Darius thought they looked just like the wafers used in church to place on the tongues of the faithful receiving the Sacrament, the bread of life. These wafers were embossed with an ankh, the Egyptian symbol for life. He wanted to ask questions about the wafers and everything else, but they were out of time. Wind gusts were beginning to pound on the windows more frequently.

"Thank you, Bakari." Shaila bowed low in gratitude. Then, they embraced, kissing each cheek. With great effort, Darius squashed the urge to yank her out of the man's arms.

The rain still held to the sky, but all around them the air colored with a strange eerie yellow.

"Hurry, my friends." Bakari called out in the sudden calm. "The darkness waits for no one."

# CHAPTER TEN

They reached home just as the first squall line pounded the city. In moments, Boston became a dark gray battlefield, barraged by nature's arsenal of wind and rain.

Shaila followed Darius to Papa Shadi's private study, which was a lot messier and dustier than Bakari's private room. Stacks of old books were piled everywhere. Thin wooden shelves bowed under the weight of scrolls, books, and small relics. A lamp with dark glass lit the room with an orange glow. Dust motes danced in front of them, swirling on light air currents.

Darius climbed over several stacks of files and reached for an immense rug hanging on the wall opposite the window. As he peeled back one of the bottom corners, he revealed a spell hastily scratched into the wall.

It wasn't particularly long, but she was frustrated that she could not read it. "You expected something different?"

"I was expecting it to be written in hieroglyphics or English. I guess I didn't expect it to be in Arabic."

"Are you frightened, Darius?"

He hesitated, drawing in a deep breath. "I would be lying if I said I wasn't." He dug out a blank piece of papyrus and a writing stick, which he flicked in the air a few times to get it working.

"What makes you scared?"

"I feel so unprepared for all of this wicked shit

going on!" He let out a heavy sigh. "Sorry. I didn't mean to shout, but I don't really feel like talking. I want to go through the layouts of Lilith's estate again, and then I want a stiff drink. In that order."

"Preparation is important to you?"

"Absolutely." His writing stick flew across the papyrus as he translated the spell. "When it comes to things like safety, it only takes one time. One unguarded moment and you could lose everything...everything that was dear to you."

Shaila could see the red aura of anger building around him.

"Papa Shadi is special to me too." She used the title Darius was familiar with.

"So special, that while my grandfather...your priest...is being held hostage by your sworn enemy, you keep secrets about the very thing that could secure his freedom?" The venom hit its mark this time.

"It is not as simple as you say! There is more at stake here than one man. Shadiki knew this." She gave him credit for his pain, but how could he not understand his own grandfather's sacrifice. Not just this one, but all of those given in the centuries he lived through as he waited for the prophecy to begin. He could have given up at any time, yet he had not.

A wave of dizziness forced her to sit down. She could feel the blood draining from her face.

"If I asked you where the amulet is, would you tell me?" She heard the brittle sound of bitterness. He did not trust her. She was too tired to try to change his opinion.

"Darius, do not make the mistake of underestimating Lilith. She is not likely to keep her end of the bargain. If she is rebuilding the army of Apophis, then she has gained more strength than she ever had before."

"It sounds like I'm not the only one who needs to admit they're scared."

"Probably." She pulled a wafer out of the pouch to study it. "Bakari said that it is stronger than the *mannah* from our time."

"What does it do for you?"

"It renews and builds our strength. It enhances our energies." Exhausted, she closed her her eyes, clutching the pouch to her chest.

"Wow. Drugs in ancient Egypt. Who would have thought that?" He was looking intently at her face, pity clearly written across his. "You need that, don't you?"

She hated seeing the judgment in his eyes, but there was no time to fight that right now. "I do. Goddess, I do."

* * *

Shaila felt some of her tension begin to melt away. The tranquility she felt in this simple sleeping room would aid her in her meditation. That and the energy boost from the wafer should finally connect her to the astral plane.

Deep rumbling announced the cat's arrival. Bessie transformed into her human form, again wearing her *steam punk* style of clothing, as she had called it.

"Where did you get this, sister?" Bessie's eyes were wide with interest as she fingered the ankh impression on the thin white wafer.

"Bakari gave that to me today. Do you need one?"

"Nope. You need it more than I do. Besides, I get some from Papa Shadi from time to time." Bessie sniffed the air. "But you can bring me a cup of that coffee I smell."

Shaila ignored the request. "Why have you not told me about Papa Shadi? That it is my own priest who is held captive by Lilith?"

Bessie snorted with impatience. "Because I know you. You are so driven to completing your mission that I you'd blow the whole thing by rushing over there to get him back."

"What makes you think I would do something so foolish?"

"You are full of questions and he's the only one with all of the answers. You would have been hell bent to get to those answers. I can tell you that Lilith has no idea you're here, and that is the best thing going for us."

Shaila could not argue with Bessie's logic, although Shaila now felt calmer since meeting with Bakari. Yesterday she could easily have chosen to leave the house to search for her priest. Being cut off from the world for so long felt disorienting. She wanted and needed his guidance.

"Bess, what was it like living through all this time?"

"Nothing very remarkable. I basically watched the world grow up. After you left, I traveled to England. I found that I liked hanging out with science geeks. Sir Isaac Newton was my favorite." Bessie snuggled on the plush chair in the corner. "You know, he discovered the law of gravity. Most people said he discovered it when an apple fell on his head. I'm here to tell you, the tree didn't drop it. I did. He deserved it. He was ignoring me."

Shaila found a fat candle and placed it on the floor. She willed a flame onto the wick. The scent of jasmine filled the air, as a tiny curl of smoke drifted upward.

"Coming over here was...different. The people

here were more liberal. They love their freedoms, and they don't hesitate to show it. They even like to share it if they can."

"You mean these people of Boston?"

"I meant the people of this country. Americans."

"Do you like it here? It is very different from Egypt."

"Very. Just wait until you experience your first winter nor'easter. That's when I'm thankful for having fur." She nearly purred the last word. Footsteps thumped above them. Bessie flashed back into her feline form.

Shaila stood in front of a tall mirror and watched her reflection. Silently, her leather clothes melted away. As she stood naked for a moment, she found Darius watching her through the mirror. He hesitated just outside the doorway. Pure desire glittered in his golden eyes. She felt a strong pull to go to him. His energies showed that emotions warred inside him. Anger clashed with desire.

Her lids dropped slowly and she willed her body to be clothed in the ancient white robes of her family. Sitting cross-legged upon the floor, she balanced her energies and cleared all thought. Her Anunnaki spirit existed on a different plane, and her survival depended upon her connecting with it.

She placed the wafer on her tongue. It tingled as it dissolved slowly in her mouth. She left everything behind. The room. The man. The house. Her soul soared through the darkness, searching for the light that would be her. Shaila a'k'Hemet, the Lady of Flame. The daughter of Inanna, and granddaughter of Tia'Mat, the Great Dragon Queen.

She would need to keep her search short if she did not want to be detected by Lilith. This dimension once held millions of spirit lights. Now, the darkness of the astral plane scared her. The sacred knowledge of the ancients had faded. The people of this time did not understand the danger they were in of losing their power...and their lives.

*Oh goddess, the spirit lights are so dim.* But there were some she could see. There were astonishingly few of her kind left. They were weak, but they did exist. She would need to find them. The humans should not have been left so unprotected. Could she have made a difference, if she had not chosen to skip across time? She hoped there was still time to lead the way.

The current shifted ahead, curving into a strange section, nearly void of light. She hesitated, unable to continue on her search tonight. She still held the element of surprise as long as they were not tuned in to her arrival.

A sudden coldness speared through her soul. Back in the direction she had come from, a swirl of dark spirits shrouded in fog fingered through the plane. *Shadow walkers!*

Her stomach twisted with horror. Someone had awakened Apophis' elite death squad. These were no simple soul-sucking demons. These demon beasts would mutilate their victims. They were pure malevolence. And they were crawling in her direction.

*Lilith, what have you done?*

\* \* \*

Fernando Mendez forced his way through the driving wind and rain. He wasn't going to miss this opportunity of a lifetime. The Alpha-Z's were throwing a party at their fraternity house, which they did almost every night. The difference this time was that he'd been invited. Sort of.

The Alpha Zeta fraternity had been banned

officially from the Boston U campus, but they still had their unofficial brownstone along Commonwealth Avenue. The property, and actually the whole block, was owned by a very old Boston family, one of whom had been an original member of the fraternity decades ago.

Nestled in between an art school and a modeling agency, the boys found plenty of fish in the proverbial sea. And fish they did, nightly. The rumor mill said that just walking inside their place was like walking through the Pearly Gates themselves. Everyone wanted to get into heaven, and everyone wanted to get into the Alpha-Z House.

Fernando Mendez was no exception.

He'd been accepted to Boston University on a full scholarship, making his family very proud. He was the first one in his family to go to college, earning that distinction by spending his whole life studying hard and making the right choices along the way.

At the age of four he'd begun his complete fascination with dinosaurs. His life's passion led him to the prestigious programs here. He especially loved Professor Marcus' classes. Professor Marcus never stopped reading about dinosaurs and anything that had to do with them. His current studies on soil were totally dry to others, but Fernando understood the passion. He was thrilled that the professor asked him to work with him on a special study for NASA.

Recently, his passion for his studies had been eclipsed by a girl. Julia McNair, the beautiful, auburn-haired daughter of a local politician, and from one of the oldest families in Boston. So out of his league. He was the son of a humble truck driver from Puerto Rico. Two people from very different worlds.

But last week, after class, she'd smiled at him. How his world had tilted from a simple smile. She'd broken up with the president of the Alpha Zeta fraternity. As they were studying for Professor Marcus' midterm, she'd asked him to join her at the fraternity house for their mid-week party.

Now, he'd found himself standing on the steps of the infamous Alpha-Z House. He felt like a major life shift was about to happen. A new world was opening up to him. The front door of the brownstone swung inward.

"Yeah. Who are you?" A girl in striped tights and a black leather sheath dress sipped from a tall glass of beer.

"I-I'm Fernando. I'm supposed to meet Julia McNair here at ten o'clock tonight."

The girl looked skeptical for a moment, but then her eyes lit up. "Wicked righteous tie, Fern. Come on in. Haven't seen Julia, but she usually shows up about midnight. Sometimes she has to wait until her dad goes to sleep, ya know."

He followed her through hallways and rooms so jammed with coeds he thought the fire codes were likely being broken here.

He nearly ran the girl over when she stopped so suddenly. She swiveled around with a fresh beer for him. He accepted it. She sipped hers again, and absently ran a finger down his tie. "I liked dinosaurs when I was girl. I really liked the raptors. I used to pretend I was one, and I'd sneak into my little brother's room and scare him."

A nearby door swung open with a bang and a couple stumbled inside, seeking a few private moments to hook up.

Fernando gulped down some beer while she looked him up and down. Her eyes showed clearly that she was evaluating and probably finding him wanting. Instead, he felt her arms snaking around his neck and her tongue in his mouth. Her lips were soft, but they tasted like strong beer. The girl giggled as he pried her arms away.

This wasn't his crowd, and she wasn't Julia. He decided to text Julia to meet him at the Starbucks down the street instead.

Before he could make it to the stairs, a guy in a Boston U sweatshirt grabbed Fernando by the arm and drew him into a room. He was about to punch the guy in the face.

"No, man. Not like that shit. Here." He indicated a room full of guys and girls gathering around a coffee table. They were all emptying plastic baggies of multicolored pills into a large glass jar in the center of the table. "It's our Hump Night Pharm Party! No better way to get juiced up for mid-terms."

Fernando didn't recognize anyone in the room, except maybe the guy sitting in the high-backed chair. He was pretty sure that was the fraternity's president, and Julia's former boyfriend. A girl stepped around the chair and sat on his lap. It was the girl who'd let him in the house, and who'd hooked up with him a few moments ago.

"So, Julia invited you here, huh?" The guy was sizing him up. Fernando did not want to fight. He could, but he didn't want to. "Sit. Join us. If Julia wants you here, then you need to stay until she gets here."

The others in the room happily poured their drinks and started popping pills from the jar at random.

* * *

The grandfather clock down the hall chimed midnight. Fernando felt each bong inside his head. He hazily remembered being pushed into a chair and having a handful of pills forced into his mouth. He'd swallowed them only after being punched in the stomach. The effects of the pharmaceutical mix hit him quickly after choking the pills down a dry throat.

As he awoke, he found himself slumped onto the couch and his stomach hurt like hell. Next to him, the party girl slumped over the Alpha-Z president. Others were scattered around the room, unconscious or giggling at some private hallucination.

He was probably having his own hallucination right now, because he was watching Julia float into the room from the balcony. She was so beautiful, floating there like a perfect angel. Her eyes scanned the room, but hesitated on him. She came closer.

He imagined her smooth skin next to his. Soft lips brushing across his jaw. Her silky, auburn hair cascading around his face. Her eyes--

"Whoa!" Fernando reined in all the strength he had left and shoved against her. This wasn't his Julia. Yellow eyes glittered above two very sharp, very evil looking fangs. Her skin seemed to have grown green scales around her throat and on her arms. It reached for him with black, bloody claws. To make matters worse, he realized several more appeared around her...just like her.

A fear from deep within bubbled to the surface. Fernando Mendez screamed and kicked with a rush of supercharged adrenaline. All of the students in the room awoke. The air became thick with fear and the pungent smell of urine.

The demons attacked, toying wickedly with the students and relishing the sounds of terror. Fernando heard flesh being ripped apart and saw beasts lapping up blood with forked tongues.

Fernando had fallen off the couch and now watched mesmerized as Julia...or what was once

Julia…sank her fangs into the party girl's neck. She seemed to take extra pleasure in tormenting the young girl. He wondered why the girl didn't struggle anymore. She had earlier. She screamed through lips that seemed frozen.

As the girl's screams subsided, Julia's eyes glowed red. She dropped the lifeless form to the floor and turned toward Fernando. He whispered a prayer and crossed himself quickly. He didn't want to give up, but his drug-affected limbs were too weak. Julia made as if to pounce upon him, but hesitated. Her bright red eyes stared at him deeply, as if trying to figure out who he was.

A window burst open with a wave of cold, wet wind. A strange fog swept into the room. Black shadows filled with evil. The beast that was once Julia peered into Fernando's soul. He felt pinned to his spot on the floor. Inside his mind, a voice rang out clearly. *Run, Fernando. Run, if you want to live. Now!*

# CHAPTER ELEVEN

Darius could not have imagined anything so beautiful before this moment. Naked she was sinfully desirable. In flowing white robes she looked glorious, like an angel from the heavens.

He had stolen a statue and discovered an angel. He felt an odd calmness replacing the anger and guilt he'd felt moments ago.

Spellbound, he couldn't leave the room. He had to stay and wait for Shaila to awaken from her meditation. He picked up Bessie and sat down in an overstuffed chair. Bessie twisted in circles a few times, nuzzled her nose in between his thighs, and fell asleep.

A slight vibration pulsed in the air. Shaila's body almost glowed with ethereal light as it hovered a few inches above the floor. He wondered why he didn't feel shocked anymore. He'd entered a Twilight Zone, and yet he believed it.

He admired the serenity in her exotic features, and envied her peacefulness. He'd been schooled in various martial arts, but he hadn't felt any pull toward the meditation or communing part. Maybe there was something to it. She looked like she felt...free.

His own eyes slowly closed.

*He was in a dark room. It felt as old and dusty as a tomb. A baby wailed from the shadows. A woman's voice curled through the stifling air, humming softly. The baby seemed to calm with each note of the song. The language was unfamiliar, but it sounded like a lullaby. A candle sputtered to life, illuminating the woman's profile.*

*She was bending over the tiny babe, rubbing its chubby little legs soothingly. She looked up at Darius, still whispering the ancient song. As she moved closer to him, he wondered why she had left the baby. He felt in his soul that there was a message in the song, but could not understand the words.*

*Standing opposite him, she cupped her hand on his cheek. He instinctively leaned into her touch. She smiled up at him, love flickering in her eyes like a candle flame. Darius breathed in the clean, jasmine perfume she wore.*

He sighed, a feeling of deep contentment washed over him.

\* \* \*

Sharp cat claws digging into the inside of Darius' thigh shattered the dream and the euphoria. "Damn it, cat!"

Bessie lunged off his lap, deftly avoiding the swat he aimed at her. She howled at Shaila's shivering form on the floor.

"Shaila!" Darius rushed across the room. Her breathing was quick and shallow. Sweat sheened across her brow, yet her skin felt ice cold. He grabbed the comforter off the bed and threw it over her. Covering her body with his, he rubbed everywhere he could, trying to create heat from the friction. "Shaila! Shaila! Wake up! Can you hear me?" He finally felt...and smelled...a long, coffee-laden breath. "Whew."

"Yes, Darius," she croaked through dry lips, "I hear you most excellently."

Darius breathed a sigh of relief. "What happened? What was that all about?"

"I did not find my astral spirit. It was so dark there I became lost. I did not expect that."

"It's not usually dark in that...dimension?" Or wherever it was she went.

"No. It used to be filled with lights. Millions of tiny lights. The light energies of the Anunnaki. Like little stars in the heavens. There are so few now, and those that are there are very dim."

"This is a bad thing, I take it."

"When light is weak, the darkness gains power." Shaila shuddered.

Darius rubbed up and down her arms to warm her up. He found her looking at him intently. Pulling one arm out of her cocoon of blankets, she'd cupped his face. As her palm smoothed across his cheek, he instinctively leaned into it. Her green eyes darkened to a deep emerald shade. The tip of her pink tongue slid across her dry lips.

Her palm tensed as it pulled his face slowly toward hers. Their lips hovered against each other, barely touching. Their breath mingling. He felt her blood pulse through her lips. His blood pumped faster in response. Every nerve in his body suddenly sizzled white hot. His lips burned. He needed...

His tongue licked across her lips, seeking an invitation. She accepted. Their tongues caressed in an ancient dance, gliding and teasing. She moaned. He pressed deeper into her. He felt her palms stroke his head and neck. Skin. This woman seemed to love the feel of skin.

Darius was so focused on conquering her mouth and feeling her dark hair slide between his fingers that he almost didn't register that in one moment he felt hot skin across his front and cool air across his backside.

Shaila was frustrated with the miniscule amount of skin exposed to her. Every nerve in her body fired to life, itching with desire to be touched. She wanted more. She wanted to feel all of Darius. So she willed away the clothes that held a barrier between them.

A burst of energy fired through her. In answer, a dying flame roared to new life in the fireplace. Shaila brought his face to hers once more and pressed every available inch of her skin against his.

Shaila loved skin. His skin. Every smooth, hot inch of him excited her. This human, who reminded her so much of the strong, determined pharaohs of her past, created such a fever in her body. Had she ever felt this good?

Her blood built to a frenzy as he licked a path between her nipples. Sucking them in, nibbling and teasing sensations in her that rippled through her veins. She wrapped her legs around him and shivered with anticipation.

Growling possessively, she bit his shoulder to control him. Rolling them over, she straddled him, poised to plunge him deep into her.

That was when she saw them...two reddened punctures in his shoulder. Shock clouded his hazel eyes. Quickly, she re-sheathed the fangs, which had extended without her realizing it. *Oh, Goddess, how did this happen?*

"Darius?" All of the fire and urgency whooshed out of her system in choking gulps. "I...I am so sorry. I do not know what came over me. I should not have..."

She expected anger. Instead, she felt two strong arms of protectiveness wrap around her body.

"It's okay, Shaila." He reached for the comforter and covered her with it once again. "You lost control. That might have been what Bakari meant when he warned you how potent it was."

"I do not like that feeling...losing control." Her teeth chattered loudly as the shivers returned. Her adrenaline must have enhanced the after-effects of the wafer. That and having been without the *mannah* for so long.

Darius continued to hold her through the worst of the shakes. "I know exactly what you mean."

She heard no judgment in his voice.

* * *

Shaila swirled her morning coffee under her nose. As she savored the earthy aroma, she gave silent thanks that the tremors had finally ceased.

Marcus stomped into the house and swiveled carefully out of a wet coat and boots. "Good morning, wicked storm out there." Marcus kissed her cheeks like they were old friends. He whistled as his eyes traveled the entire length of her body. "Leather sure looks good on you, Shaila."

"Hey, Marcus." Darius looked over at his friend's grim features. "What's wrong?"

"Haven't you been watching the news?"

"No. I've been cooking breakfast."

Marcus grimaced. "You mean you've been burning breakfast. Move over." He made quick work of flipping the food in the pan. "See? You don't stab at the omelet. Just flip it."

"What's on the news?" As Darius touched a flat screen device sitting on the kitchen counter, Shaila heard new sounds in the room.

She moved in closer and watched an image of tiny woman moving across the screen. The woman grimly described the chaotic scene: a group of college kids were murdered. Behind her, men in slick black coats entered a building that looked very similar to Darius' home.

"They're saying it appears to be another ritual murder. Wonder if the news will spark another protest in front of the State House?" Marcus ate his food, but his hands paused midway to his lips. "Could this be the work of some of those demons you talked about?"

The woman on the screen continued with gruesome descriptions and showed images of other recent murder victims. The opinion seemed to be that all were connected. Shaila thought of the dark beasts she had seen along the astral plane last night.

"There have been more of these *murders*?"

Both men nodded.

"I must go see this, Darius." She pointed at the scene in the picture device. "I will be able to tell if it is the work of demons or not."

"They'll never let us near the place." Marcus slumped into a chair.

Darius rubbed the medallion, pacing around the table. "I think I have an idea. Shaila," he pointed to the picture device, "it's like the computer signal you used."

Shaila nodded. Gently closing her eyes, she searched for its signal. It was very weak, but it hummed with loud, fuzzy noises. She felt her body shimmering away from the kitchen.

"Holy shit, that's wicked," Marcus' voice whispered with excitement.

The connection ended as Shaila appeared in full form behind a man with a huge black machine hoisted on his shoulder. The woman from the *television* stood in front of him, still repeating the same small list of details about the scene.

Remembering Marcus' reaction to her choice of clothing, she realized that she might not blend in very well. She quickly melded her clothing to match the rain-slicked black coats of the men who were allowed access into the building. She entered undisturbed.

She managed to hold her composure, but she could feel all of the blood draining from her face. Fear.

She felt the remnants of it shimmering in waves within the small room on the top floor. She feared the worst.

How could she explain to anyone that the scene before her equaled some of the bloodiest she had seen in her time? Of course, in her time Tia'Mat was the Great Dragon Queen, and she held the *shadow walkers* at bay from the humans. From time to time, a few of the dark sentinels would escape the shadows and feed from human flesh. However, Queen Tia always felt them coming, and sent her warriors to destroy them. Shaila had been one of those warriors for a while. That had been part of her training.

But nothing in her past could lessen the heart wrenching pain of seeing six mutilated young humans. Their blood painted the walls and puddled on the floor. Torn flesh barely clung to broken bones, and shredded clothing scattered across the room. A man had huddled in the hallway behind her, sobbing a prayer to his god.

"We've got a live one, here!" The sudden exclamation from the floor below made everyone in the hallway flinch. But none hesitated to hustle downstairs to assist.

Left alone for a moment, Shaila wasted no time ducking under a yellow strip of glossy fabric. Entering the room, she moved slowly around, absorbing the various energy trails left behind. She scrunched her face in disgust as she smelled the stench of demon energy. But at the first trace of the unmistakable cold energy left behind from a *shadow walker,* her fangs unsheathed and a growl of dominance vibrated in her throat.

"Those poor humans," she whispered. "They had no chance."

She could no longer deny what she was up against. What they were all up against. Apophis was somehow reaching beyond his prison. The prophecy had begun, and time was not in their favor. She still had to find the babe, but Darius was right. How would a child help them now? What had Papa Shadi seen in his visions of the future? She needed his insight.

Footsteps in the hallway alerted her that the official-looking humans were returning to the room. Pulling out the cell phone Darius had given her, she flipped it open and pressed the green button as he had instructed her to do. As he answered, she shimmered away from the bloody room and away from the cold residue of fear.

\* \* \*

"So, are there a lot of these *shadow walkers* running about?" Shaila heard more curiosity than fear in Marcus' voice.

Bessie meowed at the kitchen door. As Darius let her in, the cat bounded over to Shaila, rubbing back and forth against her legs. Panting with exhaustion, the cat flopped across the floor.

"There are always five of them."

"So, Lilith's army is a group of about five of these guys? That's a manageable number."

"No, Marcus. They are not Lilith's army. Let me start from the beginning. There are two bloodlines that carry a master cell, which is what determines the royal lines of the Anunnaki. When a new queen is enthroned, her cell becomes enlightened as well, awakening in her a power greater than any other of our kind. The cell will replicate and pass on to only her female offspring."

"A matrilinear line of succession. That's an ancient concept."

"Yes, and one that preserves the pureness of our

race. Queen Tia'Mat was obsessed with maintaining a separation. She decreed that the Anunnaki could not breed with the humans. But Apophis also carries a master cell. I do not know why, but I think it is part of the balance of life. Equality in the forces of dark and light. Neither can really exist without the other."

Shaila paused a moment, her hands still shaking from seeing the fate of those young humans. "Apophis discovered that he could use humans to his advantage. He enticed them into his cult, promising them a better path to the Underworld. They only had to give him their souls, their light energy. He absorbed this, which added to his strength. Then the human was made to drink the blood of Apophis. The result was an agonizing death and rebirth into a demon. Because they exist without a soul, demons crave them. Demons are attracted to negative emotions, like fear and despair, which is when a human's light energies are especially vulnerable."

"Then what are *shadow walkers*?"

"I do not know. My mother once told me that Apophis freed them from another world. In return, they promised eternal allegiance to him. I do know they will feed on human flesh, and they cannot be completely destroyed."

"Invincible." Marcus shuddered. "They sound like a professional hit squad."

"One that is commanded only by Apophis. He has somehow gained influence beyond his imprisonment."

"Could they be commanded by a blood *descendent* of Apophis?" Darius' brows wrinkled together as he puzzled over an idea.

"You mean Therion? If he is the son of Apophis, then he carries that bloodline and possibly the dark master cell." Shaila grew thoughtful. "That could be it.

Even without his astral spirit, Lilith can use her son's blood power to raise an army and control the shadow walkers. But I cannot fight Lilith until I regain my astral spirit."

"Then we need my grandfather. He has answers. And we only have a few hours until the gala. That may be our only chance to free him."

Bessie leaped onto the table. *I know where he is, sister. I can help.*

Shaila looked into Bessie's eager yellow eyes and nodded. "Darius, there is someone who can help us."

Marcus fell off of his chair, wide-eyed, as Bessie transformed into her human form: piercings, body paint, leather clothing and all. Never without a sweet treat of some kind, Bessie blew into a small pink bubble that grew until it popped and wilted.

"Marcus. Darius. This is my sister, Bessie."

*That damned goddess.* Darius gritted his teeth. He should be feeling embarrassed, remembering the times Bessie had curled into his lap. Instead, he aimed his irritation at the stubborn woman who always had a surprise up her sleeve. He hated surprises. When was she going to fill him in on *this* little detail? And how many more did she have?

He wanted to shake Shaila, to shout at her. Instead, he just looked over Bessie's strange outfit. She looked like a Goth teenager who'd raided a vintage clothing shop. "Well, now I see where Shaila got her taste in clothes." He didn't hold the sarcasm.

"Don't get your panties in a wad, Darius. Papa Shadi knew you weren't ready to meet me yet."

*Shit, now I have two of them?* He didn't see the humor in the situation, but Marcus did. Between laughter, he was muttering something about dinosaurs having been the wrong choice of study.

"When I get him back, I will certainly pay more

attention to a lot of things."

Shaila put her hand on his shoulder. He shrugged it off, but she was persistent. "Darius, she says she knows where your grandfather is. Bessie has been inside Lilith's home. She can lead the way tonight."

"How do you manage to roam around Lilith's estate undetected?"

Fingering the unusually large collar around her neck, Bessie filled in the blanks. "He made this for me. It masks my Anunnaki spirit, so I can move around Lilith without her knowing that I am anything other than a simple house cat."

The cat woman preened with apparent pride in her efforts. His palm wasn't itching, but she aggravated him nonetheless. Marcus was looking at her with an intensity he rarely showed unless he was talking about a recent dinosaur dig.

"Papa Shadi was certain that Lilith had found the tomb. All of his research hit dead ends, until Mr. Artie and I came along. Once the collar was ready, it was easy to go in there and snap a few photos."

"Does she have the rest of the items from the tomb?" Hope gleamed in Shaila's green eyes.

"Not that I've seen, sister. But I think there's a hidden room on the other side of the wall. The one that your statue stood in front of."

Had he missed something? He hadn't seen that on any of the architectural maps of the estate. "What makes you think that?"

"Because I felt air coming from under it."

This time when Darius fingered his grandfather's medallion, he felt a sense of excitement instead of despair. Maybe this wasn't such a bad surprise after all. For a man who preferred to take his time to prepare, tonight's plan formulated in his mind with surprising alacrity.

"Marcus, we need a limo."

"Sidekick is on it." Flicking out his cell phone, Marcus launched into his task.

"Shaila, tonight you'll be my date to the ball."

# CHAPTER TWELVE

*Damn, woman.* Darius rubbed the back of his head, searching for the right words to say. "You can't go to a masquerade without a costume."

Shaila picked at a loose gold thread on his outfit, starting a run in the flimsy material. "You call this a costume?"

"It's not like I had time to order something more authentic off of eBay." Irritated, he punched the button that opened the divider between them and the limo driver. Through the rear-view mirror, he could see Marcus completely focused on maneuvering the long vehicle.

"Hey." His skin shivered as Shaila rubbed her palm across his bare stomach, which showed between the top and bottom pieces of his pharaoh's costume. Darius actually heard her purring as she stroked his stomach. On a different day, he would make the driver spin around the block a few times.

He gave her a piercing look. "Costume. Now. But remember, this is Lilith's party. She's going to sense you, isn't she?"

"Yes, she will feel that another Anunnaki is present, but she will not be able to sense who it is."

"Then, whatever you come up with shouldn't be too close to the real thing. Catch my meaning?"

"Yes, my pharaoh." Shaila sat back into the red velvet seats, closed her eyes and smiled. Her leather outfit melted away. White linen slid from some invisible spool and wrapped around her body. It turned into crisp pleats, which hugged every curve of her body. Her hair turned to a coal black shade and divided into long, tight braids. A queen's tiara straddled her hair, and a wide beaded collar strung around her neck. "I am now your queen, the primary wife of the pharaoh."

She took his breath away.

Marcus was not so tongue-tied. "Shaila, how are you ever going to blend in dressed like that?"

Bessie's face appeared in the window next to Marcus'. "Simple. Shaila's a warrior. She'd never be caught dead in a dress. Lilith won't suspect a thing."

Darius cleared the lump in his throat and fisted the medallion. "Okay, Papa Shadi. We're coming for you. Marcus, don't park up close to the estate. Keep the limo in the back where you won't be trapped."

"Got it."

"Bessie, I think you've got your costume thing covered." He smiled at the devilish amber gleam in her eyes.

"That I do. I'll be waiting for you outside of Papa Shadi's room."

Bessie flashed into her cat form. Darius could no longer see her up in the front, but he clearly heard her tail thumping loudly on the velvet seat.

He looked at the aggravatingly gorgeous goddess-slash-queen sitting beside him. This was the most important night of his life, and he had to somehow trust this woman to help him succeed. Her unpredictability factor weighed on his mind. "Shaila?"

She put a finger to his lips. Her green eyes darted to the medallion and back again. The emotions that flickered across his face told him everything. She loved Papa Shadi too. Although she had her own task tonight, she would not let Darius down.

She leaned in and pressed her lips against his,

sealing a silent promise between them. He knew she wanted him to trust her. Each muscle in his body slowly began to relax.

"Yes, Darius?"

"Don't forget your mask."

\* \* \*

"I sense a familiar dark energy here." Darius felt goose bumps raise along Shaila's arm as they stepped into the foyer of the Troy Estate.

"Well, you should. You stood a few rooms over for many years."

"Can we skip the party and look for Shadiki now?" He could hear an edge to her voice. One that sounded like a warrior anxious to just get the hell on the battlefield.

"I'd love to, but I'm sure Lilith will know that we've arrived. We can't go skipping off through her house." As if in answer, Bessie darted past his legs, heading in the other direction toward the darkened galleries. "We must make an appearance in the dining room, and then I can figure out a good time to slip away. But even then I need to have a good idea of where Lilith and Therion are."

Shaila growled. "I look forward to seeing Lilith again."

"This isn't a family reunion, Shaila." He pulled her to the side allowing other arriving guests to continue down the hallway. "Rule number one: I'm in charge. Rule number two: we must stay together."

"Is there a rule number three?"

He smirked at her disdain. "Yes, always refer to rule number one."

"What if we do get separated?"

"If we get separated, I will stick to finding Papa

Shadi, and you can search for the baby mummy. We'll meet up at the limo with Marcus."

She nodded, and reached into the bodice of her outfit, pulling out the cell phone he'd given her. "I have this too."

He took it and programmed in Marcus' number. "Excellent. Now we have our backup plan." Lifting an edge of the cheesy gold sash, he checked his silver belt buckle. The throwing knives nestled securely inside of it. "You have to be prepared for anything in this place."

Stepping inside the grand ballroom of the Troy Estate felt like stepping back in time. Lilith had transformed the room into a lush temple garden, complete with marble floors, alabaster fountains and stone columns. Hundreds of chandelier bulbs had been replaced with candles, casting a soft flickering glow in the room.

The reception was in full swing already. Silver trays of hors d'oeuvres floated around the room, carried by men wearing only the simple twisted linen of the Egyptian working class. It was just enough material to cover their more private parts. Their chests were bare, but glistened with glittered oils. Golden cuffs wrapped around their wrists and arms.

Stationed throughout the room, models posed on platforms with silver poles reaching up to the vaulted ceiling. They all displayed Lilith's newest line of clothing, accessories and jewelry. All of it coordinated with the ancient Mediterranean theme of the party.

Lilith Troy's annual gala was one of the most anticipated events each year. This year's masquerade idea was apparently a big hit. The room was filled with guests who all seemed to share in the excitement of hiding their identities under costumes of ancient world figures.

Darius found it hard to concentrate on surveying their surroundings with so many scantily-clad ladies around, and not just the models. Behind their masks, women pranced and posed in sultry costumes. Sheer togas slung around silky shoulders. Glittery tunics and gold bustiers clung to curvy Grecian goddesses. Satiny ribbons wrapped around long legs. A tall lady dressed as the snake-haired Medusa really stuck out in the crowd.

At the next table sat a King Tut wannabe, but the leather and gold costume barely concealed the short man's very round belly. Numerous men sported costumes of gladiators, centurions, and senators. At least a dozen Caesars strutted around, some with black robes and others with white. Hercules pranced around a table of Amazons.

Darius was quite certain who was impersonating Marc Antony. The golden-haired man wore a very authentic and complete uniform of the ancient general. Therion's dark, domineering eyes scanned the crowd from behind his black mask.

Presiding over it all, Lilith sat on a gilded throne at the head of the room, raised on a tiled dais. She was absolutely resplendent in silks and gems. Her hair was pulled up in a Grecian style, golden tendrils pouring around her face and neck.

Darius felt a slight breathlessness. "She looks like the best Cleopatra I've ever seen." He couldn't stop looking at Lilith. He wondered again how he had managed to say no to that.

"She should know." Shaila elbowed him in the ribs.

"Oww. Why should she know? Was she there?"

Shaila gave him a withering look. "She was Cleopatra...or so I was told." She walked away in disgust.

"She was?" Darius questioned her retreating form as he followed her to the back of the dining room. "Wow. Now that's a celebrity." He barely avoided another rib poking. "That would explain the tribute to Marc Antony in her gallery, but I thought Cleopatra killed herself."

"You have been misinformed." She offered no explanation.

"I would like for you to fill me in on that story, but later. For now, let's--" Darius was interrupted by a trumpet call, announcing dinner. "Well, let's take our seats."

\* \* \*

"Therion, I feel the presence of another..." Lilith let her thoughts trail off as she searched the room. She wouldn't be able to find the source of her discomfort by sight. This was an A-list crowd. Her wealthy clientele and business associates had plenty of money to spend on lavish costumes. Thus, the costumes in the room were visually authentic, down to the last beads, cuffs, and wrapped sandals. The themed masquerade had been a fabulous idea.

"Mother, you've known that some of your *family* is about." Therion patted her hand sympathetically. "Have you forgotten?"

She withdrew her hand with a vicious glare. "I am not a doddering old woman. I have not forgotten."

"Well, you are several thousand years old."

She curled her lips into a snarl that threatened lethal consequences.

Chuckling, he leaned in and kissed her on the corner of her mouth. "And yet, you don't look a day over twenty-nine."

She softened her lips to smile with self-appreciation. She stood and graciously welcomed her guests to the party. She pointed out several of her favorite costumes and tactfully refrained from revealing their masked identities.

Gesturing to the runway, which pierced straight through the center of the dining room, Lilith announced the start of the fashion show. Again, the half-naked men entered the room to pour wine and serve the first course.

The centerpiece of her collection would be revealed during the dessert course, the climax of any good dinner. She couldn't wait to see the effects of the designer fragrance she'd created. Her breath caught as a shiver of anticipation spread across her skin.

The meal was presented as authentic fare, albeit with a modern eye for detail and flavor. A band in the corner played modern new age music, highlighted with instrumental sounds from ancient times. With each course, the clothing of the runway models became skimpier and skimpier.

Just before the dessert was served, the finale of the new Troy Collection began. The models pranced down the runway in time to the sultry music. They wore matching coal-black Cleopatra wigs with gold beads. Instead of clothes, each model wore only wide gold ribbons wrapped around their bodies. Each one wrapped slightly different, depending upon which piece of jewelry they were displaying: rings, earrings, necklaces, anklets and various piercings. They were adorned with glorious jewels of all kinds...and in all places.

A few guests shifted in their seats, heated over the naughtiness of the display. The music changed slightly, but enough to alter the mood. The servers appeared with the desserts. Beautiful dark chocolate pyramids glittered with edible gold lace. Each tiny temple sat in a pool of raspberry coulee and a myriad of fresh berries. The top third of the pyramid was removed for each guest, revealing a small vial of perfume nestled on a cushion of sweet marzipan.

"My honored guests, you are the very first to sample our premier line of perfume. It is the nectar of the ancient gods and goddesses. A scent so pure and ethereal, it enhances each individual's core scent. It is a perfume made for both women and men. We call it simply...*Ambrosia*. I hope you find it...arousing."

Lilith seated herself back upon the throne, overlooking all of her guests like the Queen of the Nile, presiding over her minions. Seated on a slightly smaller throne to her left, Therion joined her visual search through the crowd.

Lilith's suspicions grew as her eyes fell on an unknown profile. "Who's that black-robed Caesar right there?"

"He's our soon-to-be-mayor's attorney." Therion raised his glass in the man's direction. "He's here representing Steven McNair while the candidate splashes posters all over town for help in finding his missing daughter."

Lilith sipped slowly from a golden goblet. "I can imagine."

"Duty before family."

She ignored her son's callousness. "Should I be flattered that you think my party qualifies as a civic duty?" Scanning the room, she found herself admiring a very lithe pharaoh. She preened with a surge of desire. Instinct, and his energy trail, told her that the man behind the gold mask would be Darius Alexander. He was watching her just as intently. She raised her goblet in silent toast to him.

"Lord, mother!" He coughed into his fist. "Does everything in your life revolve around sex?"

"Don't be a prude, son. There is nothing on this earth more sacred than sex." She smiled sweetly at him, but behind her goblet the smile disappeared. Lilith Helene Troy knew all about sex. She'd been made for it. It had been her station in her miserable past life. "The blood of kings passes by birth. It is the woman's line of succession that preserves the bloodline. Don't ever forget that."

"That's an ancient concept. Those ways are over." Therion grabbed a cognac from a passing tray and downed it one gulp. "It's a whole new world."

"Yes." Her lips spread with a wide smile, and she looked proudly at her son. "Yes, it is. It's *my* world now. It will be my bloodline that rules."

Throughout the ancient world, she'd been subservient to the lords of her kind. She detested being so lowly. Among the humans, however, she was a goddess. A goddess on earth. Being Helen of Troy had been fun, but even then she became little more than a piece of property to the human men who ruled their people.

As Cleopatra, she'd found true happiness. Her people loved her and worshipped her. Men sought to please her. But humans fought constantly, and she'd found herself seeking the counsel of Julius Ceasar. By seducing him, she'd secured the safety of the Egyptian people, whose country was on the brink of being conquered by neighboring humans. She'd only cared because the conquering groups were filthy and passionless, lacking the pageantry and glory of the Egyptians.

She'd won peace, but again at the sacrifice of her body. Then, Marc Antony entered her world. Sweet goddess, but he'd been the perfect image of her dreams. For a human, his sexual appetites were divine. His sensitivity and skill had pushed her astral spirit to new heights.

Lilith could barely catch her breath as the image of her lover was so vivid in her mind. But they'd both been betrayed. Betrayed by her own kind. She seethed with ancient anger.

However, revenge was sweet. Her pulse calmed as she thought about the twist of destiny that had freed her from her eternal prison. When she found herself in this new time, she discovered that most of the Anunnaki had left. Those that remained were weak, leaderless, and scattered across the world. Once again, she'd found ways to be adored by millions of humans. Survival alone was a form of revenge, but she longed to avenge the murder of her most cherished lover.

\* \* \*

Shaila watched the party guests give themselves a little touch of the exotic scent on their throats and wrists. They continued enjoying their desserts, many saluting Lilith who sat regally on her throne. A new round of wine appeared. A very sweet wine. The humans slowly came under the spell of the heady tonic that she realized must be in the perfume.

"Darius, we must get out of this room." She saw that he was focused on Lilith. Too focused. "Now!"

"W-what?" He rubbed his neck. "Why?"

"So you do not come under the spell, too." She resisted the urge to send a pulse of energy at Lilith to knock her off her throne. Shaila did not have enough strength to put a lot of power behind it, and Darius would be furious with her for risking her identity.

"The spell?" His voice dropped to a husky whisper.

"Precisely. It is in the perfume, and I suspect it may be coming through there, too." Shaila pointed discreetly toward a couple of rectangular metal grates on the ceiling. A slight haze floated into the room between the bars.

"You know what's in this stuff, don't you?"

Shaila nodded. "I suspect that it is a highly concentrated form of *mannah*. Like the wafers Bakari gave me, but in a liquid form."

"It's good for your kind."

"Yes, it is. But it could easily overpower a human."

"Lilith's drugging us?" The last word came out with a slight slur.

"More like she is testing it on you." Shaila didn't even try to hide her annoyance.

Darius kept rubbing his neck and fanning his face. The effects of the perfume would soon cloud his mind. She needed him to stay focused on finding the mummy and his grandfather.

"Come," Shaila tugged at his arm. "Come, Darius. We must reach the balcony. Fresh air. Come."

He complied sluggishly, nearly tripping over the leg of his chair. Fortunately, they had picked a table at the back of the room and the balconies were not far away.

She stole a glance at the golden queen on her throne. Lilith seemed to be watching them intently. Even from across the room, Shaila could sense the woman's heated interest in Darius. Her energy radiated desire. As they neared the balcony, Shaila felt the crisp breeze blowing in through the opened doors.

She did not need the effects of a perfume to feel desire. The hand Darius held tingled, reminding her how much she wanted to touch the rest of this man. She remembered the way his skin felt against her own. She hesitated in the doorway, watching Darius take deep breaths of the fresh air.

If she did not start showing some sign of the perfume's effect, Lilith would begin to suspect something. Shaila had to protect her identity. She had to mark her territory. Growling possessively, she swayed her body against Darius and crushed her lips against his.

The cool breeze had indeed begun to clear the strange haze from his mind, but Shaila's quick kiss ignited him, launching his body into autopilot. He swung them both underneath a cascade of blood-red curtains, pressing her back against the wall. Hidden behind the thick dark material, Darius felt like he was inside his own private dream. As dreams went, this one tasted very real. It tasted like sweet wine. *Shaila.*

The name echoed in his mind, and whispered from his lips. He felt her purring when he called her name. Capturing her mouth, his tongue explored and captured in a war he wanted to wage forever.

Until a thin gray man appeared beside them, clearing his throat to gain their attentions.

"Madame Troy insists that you join her in her private sitting room."

Recognizing the demon doorman, Darius grabbed him by the throat and growled. "Go away before I cram your forked tongue down your slimy throat."

Shaila redirected his face toward hers. "We must go," she whispered in his ear. "You know that."

He shook his head to clear the fuzziness away. In a gravely sarcastic voice, he agreed. "Let's go pay homage to the Queen."

The queen blew him a kiss from across the room as she stood. As they crossed the hall, the band struck up a new beat. The tune slowly dissolved the sexual mood in the room. Guests disengaged themselves from each other, smoothing their clothes and collecting their dignities. The dining hall buzzed with conversation once again, along with the sounds of silver and china tinkling.

Therion now stood alone before the crowd and announced the opening of the galleries to all of the guests, inviting them to browse the Troy Estate's private collection of antiquities and to dance the night away. As he exited the dais, the band began playing more lively dancing music.

Shaila had slowed down during Marc Anthony's speech. "Why is that voice so familiar to me?"

Darius leaned into her ear from behind. "Possibly because he is Lilith's son. That's Therion, the one you've been entrusted to keep the amulet away from."

He felt a shudder pass through her body.

# CHAPTER THIRTEEN

"Good evening." Darius felt awkward standing in front of Lilith Troy wearing a pharaoh's getup, while she was regally decked out as Cleopatra, a pharaoh's queen. The irony was not lost on him, and it spawned a wicked headache. He pulled his mask off and briefly pressed the back of his hand to his forehead.

"Hello, Darius...and guest?" Lilith couldn't have looked at Shaila with any more venom. She looked ready to unfurl her talons and sink them into her competition.

"Ms. Troy, I would like to introduce you to my date...um, Shelly."

"Hello." Lilith circled *Shelly* like a falcon circling its prey. "Why don't you take off your wig and mask. Come, girl. Show us your pretty face. Let's see the beauty of the one who's managed to catch the attention of our elusive adventurer. Come, show us."

He was certain she would rip the accessories from Shaila's head if he didn't intervene quickly. "Lilith, thank you for inviting me. Your parties are famous for their bling, but what exactly was going on in there?"

"Did you like my new fragrance?" Lilith licked her upper lip and looked at him coyly from under her lashes.

"Was it entertaining to you, using your guests as guinea pigs in your little mass orgy experiment?" He let his disgust show.

"What's wrong with spreading a little love,

Darius?"

"Then why stop it?"

"I can't very well ruin the dignity of my guests. It was only a test...to see if it really did have an aphrodisiac effect."

She glided toward him. "You really do look like a stunning image of a pharaoh. You're a natural."

"Yes." A dark voice slithered into the room. "King Darius. Weak and inefficient. His army decimated, and he himself killed by Alexander the Great."

Darius instinctively fingered his belt buckle. He also noticed Shaila's jaw clenching and grinding. A memory surfaced of Therion groping the statue.

"Actually," Darius moved between Shaila and his rival, "that was Darius the Third. Tonight I'm Darius the First."

"A Persian thief, either way. Hmm. Sounds familiar."

"Darius the First was known as the law-giver." Darius moved into Therion's personal space, looking the big man up and down. "But Marc Antony's legacy was...cowardice and suicide."

Big hands suddenly encircled Darius' neck and lifted him a few inches off the ground.

It took all of Shaila's strength to stay put, keep her fangs sheathed, and not assist Darius. She felt useless standing there like some child. Had she interfered, Lilith would surely begin to see through the costume and discover her true identity. She already had little confidence that a costume and mask could make much difference, but it had been over three thousand sun cycles since Lilith last saw her. That had to count for something.

"Put him down." It was Lilith who intervened. "Now!"

Therion growled at Darius, but reluctantly let go.

"Careful big guy, you're drooling."

Therion responded to the insult with a blow to Darius' stomach.

"*Therion!*" Lilith's eyes glowed red with anger. Therion apparently understood her veiled threat, and he moved away toward the liquor bar.

"Mother, you don't need this piece of gutter trash to help you. I'll bet he's failed to find the amulet." He poured himself a drink and pointed the bottle toward Darius. "I still want my statue back, and I'd love to beat it out of you."

"Hush. The statue is of no importance." Lilith swept the air with her fingertips.

Shaila stood a bit taller, unsure whether she should be insulted.

The movement seemed to remind Lilith of her presence in the room. "Shelly, I apologize for my son's rude behavior."

"Go have your little chat, Mother." Therion turned toward her with a hand over his heart. "I promise to improve my behavior."

"Yes. I have something infinitely more important to discuss with you, Darius." Lilith moved toward the door and waved at Darius to follow her. "Please. Walk with me. Therion will accompany your date back to the party. I need to speak with you privately."

Shaila watched Darius' eyes shadow with tension and anger. She envisioned him ripping Therion's throat out. She gave Darius a quick kiss on the mouth and smoothed his beaded collar.

"Look for Bessie," she whispered in a voice strained by her own rise in temper. "Be careful."

\* \* \*

"I know you, don't I?" Therion murmured next to

her ear after Darius had left with Lilith. He stood behind her, brushing his chest against her shoulder blades.

Shaila felt his breath hot against her ear. She could hear him inhaling her scent.

"You know nothing of me." She did not fear him recognizing her voice like she did with Lilith. She put distance between them, but her eyes remained fixed on him. For a man of his imposing size, he seemed nimble on his feet. She would be wise not to underestimate him.

His dark eyes gleamed with frank desire. A spicy aroma hung around his face as he leaned in closer to her face. "Darius is a pussy. He's not man enough for you."

The sound of his voice brought unwelcome memories of cold hands fondling her frozen skin. Instinct told her this man would not enlighten her spirit. He would imprison it in darkness. He would possess her in every way and use her energies to strengthen his own. That was not the Anunnaki way. Energy was a shared force.

Shaila ignored him, focusing instead on determining his weaknesses. He was not going to allow her to leave this room. The lustful glitter in his eyes told her he would try to take her any way he could...even by force. Like his father, revenge colored his aura with dominant red and purple hues.

She felt a surge of her old spirit around her. Though she could not seem to connect with it, she felt its power...its strength. The warrior in her would not yield. The crusader in her would die before submitting to this twisted son of Apophis.

His dark laughter infused the room.

Moving to the far side of the room, Shaila kept her eyes on him.

"You watch me like a fighter watches an opponent. You're not a simple female." He leaped over a long chair and strode arrogantly to her side. "Yes, I was right. Your eyes are angry and your breathing is shallow. Right now you want to fight me, don't you?"

*I want to destroy you.* Shaila felt trapped, like a caged lioness. Looking for the most advantageous spot to defend herself, she stepped behind a tall chair. Slowly, she reached under the linen of her costume and loosened the snap of the leather holster, which held the dagger to her thigh.

Therion couldn't remember ever feeling such excitement as the moment his eyes had fallen on her. Even with that ridiculous mask, recognition and desire had flooded his body. Had she stepped out of his dreams? Or had his dreams been preparing him for her arrival? Either way, he wasn't going to remain in a crowded ballroom to play host to a bunch of local yahoos.

With Darius and his mother gone, his mind flipped through the various strategies he could employ to conquer her. Slowly circling the room, he visually drank in every detail about her. But he wanted more. He wanted to see everything she had to offer.

She did not shrink away from him. Her eyes remained alert and she flexed her muscles. He recognized the signs of someone preparing to fight. He felt her surge of adrenaline. He breathed in the scent of her anger. He watched every muscle move with the lithe grace of a cat.

"What a little lioness you are."

She halted.

Therion used the opportunity to catch up with her, watching her fantastic green eyes widen with shock. He desperately wanted to see her face and to look upon the features of destiny. Whatever he'd said that bothered her, it presented the opening he'd been looking for.

He lunged and trapped her against the wall, pinning her wrists together behind her back. The position pushed her breasts forward and unprotected, but one thing still stood in his way: the beaded collar. He freed a hand to rip the offensive item from around her throat, leaving luscious skin open for his assault.

Therion took advantage of the opportunity and kissed the base of her neck. His lips felt her blood surging furiously just below her skin. She struggled like a wild feline, growling and hissing for a fight. Launching his battle plan, he sought first to conquer her lips.

*Oh goddess!* Where was her astral spirit when she needed it? She was on her own. Her neck stung from the force of the necklace breaking around it. Therion's breath felt hot and wet on her skin. She choked back a wave of bile rising up her throat.

Shaila roared out with pain and disgust. Her fangs began to extend inside her mouth. She needed to keep them hidden. Impatiently, she awaited the right moment. Finally, his rough possession of her wrists lessened enough, and she felt him repositioning himself to kiss her.

From deep within her chest, a growl vibrated menacingly as she struck out with every ounce of force she could gather. The hardest part of her knee connected with his groin. Therion howled with pain and dropped to the floor.

His scream of pain turned into dark laughter all too quickly. "Ah, you're a smart one. You presented your pretty breasts out there for me like a sacrifice. You manipulated me into putting my obvious weakness right into your path. I love the way your mind works."

"Men are foolish with their lust."

"Yes, our brains are in our cocks. I know." Therion hefted himself to the closest chair. "But I am not like most men. I'm a fast healer."

His large body launched toward her, but she easily avoided his reach, leaving him to crash into the liquor bar. She had expected a quick move. Even without his Anunnaki spirit to aid him, he was still the son of Apophis. Shaila would never underestimate him for that fact alone.

"You aren't running away. You're tough. But make no mistake. You will be mine. And for once, my mother will not interfere."

The vehemence of that statement shocked her. Did the devoted son of Lilith resent his mother? Shaila did not have time to ponder that. Right now, running away from Therion was the best course of action. Time was growing short, and she needed to look for the hidden room that might hold the infant mummy.

Before Therion could readjust from the momentum of his hurled body, she was out the door and running down the long hallway that hopefully led to the staircase.

He was quick. She could feel him close behind her. His laughter heightened her resolve to escape him. She found a curved staircase, but it didn't lead to the lower level. She hurled herself upward anyway, avoiding his hands as he tried to grab her ankles between the rails.

Desire for the mystery woman enflamed Therion, boosting his own natural rush of adrenaline. Like a wild cat, her body was taut and wired for flight, springing out of his reach time and time again. His predatory blood sang with the thrill of pursuit.

He couldn't wait for those long legs to be wrapped around him. The next time she was breathing heavily, it would be from the intensity of his sex inside of her. Visions of taming and possessing refueled his muscles, giving him a surge of energy.

Shaila sprinted around a series of corners, finally out of her pursuer's line of sight. She quickly dodged into a darkened room, waiting for her eyes to adjust and for her breathing to calm.

The lock on the door clicked, but she had not touched it. She tried to open the door, but it held fast. She was about to will it to unlock when he grabbed her from behind. There was obviously another way in.

In the darkness, he dragged her deeper into the room. She tried to slam the back of her head into his jaw, but all she could feel was his body shaking with wicked laughter. His arm wrapped around her too tightly for her to reach her weapon.

Hearing a small snapping sound, she felt a fire flicker to life. It sent an orange glow throughout the room.

"Ow." The heat nearly scorched her leg. As he turned her into the room, she felt the blood drain from her face. She had escaped to a room with huge bed in it. "Oh goddess, no."

"Oh, yes." He laughed wickedly.

\* \* \*

"Darius, darling. Where is my amulet?"

"I've been busy."

"With your…girlfriend?" Lilith trailed a polished fingertip across Darius' bare stomach.

He wished he'd picked a costume with more coverage to it, like maybe a suit of armor.

"I don't have time for you to dally around with a woman."

"Unless it's you?" He cursed himself for his stupidity. Shaila had warned him about toying with this woman.

"You could say that." She licked her polished lips. "Are you offering?"

"I'm only interested in one thing."

Her eyes darkened with impatience. "Yes, and you seem to have forgotten about him."

"Never."

"Then you are choosing to ignore our deal?"

"Let me see. Is that the one where I sold my soul to the devil's wife?" *Damn.* He felt the heat of the energy blast even before it slammed him against the wall.

"Maybe you have time for joking, but I do not. Follow me." Lilith thought of the woman who'd accompanied Darius to the party. Her fists clenched involuntarily.

Sex was nothing to be jealous about, but jealousy pierced her when she saw the look between the two. It was a look that spoke volumes. It spoke of trust and companionship. That was a level of feeling that Lilith had never found her whole life. And it had been a very long life. The closest companion she'd had was her son, but deep down she didn't trust him. He was the spawn of Apophis, and had his father's deceitful nature.

She called the shots now, and she'd raised her son to adore her, for when the time would come that he was reunited with his dark astral spirit, she needed to be strong enough to control him. She could never truly rule without his full spirit at her command.

She brought Darius up the spiral staircase to the top floor.

Down the hallway, Darius could see the outline of a cat pacing in front of the last door. Lilith led him into the first room, which turned out to be another sitting room. But this one was attached to her bedroom, which he could clearly see through a columned archway.

"Yes, Darius. You have sold your soul to me. The deadline is now. Give me the amulet."

"Why is this amulet so important? You spoke only of its value, not of its power. So, what does this amulet do exactly?"

He felt her sliding up behind him, drawing designs on his back with her fingernail. "There is an ancient power within the black diamond."

"One that could be used to free Apophis?"

She actually snorted, as if he'd said something funny. "I am not that stupid, Darius. I have no wish to free that evil bastard."

"But that is the prophecy, isn't it?"

"So, your grandfather really does know about the amulet. I don't believe in prophecies."

He knew she was full of shit. "The power in the amulet belongs to the son of Apophis. Your son is the destroyer, isn't he?"

"Inanna is the destroyer. She and her daughter. They destroyed my life."

"Lilith. There is a lot of history to your name. An ancient Summarian goddess, consort of the Underworld."

She looked like she wanted to claw his eyes out. He wondered if putting her on the defensive was a wise course of action.

"And of course, there's the story about a woman named Lilith who supposedly dumped Adam out of her bed."

"Don't believe everything you hear." Flame sprang to life above her palm and she threw it violently into the fireplace. It flickered anxiously. "But it does sound like me, doesn't it? I would have refused to be subservient to a man like him. Let all men like him go slinking off to find solace with petite and docile little creatures like Eve."

"What does Inanna have to do with the prophecy?"

"As her handmaiden, I knew all about her true nature. How evil she was and how she had everyone fooled, especially the humans. She and that war goddess daughter of hers. They are the destroyers in the prophecy."

"Where are they now?"

"I don't know where Inanna is, but her daughter is dead. In the wrong hands, the power of the amulet could resurrect them. That is what the prophecy means. If I possess the amulet, the power will be mine to protect."

The irony of that nearly blew his mind. He bit his lip to keep from smirking at her. It would be more enlightening to allow her to play out her little charade.

"How do I know I can trust you after I bring you the amulet?" He moved purposefully toward the tall mirror. "Show me my grandfather again...please."

A new image of Papa Shadi shimmered in the mirror. This time he looked comfortable in a bed with many pillows under him.

"I'm sorry that my interest in your grandfather sounds so selfish. But it's for the best interests of everyone, and possibly the world. Wouldn't you like to be the savior of the world, Darius?"

He'd been so focused on the image in the mirror that he'd not been paying attention elsewhere. The fire was roaring with renewed vigor, and the Queen of the Nile was sauntering in his direction. Lust blazed openly in her eyes.

"I showed you mine." Her lips parted invitingly as her hands rubbed up his arms. She leaned her whole body against his. "Now, you show me yours."

Darius held his tongue and tried to think of a

way out of this room. He had nothing to subdue her with, and he'd be damned before doing…that.

Fortunately, he'd needed nothing at all to distract Lilith, because a war-like shriek echoed from down the hall.

# CHAPTER FOURTEEN

Shaila struggled to free herself from Therion's grip. Her futile attempts only seemed to inflame his lustful fury. Therion gripped her by the throat, lifting up until her toes barely held on to the floor. She managed to pull a small hiss of air through her nose.

"Now, woman. I will not be sidetracked from taking a good look at you." He ripped the mask off of her face. She suffered a thorough inspection of her face. His black eyes darted across all of her features. She was ready to spit fire at him.

He laughed, the sound rumbling deep in his chest. "You look so familiar, like you really could have stepped out of my dreams."

"Let. Me. Go." Shaila enunciated each word slowly, her voice strained by his grip on her throat, but she knew he heard her.

"Make me." His eyes blazed with the thrill of a challenge, but he lowered her solidly onto her feet. "Fight me. Fight me with all your strength. Kick. Hit. Whatever you've got." He smiled wickedly. "But then, my little hellcat, it will be my turn."

"You disgust me, Therion. Son of Lilith." Shaila spit in his face, still being careful to hide her fangs inside. He laughed again. Then, he smacked her across her cheek. Not only did it sting, but it pushed one of her fangs into her lower lip. A trickle of blood slid from the corner of her mouth.

His pupils dilated with excitement. He leaned in and licked the dark red droplets away. She shivered with revulsion. She had to get away before she betrayed herself, which would ruin Darius' opportunity to help her save Nefertiti's child.

Well, if he wanted a fight, she would give it to him. But first, she needed to get over her disgust and let him in a bit. Shaila forced a moan from her lips as she lifted one leg to rub up and down his thigh. She couldn't bring herself to kiss him on the mouth, but skirted around it with little nibbles. His beard scratched her lips. His costume armor cut into her ribs, but she ignored it.

Slowly, Therion took the bait, sliding his hand down to her thigh, but she stopped him before he reached her hidden dagger. Instead, she lifted his hand to her chest. With one free arm and one free leg, Shaila had all she needed to get the upper hand. In one quick motion, she swept his feet from under him and pinned his face down into the floor.

Whipping out her dagger from its sheath, she pierced him between the shoulder blades, letting him know she was in charge now.

"My little lioness has incredible speed and power. Mmm. That's wonderful." It was his turn to catch her unawares. He kicked out, tipping her sideways. The dagger slipped from her grasp momentarily.

She quickly recovered her grip on it, but with her attention shifted, Therion was up and in a fighting stance. He gave her no time. He launched at her with a kick to her head. She blocked with her forearm and swung the dagger with the other.

It slipped swiftly under his breastplate and cut a swath across his stomach. A trail of dark blood oozed through his costume.

"Bitch!" He spit at her.

"We are even." Shaila touched the back of her

hand to the corner of her mouth.

Therion grabbed a pillow from the chair and threw it at her. As she blocked it, he had followed the pillow's path and was right there with a punch. Shaila had enough time to move slightly, but the blow grazed her temple and spun her off balance.

As he shoved her backwards, she felt the wall slam into her back. He used his weight to push her hard into the wall. Before he could readjust his stance, she bit into his neck and landed a quick punch to his bloodied stomach.

He shrieked with pain. She cringed from the very unmanly sound. Before he could gather his senses and run her down again, she managed to duck around a chair.

"You are the ass of a jack!" Shaila shouted at him. Someone came crashing through the door behind her.

*The mask!* She couldn't let anyone else see her. She spotted it on the floor beside the fake fireplace.

"Mother!" Therion growled angrily, obviously displeased at having his mother interfere.

Shaila stayed behind the chair and willed the mask back onto her face. Strong hands gripped her shoulders, and she whipped around to strike.

"No, it's me."

Shaila fought the urge to throw her arms around Darius, but she hoped her eyes showed how grateful she was for his timing.

"Therion!" Lilith looked disgusted, her eyes darting from her son to her guest. "How dare you do this? What part of your body do you think with?"

"She's mine. You will not spoil this one, so don't you dare touch her."

The argument between mother and son seemed to swell from deep within them, like a fight that had been a long time in the making. Completely engrossed in their fury, they did not seem aware that Darius and Shaila slipped quietly from the room.

* * *

Darius chuckled softly as they quietly made their way down the long dark hallway.

"What are you laughing at?"

"You're right. He is a jackass." He gave her a lopsided smile.

Bessie paced frantically as they dashed around the last corner. Her eyes brightened with anxious excitement.

Opening the door, Darius flipped on the lights. Startled, the gray doorman stood up from a chair next to the bed. The demon barely had time to flicker his forked tongue before a small knife sliced deeply into its forehead. Darius smiled for the first time that night. "I've been dying to do that."

As the demon disintegrated on the floor, Darius ran to the bed and scooped up his grandfather's unconscious body. Shaila retrieved his knife from the floor and raced out of the room behind him.

Bessie darted quickly down the staircase to the gallery level. A small group of party guests lingered in nearby rooms. A set of large clay pots prevented guests from entering the darkened gallery rooms at the far end of the house.

As they followed the cat, Darius nodded toward the empty platform. "That is where you stood for many years, Shaila."

Shaila smirked at the idea that she had been there all that time, right under Lilith's nose.

Darius shifted his hips, adjusting to the extra weight he carried. "Hurry, we don't have much time. Her hidden room should be behind this wall. How do we open it?"

Bessie paced nervously at the foot of the staircase. Her ears pinned back and her tail flicked back and forth in jerky movements. *I don't know.*

Shaila would move the universe if it could help her find the infant. Squaring her shoulders, she concentrated on the wall. Sending a pulse of energy toward it, she sighed with relief as it cracked open slightly in the middle. Pulling in a huge breath, she pushed two energy pulses at the door until it slid open.

Stepping into the room brought back intense emotions and vivid memory. It was the tomb in which she had spent an eternity guarding the hiding place of Nefertiti's son. The walls still showed the prophecy in bright colors. The limestone felt cool to the touch.

But only one thing really interested her. The sarcophagus carved with her name on it. Reverently, she lifted the lid and slid it over to the side.

"Oh Goddess." White hot pain zinged through her chest and pricked the backs of her eyes. A large tear blurred her vision briefly, before slipping down her cheek. Two mummies lay inside of it in eternal rest. The adult woman was the wet nurse chosen to wean the child after his rebirth. She still cradled the infant, but both were black as soot. Shaila reached toward one of the woman's tiny blackened toes. She had barely touched it when it shattered into a cloud of charred dust.

Now, her failure was complete. Her hopes shattered into gray ashes. But her sorrow quickly turned to anger. Her fangs slid out as she roared out her despair. "How dare she? How dare she keep these poor souls like trophies?"

"Shaila, she doesn't have their souls, only their bodies. Their souls are free in the Afterlife."

He was wrong. Their souls weren't free. Without

their bodies to return to, they were trapped forever in the thin veil between life and death.

*Sister, she is coming!* Bessie warned from the gallery door, crouched in the shadows.

The witch was near. They didn't have time to dwell on anything else. "Lilith is coming." Shaila sent another energy pulse to slide the door shut, trapping them inside. They could hear muffled sounds of footsteps on the other side of the wall. "We have to get out of here, Darius. I am too weak to fight her now."

She was also scared and riddled with guilt. Two feelings a warrior should never admit to.

"Okay then. Time for our backup plan. Pull out your phone and push that green button like I showed you."

"I will not leave you. I will stand with you."

"Get out of here, Shaila. Press the damn button."

They could hear Lilith and Therion yelling and beating on the door. Shaila's spell would not hold the door closed for long.

She pressed the button. "Oh Goddess, hurry up!" The phone rang a second time with no response.

The wall began to rumble sideways.

On the third ring, Marcus answered. Shaila wrapped her arms around Darius and his grandfather, and used the last of her energy to move all three of them through the satellite signal. She screamed from the effort. The movement through the signal seemed to go on endlessly. At first, it was a cold darkness. Then, colorless vibrations and excruciating sounds attacked her senses, nearly caving in her conscious mind. Feeling the soft velvet seat of the limousine underneath her, she finally allowed the darkness to consume her.

* * *

"She was right. You *are* a jackass." Lilith stood

proud, regally staring her son down. She realized that Darius and his woman were no longer in the room, but she could still feel them present in the building. "I know you hate Darius, but to rape his date in my home is unthinkably stupid."

"Mother." The word dripped from his lips like a poison. "She is destined to be my wife. She's the one from my dreams. I feel her in my blood."

Lilith sighed and approached her son, tsking at the bloodied mess of his shirt. She slowly removed his chest plate and unbuttoned his shirt. Like so many times before, she slid her palm across his wounds, healing him back to unmarred perfection. She admired the firmness of his muscles and smiled with maternal pride. The smile died from her lips.

"Of course you can feel her in your blood." Lilith held back the shoulder cloth of his costume and glared into his dark eyes. "She bit you."

"Yes," he chuckled with the delicious memory. "She did bite me. That vicious little lioness, she wants me."

"She doesn't want you, you fool. You have two puncture wounds, which means she's one of us."

"You mean she's one of you."

"Therion, you are Anunnaki too."

"Until my powers are returned to me, I am no more than a human, weak and imperfect."

"Stop saying that." Several recently-replaced wall lamps exploded with her temper. "You are my son, and the son of Apophis. You are the heir to the Underworld! We are destined to rule side by side. To be loved by all."

Therion advanced on his mother, his eyes black with venom. "You will not touch her, Mother Dearest. You have made every woman in my life strangely disappear or suddenly become sterile."

"They were not worthy of you. None of them." She shivered as a cold finger of dread wriggled up her spine.

Therion backed away. "I have let you control my entire life. I didn't mind it before, but I mind it now."

"But Therion, darling." She reached for him, but he swung his arm away. "I think it's not a coincidence that she showed up here tonight, and with Darius Alexander. We cannot escape the idea that she could ruin all that we've worked for."

"All that *you* have worked for. She will not destroy me. She is my soul mate, my choice."

"Therion." Memories of her first conversation with Darius haunted her. She refused to accept Darius' prediction that Therion would not long stay under her control.

His pent-up frustrations exploded. "No. This is not a Greek tragedy, and I am not going to marry my mother."

"Therion, if you do not stay away from her," Lilith's voice dripped with venom, "then I will kill her."

"I thought you were forbidden to kill your own kind."

"The Great Dragon Queen isn't here keeping tabs anymore, now is she? She left this planet thousands of years ago, leaving us here to fend for ourselves."

"So, who is she then? Who is this relative of yours who waltzed in here with that thief?"

"I need to find Darius. We need to know exactly who she is." Fear clawed at her, making her gasp for breath. She had missed something. The truth was right there in front of her, but she couldn't grasp it. "I can still feel his presence. I believe they have not left the estate yet, and I think--"

Leaving her thought unfinished, she sprinted to

the mummy room. The door rumbled to a close as she and Therion reached the room.

"Gods in hell." She threw a fire blast at the wall, but it had no effect. She used all of her energies, but the door wouldn't budge. Something tickled the air around her. "There's a spell on it."

"Who could produce a spell strong enough to keep you out of your own room?" Therion grabbed a spear from a nearby display and tried to pry the door open.

The truth pounced into Lilith's mind like a lion...or rather, a lioness. *His little lioness.* Straight out of Therion's dreams. She'd been there in front of them all these years. Darius hadn't done anything with the statue, because it wasn't a statue. The empty platform in front of the wall mocked her. Yes, who indeed had power enough to keep Lilith out of her own room?

Fury flew from her fingertips, scorching the wall. Screaming with an anger thousands of years deep, she threw blast after blast. Breathless from the assault, she dug into her deepest energy source and directed it at the hated door. Finally, she broke through the spell. The door slowly rumbled to the side.

The room was empty.

# CHAPTER FIFTEEN

Shaila drifted in a deep, dreamless void. She awoke in a strange room, but she was too groggy to get up. As her eyes adjusted to the darkness, she recognized the padded floor and walls. She was in the weapons room of Darius' lab.

The faintest sound of deep breathing next to her drew her attention. *Shadiki!*

She crawled to him. With a palm on his face, she mentally reached through his energy, searching for his mind. She needed him...needed to talk to him. But he seemed lost to her.

Now she knew the child was lost to her too. The memory of the burned bodies slammed into her with the force of a chariot. Her breath expelled in choking sobs as she hugged her priest's unconscious body.

Voices drifted toward her from the other room, along with the aroma of coffee.

"I hope Bessie made it out of there." She could hear the concern in Marcus' voice.

Mentally ridding herself of the hated queen costume, Shaila whisked on her black leather clothing. As she padded barefoot into the room, both men openly stared at her, slack-jawed.

"Uh, Shaila?"

"Hello, Marcus." She turned her back on them to pour herself a cup of hot coffee from a tiny machine.

"I, uh, think you forgot to fix your hair?" Marcus nervously pointed to the unusual direction some of her hair had worked its way into.

Absently sipping her coffee, she mentally smoothed the strands and wrapped them into a thick braid down her back. "Does this meet with your approval?"

"Knock it off, Shaila." Darius pushed a chair out and indicated for her to sit down. "Marcus is not the target of your anger."

"Maybe not," she directed a nonchalant look in his direction, "but he'll do for now."

"Hey, don't bite the hand that feeds you." Marcus leaned in closer but kept a discreet distance. "I'm sorry about the mummies."

She nodded. It was not his fault. It was all her fault for not being there to protect the babe. She had failed them all: Nefertiti, the babe, her kind. A lump formed in her throat."Darius, it will not take long for Lilith to put it all together. My blanket will be blown."

"I agree. Your cover is probably blown."

"How long was I..." She pointed to the back room.

"For only an hour. It's not yet midnight." Darius put his hand gently on hers.

"They will come, and I will need my full strength to fight."

"How do you get your full strength back?" Marcus asked.

"Part of the process of preserving me in the statue was to remove my astral spirit, so that my soul would not decay along with the body. As weak as I am, I cannot stay in the astral plane long enough to find it."

"Without it, she's running at half power, so to speak." Darius flicked out his cell phone and tapped away on it.

"Maybe that's what saved you from being detected by Lilith for all those years."

Shaila sipped thoughtfully. "My priest will know how to reach it."

"You know, many ancient concepts of the soul involved the merging of masculine and feminine energies. It was very prevalent in ancient Egyptian mythology. Gods and goddesses were always paired as a husband and wife. The yin and the yang. The ouroboros, the eternal soul of the world." Marcus drew his hands in a circle to demonstrate his point.

"There is someone who can help." Darius cradled the phone against his face. "Hello, Bakari? We got him. We need you to--"

Before Darius could finish his request, Bakari shimmered into the room. "Where is he?"

Darius brought the man into the far room. Bakari knelt, honoring his unconscious friend. Briefly, he touched Papa Shadi's face. A hesitant smile pulled at his lips. "Darius, your grandfather is not in a coma, but he is incredibly deep in a meditative state. I cannot reach him. He's built massive walls around himself, probably to keep Lilith out of his mind."

Shaila smiled at the resourcefulness of her priest. The time for despair was over. The warrior in her knew it was time to move forward. "I could reach him, but I need my full power to do it."

Bakari put his hands on her cheeks, and smiled. "You will need the energy to fight soon."

Darius moved to stand next to her, his expression a weak attempt at indifference. Shaila pulled Bakari's hands down from her face, but held them in hers.

"Bakari, trusted friend of my mother, can you help me connect with my spirit? Can you help me regain my full energy?"

"No, my goddess, I don't know how to help you."

Shaila sighed dispiritedly.

Darius reached for one of Shaila's hands, placing the *Eye of Ra* medallion into her palm. "Try this. You used it to give him long life, Shaila. It has his energy in it. I've felt him with me ever since I put it on. I think you can use it now to reach him."

Darius looked to Bakari and held out one of Shaila's wafers. "This will boost her energy, and I'm wondering if you can add your energy to hers to help her buy some time."

Bakari smiled with pride. "Yes, I think I can do that. Shaila, the rest will be up to you and the will of the gods."

"I *am* one of those gods, and I do indeed will it."

\* \* \*

Shaila and Bakari sat cross-legged on either side of Papa Shadi. She placed the wafer on her tongue, welcoming the warm sensation it spread through her. Laying the gold medallion over her priest's heart, she held it there with her palm. Through her skin, she felt his pulse vibrate, weak and slow.

Bakari cupped a tiny ball of wispy light above his hands. "I'm ready. But remember, Shadiki's built a wall to keep meddling goddesses out. Find the door, and I will help you get through it. Trust in that."

Leveling her own vibrations to match her priest's, she closed her eyes and lifted her spirit into the darkness. The astral plane greeted her with a blast of cold fog. She shivered, but pushed onward, searching for Shadiki's light. It felt like she traveled for an eternity, but finally a long dark wall loomed before her. She raced along the edge of it until a door revealed itself. A sliver of yellow light shone around a golden door engraved with the *Eye of Ra* symbol.

Shaila tried to open the door mentally, but it

wouldn't budge. Blasting it with energy pulses had no effect on it. She tried to tamp down her frustration, knowing the negativity would hinder her chances of succeeding. Another futile attempt brought tears to her eyes.

*Goddess, help me,* she screamed into the shadows. Digging deep into her remaining power source, she forced a continuous pulse toward the barrier.

Sobbing, she felt herself slipping away. Furious at the prospect of failure, her nails turned into talons, scratching at the door and shredding its outer layer. Exhausted, she felt her body begin to float away.

Quickly grasping the handle, she drew her face to the engraved symbol and pressed her lips to it. Behind her, a warm white light appeared. It surged into her, heaving her body into the door.

The golden barrier finally gave way.

Shaila found herself sitting in a room identical to Shadiki's private study. The walls were filled with dusty scrolls and faded pictures. Her nose inhaled the smell of old leather and apples. Relief brought tears of joy to her eyes.

Shadiki sat in a cozy, patched-up chair, smoking his pipe. With an expression of sheer pleasure, he hugged the long water pipe to his chest with the tip of it resting on his lips. A cloud of apple-scented smoke plumed in her direction.

His wizened face was covered with a short white beard and mustache. But she recognized his eyes, bright blue and sparkling with the wit and humor befitting a mage.

"Ah, nefer, you finally made it!" He spoke in English with an accent as thick and strange as hers. "Come, let me see you."

She knelt in front of him, and he cupped her face gently. He had always been like a father to her, giving her more compassion and guidance than she had allowed any other human to do.

"Thank you for bringing this back to me." He chuckled and held up his medallion. "I lived through so many ages of time that I had almost forgotten what to do."

"Yet, you did remember, Shadiki. I am here now." She laid her head in his lap. Strangely, she felt warmth from him, even in this cold realm of unconsciousness. "You sent your grandson, Darius, to find me."

"Ah, that boy. He is so troublesome." But the pride in the old man's eyes betrayed his true feelings. "I have been trying to prepare him for the future."

"What is the future, my priest?"

"Destiny, of course."

His cryptic answer did not please her. "And what is our destiny?"

He stroked her hair absently. "I can no longer see that, *nefer*, my beautiful one. My visions ceased long ago."

Shaila looked up into his eyes. "Well, there must be a destiny in that too."

Shadiki drew in another deep breath through his pipe and blew a puff of smoke above them.

"My priest," Shaila pulled herself upright and leveled a serious gaze at him, "I do not have much time. My powers are weak. Darius managed to resurrect my body, but I cannot seem to connect with my astral spirit."

He stroked her cheek, his smiled broadened with pride. "Smart boy, that one." He puffed again on his pipe.

"How do I connect with my spirit?"

"It has always been within reach, Shaila."

"How? It will not come to me."

"He will deliver it to you. You are the protector. He is the deliverer."

"No, priest. The deliverer is gone. He is destroyed."

Papa Shadi looked puzzled at her tears.

"I saw the sarcophagus in Lilith's room. I saw the wetnurse and the babe. She had burned their bodies years ago. I have failed."

Papa Shadi's eyes sparkled with mirth. "Ha, serves that witch right."

"What?" She wiped the wetness from her cheeks.

"The babe you saw was not the deliverer."

"He was not? But I saw him, still cradled in the wetnurse's arms."

"You saw what I wanted Lilith to see." Slightly yellowed teeth grinned from behind the white beard.

"Tell me."

"The world we knew is long gone. When you walked this earth, that part of the world was advanced. Our peoples were revered for our knowledge and power, but time has changed. My beautiful Egypt has fallen behind the rest of the world. Her people have been left in the dust." He chuckled to himself. "I'd been waiting for a sign. But I finally tired of waiting. On my next trip to Cairo, I took a cruise boat to Karnak. While the rest of the tourists spent the day in the Valley of the Kings, I made my way over to Deir el-Bahari, your mother's temple."

"I remember it well, being in that room while you embalmed me in the statue." A shiver fingered up her spine and goosebumps rose along her skin.

"I am sorry, I wish things had been different. I was so pleased to have remembered how to find the hidden room. Miraculously, it had not been discovered yet. I managed to push the lid of the sarcophagus over enough to remove the infant and replace it with one I had brought from a nearby cemetery. No one in particular, just a tiny body destined to help me."

"But you left me there."

"Yes, my goddess. I had no choice. I was out of time, and I had no way of carrying you." He sucked in another puff of smoke, the scent of apples curled around his face. "The gods were with me. I do not know how I made it through U.S. Customs without that mummy being discovered."

Shaila did not know what that meant, but she understood that he made it back here to Boston with the babe. "So, where is it? Where is the babe that I am to train and protect, Shadiki?"

He looked at her puzzled. "You don't know?"

"I would not be here in your mind if I knew."

"I already gave him life, Shaila."

She drew away from him in shock, instantly aware of what she had missed. He had been there all the time. "Darius."

"Yes. Darius Alexander, my grandson. Although we both know that he is not truly my grandson."

"No. He is the only son of Nefertiti."

"She understands, *nefer*. She sends her blessings to you."

"She cannot."

"She can. She does."

"But I failed to protect her."

"You did nothing wrong. She knew her time was almost at an end. The priests were not going to allow her to live, or her son. Lilith did her part too, in fueling the priests' lust for vengeance."

The room began to crumble away, slowly at first. Shadows slithered through the room.

"Beware, my goddess."

More pieces of the room swept away with the cold winds.

"I am ready for Lilith."

"Beware of the Death Beast!" His pipe shattered, and he gripped the medallion fiercely. He struggled to rise from the chair. "Keep the amulet safe."

"How do I fight? I am weak. How do I reach my powers?"

The last of the walls tumbled away. Just as the inky shadows wrapped around him, Papa Shadi screamed in pain. One word echoed in the darkness. *Love.*

What about love? Frustrated, her mind questioned why everything had to be mazes and riddles with a mage.

The darkness finally consumed her.

# CHAPTER SIXTEEN

A half hour had passed while Shaila sought to help Papa Shadi, but to Darius it felt like an eternity. He crushed a circular path into the carpet around her meditative form. The only break he took was to briefly help Marcus on the computer. Marcus was absorbed with research on ancient cults, demons, and shadow walkers.

As Shaila's body slumped over, Darius rushed to catch her. His heart pounded in his chest. He prayed she'd been able to find and talk with Papa Shadi. He was thankful to have his grandfather back, but he cursed the detour his life took only a few days ago.

"Shaila," he whispered gently into her ear. "Come on, honey. Wake up."

Her eyelids fluttered open, but she cringed at the bright fluorescent lights. He waited patiently for her eyes to adjust and her body to relax. His own body was strung as tight as a bowstring.

Finally, he could see a sparkle of recognition in those large emerald eyes. But something had changed. She seemed to draw away from him. A look of shame crossed her features. Why?

"Shaila, what's wrong?"

"I...N-Nothing." She avoided meeting his gaze.

"Shaila?"

"What?" Now she almost sounded irritated. "I feel a little fuzzy, that is all."

"Why do you smell like apples?" He could tell that she was trying not to, but she smiled anyway.

"Smoky apples. You did find Papa Shadi!"

Darius felt a small prick of jealousy that he couldn't have been the one to go to his grandfather. Yet, he found himself smiling too. Memories flooded his mind of Papa Shadi hugging his shesha pipe and puffing out clouds of fragrant smoke. He drew Shaila into his arms and whispered his thanks into her dark hair.

"Yes. He seems in good spirits. I think he was enjoying the solitude."

"Were you able…to speak with him?"

"Yes." Shaila stood up and retreated to the outer room. She hesitated at the doorway, glancing back at his grandfather's body. "Bakari was right. He really knows how to build a strong wall. He was sitting in a room very much like the one at your house. It must be a place that gives him comfort." Sadness overcame her. "But I must have weakened his defenses, because the darkness surrounding the room eventually closed in on us."

"So, did he help you figure out how to connect with your spirit, Shaila?"

"No, Marcus. I am afraid I am still left to figure that one out on my own. All he said was to be wary of the Death Beast, but I already know I must prevent Apophis from escaping."

Darius wondered why she purposefully avoided eye contact with him. "Tell me what he said. What else did you learn?"

"I must get back to the house, Darius. I must look through his study once again. He said it was within reach."

"Shaila, answer me, damn it. What else did Papa Shadi say?"

"Nothing."

She was lying, damn her. His palm itched. He

took a step in her direction, but she bolted for the stairs and disappeared through the grate. Darius looked at Bakari. "She's lying to me, I know it. I feel it. Why does she refuse to trust me? I just don't understand what makes her keep things from me."

"Our Lady of Flame is entitled to keep her thoughts to herself. Maybe you should trust her?"

*Asshole.* "Don't patronize me, Bakari. I have trusted all of you at pretty much face value lately. I think it's time *I'm* trusted around here too."

"Then, go. Go after her. Make her understand that she can trust you. Even a goddess can feel vulnerable." He motioned toward the stairs.

"How do I convince a goddess to trust me?"

"Tell her the truth."

"And which truth is that?"

"The one that ends with…I love you."

Darius was speechless. Was he in love with her? "Bakari, will you…"

"Of course, I will look after your grandfather here. I'll call your cell if anything changes."

"Thank you."

"Marcus…"

"Go, man! Don't let her walk the streets of Boston alone at night. I'll hang out here and play around with ALICE. She's been pretty good to me so far."

Darius dashed up the stairs, through the crowded game room, and into the darkness. Cold air seeped into his body, but it wasn't the air that made him shiver. A red moon hung low in the sky. It was the kind of night that felt heavy with evil malice and raised the hairs on the back of his neck. Tomorrow night was a full moon. A hunter's moon. *All Hallows Eve.*

* * *

It didn't take long to catch up with Shaila. He

found her in the alley four blocks away. Two demons in leather trench coats flanked her. He was really not in the mood for slimy fangs, green scales and bad breath.

"Well, you guys sure dress better than your buddies." Already airborne by the time both demons swirled around in surprise, Darius kicked the neck of the first one, and followed his foot through into the ear of the other.

He wasted no time in waiting for answers. These demons recovered far too quickly. Shaila responded with her own attack. With only one to concentrate on, Darius focused on avoiding the fangs. "Grandma, what big teeth you have."

"All the better to eat you with." The demon leaped toward Darius and narrowly avoided another kick to the head.

Darius shifted his stance and started to reach for his throwing knives. He paused as an interesting new weapon came to mind. The moonlight revealed a rusted iron fence up ahead. He ran at the demon and used him like a springboard. Flipping over and landing on his feet next to the fence, he used his heel to knock a loose bar off.

With no time even to turn around, he flipped the rusty bar to his better hand and stabbed backwards. He could hear gurgling behind him. "I always hated Little Red Riding Hood, but I loved the ending where the woodsman chops the wolf's head off."

Swiveling around, he ran the demon backwards until the tip of the iron bar impaled it to the wall. He wouldn't be going anywhere just yet. Darius took a moment to check in on his goddess-slash-warrior.

Shaila had picked away the other demon and slashed his throat with her dagger. The exposed artery gushed dark blood down its neck. He cackled, flicking his forked tongue at her.

"You can't kill me, woman." His voice turned raspy as air entered the wound. "I am already dead."

Shaila smirked. "You only think you are dead. When I sever your head from your neck, you will be going to the Underworld for good this time."

The demon started to cackle again but choked on blood. Shaila flashed a wicked feline smile. "Oh, I hope I do not get a scale caught between my teeth. I really hate it when that happens."

Darius almost laughed as the demon's eyes widened in surprise and fixated on her fangs.

"Did they forget to tell you that your prey was a goddess?"

He barely had time to shake his head before she attacked. She roared like a huntress thrilled by the smell of blood and fear. He ran, but she bounded after him until she caught him. Shaila sunk her fangs into his shoulder, and with her dagger she slashed at the muscles in his neck.

As his eyes bugged out, she ended his torture with a mighty kick sending his head tumbling along the gutter. Both the head and the body burst into a blue flame, and within seconds the demon vaporized.

Darius grinned. The sight of Shaila sauntering toward him like a predator frightened him, and yet it really turned him on. Those friggin' long legs in skin-tight leather.

Shaila grasped her dagger by the tip and hurled it in his direction.

He froze as it whined past his ear. He heard a slight sigh and felt the heat of a flame on the back of his neck.

"Damn, I am really starting to like those bad-ass leather boots." He winked at her.

Her fangs had retreated, but blood remained on her chin. Reaching for her face, he wiped the blood off with the pad of his thumb. Her breathing slowed, but then he heard a slight hitch in it.

"Hurry, Darius." She slipped her dagger back into its sheath at her thigh. "We must go. *Now!*"

* * *

Demons screeched in frustration on the other side of the front door. Darius's lungs burned from the all-out sprint to get home. Shaila stood beside him, gulping in air and steadying herself with the banister.

"Deja vu."

"What does that mean?"

"It's something we say when we feel like we've experienced something identical before."

"Then, yes. I do believe we have experienced the deja vu." Hissing and clawing continued on the other side of the door. "Do not worry, Darius. His spell will keep them out. In my time, Shadiki was the most powerful wizard among the humans."

"I'm not worried about the spell. I'm worrying about Papa Shadi's front door. He's gonna be really torched about it."

Some of the tension eased.

"I've never known my grandfather to be very wizard-like."

"Shadiki has many talents. His spells were strong and his visions were uniquely prophetic, which made him a talented priest in my temple."

"So, my grandfather was a priest in ancient Egypt?" Darius helped her to her feet. "That would have gone over great at career day."

He ignored her look of confusion.

"You know, I think I have inherited some skills from Papa Shadi. I have always been able to see very clearly in darkness."

Shaila looked away from him. "Not a usual human skill."

"No, it's not. There's more too." He grew frustrated at her refusal to look at him. "I can tell when someone is not being truthful. When they are lying."

She did finally look at him. "Truly you can?"

He nodded. "My palm itches when someone is lying to me."

"Is it itching now?"

"No, but it did back at my lab, when you said there was nothing more that my grandfather told you. You were lying then."

Shaila made her way up the stairs. She paused halfway up. "I did lie to you. I am sorry, but I cannot explain it. I do not know how."

He heard the water begin to spray in the shower.

Twenty minutes later, he realized the water was still running. That's when it occurred to him. *She's gonna run.*

He dashed up the stairs and threw open the bathroom door. Steam curled out of the small room and into the hallway. A rumpled towel lay on the floor. He relaxed slightly, until he realized she wasn't in any of the rooms on the top floor.

"Shaila!" Each room proved to be empty.

He finally found her in Papa Shadi's study, weeping over a stack of dusty journals.

"I was going to leave because I cannot face you. But I could not. A warrior does not turn away from what must be done."

"Is that why you're crying?" He tried to wipe a tear away but she turned her head aside.

"No, I am crying because I cannot figure out what Shadiki said. The answer is here somewhere...within reach. But I cannot read this language."

"It's okay, honey. It's okay." He tried to soothe her. "We'll find it together. Whatever it is."

"Darius, I have to find my way back to my spirit. I have to. How can I defeat Lilith without it?"

She was so distraught, he wanted to smooth away her fears. His chest tightened painfully. "Shaila, it'll work out. I believe that. I'm here. I know I'm only human, but I can protect you. I have to."

Shaila's heart swelled almost painfully, sending strange sensations throughout her body. Stroking his face, she pulled his head towards her and kissed his forehead. Pushing him back, she admired his features, so strong and commanding. He looked like the pharaoh he should have become. His features resembled his father, but his eyes were a nearly identical shade to Nefertiti's. How could she have missed it all before?

"Darius, it is my job to protect you."

"I don't need protection."

"Yes, you do." She made sure he was looking into her eyes. "You are the deliverer, Darius."

"What?" He pulled away from her. "That's nonsense."

"Is it? Is it really?" Fresh tears sprang to her eyes. "Is it any crazier than a human from Boston resurrecting an ancient goddess from a statue?"

She watched his eyes dart from side to side. Silently, she waited for him to gather the puzzle in his head and process all of what he had known and what he now knew.

"At the moment, everything seems crazy. Yet, nothing seems crazy. I--I am not sure what to think." He picked up a picture of himself with Papa Shadi. They were standing next to the Sphinx in Egypt. "I'm not really his grandson. Am I?"

"Not by blood." She leaned into him, whispering

the answers to his past. "Many years ago, he went back to Egypt to find the tomb. He opened the sarcophagus and switched the infant mummy with the bones of a much newer infant. He brought that mummy home, here to Boston. He used his own wizard's skill to resurrect you."

Darius remained silent. His thoughts returned to the dream he'd had the other day, during Shaila's meditation. In the dream he'd stood in a room with a woman who'd seemed vaguely familiar. She'd kissed him on the cheek, and then smiled like a mother proud of her son. Unconsciously, his hand lifted to the cheek she had touched.

"Darius, you are the only son born to Nefertiti, Queen of Egypt. She entrusted you to my care over three thousand sun cycles ago, so you could fulfill a destiny prophesied by my priest." He watched fat tears slip down her cheeks. "Days after giving up her beloved son to me, Nefertiti was murdered. I should have been there to protect her. I had promised on my life to protect her. She was my best friend in the world, Darius, and I failed to protect her."

Darius lurched towards Shaila, grabbing and shaking her. He didn't know why. Blood rushed loudly through his head.

"Goddess, help me, but I love you. I have no right to, because I have failed in every way." She flicked open the hilt of her dagger, exposing the small black diamond amulet which had rested inside of it for several millennia. "I never even trusted you enough to give this to you."

He pulled her into a tight embrace, feeling her hot tears searing through his shirt. He should be angry. Yet, he wasn't, and he suddenly knew exactly why. "Shaila, I trusted you enough not to ask for it."

\* \* \*

Darius picked her up in his arms and carried her upstairs to his bed. Lighting the fireplace, he unbuttoned his shirt and tossed it absently to the floor.

"Do you trust me now, Shaila?"

"I love you." She propped herself up on her elbows, eyeing him curiously.

"But do you trust me?"

"Completely."

Darius crawled towards her from the foot of the bed until his lips hovered barely above hers. He could feel her breath mingling with his.

"I've heard others refer to you as *my goddess.*"

"Yes."

"You are Shaila a'k'Hemet, of the Anunnaki. You are a goddess to the people of Earth. As a goddess, you deserve your full powers." He gave her his most wicked smile, and teased her lower lip with his teeth.

"Yes, I do deserve my full powers."

He captured her full lips with his in a brief but deep kiss. She moaned when he pulled up away from her.

"I know the way, Shaila." He leaned in again to nibble an earlobe. "I am the way."

"You are the way?"

He chuckled at her confused look. "I am the masculine. You are the feminine. My job is to *deliver* you to your astral spirit."

*Love.* That was the last word Shadiki said. Could it be that simple? She looked deep into those brilliant hazel eyes the color of the dunes at dusk. He was a pharaoh. He was *her* pharaoh.

But did he love her? The depth of Darius' feelings would have to mirror her own. There was only one delicious way to find out. She moved to claim his mouth, but he held aloft.

"Shaila." He whispered in her ear. "From now on, you are only *my* goddess."

The possessive gleam in his eyes sent a shiver of delight all the way to her toes. "Yes, my pharaoh." She would no longer be denied. She felt the rumble of laughter in his chest as she flipped him over with her powerful legs.

"Déjà vu," he whispered. She too thought of the first time she had flipped him underneath her. The day she had that wonderful bath.

"I need to feel skin, Darius. I grow tired of all the clothing people wear in this time." She willed away their clothes instantly.

She lowered her body over his, sliding up and down slowly. Nerve endings shot hot energy spikes across her skin. She withstood the pain, knowing what would come behind it. Her skin flushed, and then dampened with restrained need. It had been so very long. An eternity. Now, she wanted him desperately, but she held herself in check. She wanted this first time with him to last an eternity.

In the fireplace, flames licked and snapped furiously. His hands burned a path across her back as they slid downward. She purred with excitement when his palm smoothed around her thigh, cupping her center. Her muscles shivered as his fingertips explored her deep and slow. Her womb clenched as he teased a quick hot release.

Shaila pulled away from his fingers, and licked a path down his chest, laving each nipple in turn. His moans sent her further downward along his stomach. His muscles twitched with tightly controlled laughter as she found a ticklish spot. She licked along his inner thigh until he grabbed a hand full of her hair and guided her mouth in a different direction.

Darius nearly launched from the bed when she

took him fully into her mouth. She could feel his energies warring with pleasure and pain, but he wasn't there yet. With her lips and tongue, she massaged every inch of him. Until she felt it...

She looked up to see his face. He was mesmerizing as he balanced on the edge of bliss. A very faint blue glow enveloped him. He thought only that he was giving her the way to her full power, but he didn't realize that she would be giving him the same path.

*Damn, this woman doesn't play around.* Agony and ecstasy warred within him as she slid long and slow back up his body. It was his turn to prowl. He flipped her back underneath him, where he could keep her under his control for a while. He felt warm and strangely powerful. Every cell tingled throughout his body, as if they were awakening for the first time. Shaila was smiling up at him, almost proudly.

Growling his desire, he grabbed her chin with his teeth. He rubbed her center with his erection, but denied her his entrance just yet. As he moved downward, he traced a lotus tattoo with his tongue and captured her nipple between his teeth. As she cried out her desires, he felt her nails clawing his back.

She growled and hissed when he finally dipped his head even lower, tasting her. She was swollen with desire. He flicked her gently with his tongue, and she bucked and tensed frantically. He looked up to see her face glowing. She was so beautiful, and she was his. His goddess. His woman.

Firelight flickered in her eyes. Her body stilled, but her skin burned as if it were aflame. *My lady of flame,* he thought. He suddenly brought himself back up to her, capturing her lush mouth in a deep kiss. Then he clenched her jaw with his teeth again, but more gently this time. Her long legs wrapped around his waist.

He plunged into her. With deep thrusts and slow withdrawals, he pushed them both into heaven. He could feel them rising above the bed. Shaila was urging him for more. "Please, Darius. Oh goddess. Darius, I need you with me."

He felt like he was in a dream. Floating. Little wispy white lights drifted toward them. Quickly at first, but then their pace slowed. He wondered what they were and why they hesitated.

"Darius." He heard her voice calling out to him urgently. "Darius?" He looked down at her, his beloved immortal goddess. She was reaching for him, but he felt like something was pulling him away, tearing him from her embrace. Growling viciously, he vowed that nothing would take her from him.

Shaila was wrapping herself tighter to him, and he felt earthbound once again. He was still inside her, and still painfully full. Gritting his teeth, he withdrew. She started to moan desperately, but in one swift move, he flipped her over onto her stomach and entered her from behind.

Rubbing her inside with his erection and outside with his fingers, he sent her just where she needed to go. A feline scream burst from deep inside her, and her skin flamed with the blue light of pure energy. He felt his own skin burn with a bright light as he released inside her.

Utterly spent, they lay together motionless. Breathing. The blue glow slowly faded.

"Darius." She sounded gloriously tired. "It came to me. I did not have to go looking for it. My spirit came to *me*. It found *me*."

Darius felt a strange vibration through her skin. He slowly drew her back around to face him. "Are you...purring?"

She laughed as she nodded sleepily.

"I hope that's a good thing."

Shaila responded by snuggling into his chest and fingering one of his nipples. "I feel like a hot, bubbly bath."

"I always thought cats hated water."

"Wherever would you get that idea? I love water." Her emerald eyes darkened with renewed mischievous energy. "Let me show you what a cat can do in water."

He let out a long, tired sigh. "Okay, if I must."

*Hell*, he would let her show him anything. Anytime.

# CHAPTER SEVENTEEN

Barely a few miles away, demons gathered by the dozens in a basement deep beneath the Troy Estate. Once used in aiding fugitive slaves and later in trafficking booze, the estate now served a new darker purpose. Stone floors lay bare and dusty from years of neglect, but the walls had been given an eerie makeover.

On three of the walls, hieroglyphs had been painted in bold colors accented with gold. The pictures depicted the darkest part of the prophecy, the *Age of Awakening*. The frightening imagery showed the resurrection of millions of souls who would serve the dark lord as his demon army. Other scenes depicted horrific battlefields and bloody rituals of sacrifice.

On the fourth wall hung a massive black tapestry. Strange alien symbols were stitched into it with gold thread. In front of the tapestry, the floor was raised a couple of feet higher. The right side of platform held a white granite altar already stained with the blood of sacrifices. The next victim lay motionless under a dark red blanket.

A massive black granite throne loomed in the center of the dais. Currently, it was occupied by a large figure cloaked in a blood red silk robe. The robe shimmered as if blood actually flowed through its threads. From underneath a large hood, bright red eyes glowed with malice. Fury radiated from the form.

Gathered in front of the dais, the small force of demons stood waiting for the next sacrifice or mission.

From somewhere in their midst, twelve sharp beeps announced the arrival of the midnight hour.

The dark figure on the throne grew agitated at the sound. Bony, gray fingers snapped angrily, followed by an anguished cry from one in the crowd -- a demon in preppy college clothes who still wore a new Fossil watch on his wrist.

Until now. The watch imploded on his wrist, sending his hand skittering across the dirty floor. Looking up at the evil one on the throne, the demon wisely held back further screams.

Shivery darkness seeped into the room. Demons scattered to the sides to give a wide berth to the eerie figures that entered from the outer corridor. Five malevolent beasts slithered up to the cloaked leader. Robes of black fog cloaked their forms, but torchlight reflected off of shiny talons and teeth.

"Your Grace," a screechy voice echoed indignantly. "There is new light in our dark world."

"How did you not stop her?"

"The spell on the house prevents our entry. We regret the failure."

"You regret nothing."

"As you wish, your Grace."

"She will fight to the death to protect the humans." The cloaked leader paced across the dais. "But we can still control the prophecy if we have her under our command."

"Yes, your Grace."

The skeletal fingers appeared again, pointing toward an alcove. "Bring me the box."

A demon appeared from the alcove carrying a gold pyramid the size of a lampshade. His progress slowed until he was dragging his feet. His hands carrying the item sagged downward with each step.

"Come quickly, you idiot. We haven't got all

night." Bony fingers reached up and tossed the hood back. The demon with the box nearly stumbled at the true sight of their leader. Gray skin barely stretched over the bones of the skull. Jagged teeth and four glistening fangs protruded from a lipless mouth. The blood red eyes glittered under translucent eyelids. Black ears hugged the skull, pointing back like arrows.

A hush spread through the demon horde as their leader transformed in front of them. The skin grew soft and supple, and took on a more golden glow. A beautiful mane of blonde hair grew out of the skull. Malice still glittered but now in tawny colored eyes. Pearl white teeth flashed from behind full, luscious lips. Lilith smiled at her minions.

"If I want something done right, I apparently have to do it myself." She snatched the pyramid box out of the demon's hands. Removing the lid, she held up a very delicate pair of golden wrist cuffs. The torchlight flickered in her eyes. She laughed bitterly, before smashing the box on the floor.

She faced the five stygian souls in front of her. "I have an important task for you, and you will not fail me. Go to the astral plane and find the old man's soul. Make sure Shadiki Aria never awakens. Go."

"As you wish, your Grace." They disappeared through the back corridor from whence they arrived, as she turned to face her small army.

"I have promised Apophis an Anunnaki soul." She thrust the golden cuffs in the air above her head. "Tomorrow night, we celebrate the birth of a new age."

Cheers hissed and growled from the demon horde. "All hail, the Great Dragon Queen!" The crowd took up the chant, while the object of their cheer retreated into the hallway behind the tapestry.

Nervously, Bessie slunk from her spot in the shadows. Her ears pricked back in annoyance from the bloodthirsty din in the room, she leapt on to the altar. Nostrils flared, she gathered the scent of the victim hidden under the blanket. Silently, she retreated through the same hallway behind the tapestry.

* * *

Shaila smiled as the fresh aroma of creamy coffee wafted under her nose. She had to put some effort into prying open one eyelid and attempting to sit up. From the open window, the frosty morning air chased her back under the thick cover.

"I hate being cold." She moved to curl up next to Darius as he sat on the edge of the bed. "I think I was cold inside that statue."

"Papa Shadi loves the snow, although he hates the wicked winter storms. They can be pretty nasty."

She finally braved the chill to reach for her cup of coffee. She had to. Darius made no move to hand it to her, the big tease. And, he showed no sign of being bothered by the cold. She stubbornly refused to show weakness of any kind.

Snatching her cup from the tray, she noticed that it was accompanied by a bowl of fruit and slightly burned omelets. "What is this?"

"It's called breakfast in bed."

"It is burnt."

"If you're going to criticize," he started to pull the plate away from her, but she held on tight.

"I meant no affront, Darius." She leaned forward and kissed him soundly on the mouth. He generously released the omelet for her enjoyment. She had a mouthful of egg when she continued. "I think you might want to consider taking some cooking lessons from Marcus."

Darius made as if to pounce on her, causing her

to laugh, nearly dropping the eggs.

Instead, he leaned in and nibbled her neck. Shaila moaned as little goose bumps spread across her arms. *Oh, goddess, to hell with the eggs.*

She reached around his waist and drew him down on top of her. Even through the thick down covers, she could feel his desire pressing against her. A familiar sensation vibrated against her hip. She planned to ignore it, when it happened again.

"Damned timing. That's probably Bakari." He sat up and flipped open his cell phone. "Hey."

During the call, Darius paced up and down the hallway. Within a few moments, he appeared in the doorway.

"Hey, Shaila, we need to get ready to....go. Oh. You're already ready. Damn, I hate that you can do that."

Shaila looked down at herself. She had flashed on the usual leather pants, boots, and halter. "Yes, I am ready to go."

Darius licked his lips. "Those boots really are a huge turn on. Remind me that tonight I'd like to see you wear nothing *but* the boots."

It was going to be a great day. She finally felt powerful again. Her skin tingled with renewed energies. She double-checked. Yes, her dagger was safely tucked into its sheath and strapped to her thigh. Soon, she would face Lilith, and destroy that witch's plans.

Darius joined her downstairs. "We're going to meet up with the guys at the lab. ALICE has found some interesting facts for us. Apparently, my computer is flourishing under Marcus' charms. Okay, let's go."

Dashing out the door, Darius hesitated at the bottom of the stone steps thoughtfully. "Let's go the long way by Beacon Street. That way we can bring fresh coffee and bagels for the guys."

As they turned onto Beacon Street, they were swamped by a huge crowd of humans. They poured down the street in an angry wave, engulfing everything in their path. The swell of the crowd forced her in the opposite direction. She nearly tripped over one of the young people in front of her. The energy of the mob around her sizzled red with fear. They were carrying signs and shouting for more protection.

A tight sensation squeezed her senses and her mind flooded with memories of being trapped within the statue. She mentally shook off the images before they clouded her mind. The crowd continued sweeping her along its current path. When the rush finally slowed and started to spread out, she caught her breath in large gulps. Turning around, she found herself in a large space filled with green grass and tall trees. The buildings of the city towered beyond the treetops. Dozens of fat brown birds skittered across the ground cooing nervously.

But there was no Darius. She swirled around and around, searching the thinning crowd for him. She spotted a shaven head, but the bearer of it had a green beard. Definitely, not Darius. By now, she had turned around so many times, she had lost her bearings. Shaila had no idea of which way she had come.

Instinct drove her to keep moving along the path. She would find her way out of this place and back to Beacon Street. She paused next to a large object with small children crawling over and around it. She smiled at the small humans bundled up against the chilly morning.

Finally, she spotted a man with an official-looking coat. She tapped on his back. "Excuse me. Can you help me find my way back to–"

"My dearest little goddess. How good of you to

show up...Shaila." As he turned her way, her name spat from lips like snake venom.

Shaila turned to run away, but he caught her arm.

"Let me go, Therion. Or-"

"Or what? Look up in that tree." He pointed to a limb half way up. A dark figure perched there. The demon did not scare her, but his location above a little red-headed child did. She understood the threat.

"Make him go away, and I will go with you." But while she watched the demon fade into the shadows, she felt something cold wrap around her wrists. "What are you doing?"

Therion snapped golden cuffs onto her wrists. The searing pain she felt from them took her breath away. She gasped for air as she sagged to the ground.

"I am making sure that you cannot use your newly-engaged powers on me." His evil black eyes flared angrily at her. "Yes. I know who and what you are. I also know what your powers can do for me." He pulled her fully against him, breathing heavily into her ear. "I can offer you so much more than that pathetic thief, Darius."

"But you are human too."

"Not for long." His mocking laughter echoed off the trees. "You are going to give me back my god powers, Shaila. There's an easy way, and a hard way. I am so hoping you pick the *hard* way."

She spit in his face, a useless gesture but the insult was acknowledged as he yanked her towards a big, black vehicle.

Looking through the back window, she finally saw Darius. He sprinted toward them, but then he suddenly dropped to his knees, his face buried in his hands.

*I love you.* Shaila was certain Darius would find

her. She prayed that they would all make it through this.

* * *

Darius finally found her, but it was too late. He was just in time to see Therion shove her angrily into a van. He swore every kind of vengeance possible on his rival.

His blood pumped violently through his body as his fury reached a level he'd never felt before. His skin prickled as if it were energized by a strong current of electricity. His jaw ached miserably, like he'd been punched a hundred times. Then, the pain turned sharp and zinged through his skull.

*What the hell's happening?* The pain dropped him to his knees and nearly blinded him. He rubbed his jaw, trying to ease the torment. Blood rushed loudly in his ears, drowning out the sounds of city traffic. Darius stumbled out of Boston Commons and headed as quickly as he could towards his lab.

Darius collapsed down the stairs as dozens of light orbs danced around in his vision. Marcus caught him before he crashed into the computer. Darius gulped for air through jaws that now felt on fire. He screamed in blind torment.

"What the hell, Dare?" Marcus let him go and backed away very quickly. "What are those?"

Bakari rushed in from the back room, his jaw dropping in shock. "Gods in Hell, Shadiki, you cagey old mage. How come you never told me?" He rushed to Darius and grasped him on the shoulders.

Warmth spread from Bakari's touch, and finally Darius began to feel his body calm. His vision cleared, and the pain in his face ebbed to a dull ache. Bakari pulled out a linen handkerchief and dabbed away a trickle of blood on Darius' chin.

"What the hell just happened to me?"

"Destiny." Bakari chuckled like someone with an inside joke.

"What's so funny?" Daruis looked at both of them, their faces a mixture of shock and awe. "Somebody tell me something or I'll start slamming all of you."

A familiar voice rang out clear and strong. "Don't pay him any mind. He is just angry that he didn't start believing me a long time ago."

"Papa Shadi," Darius whispered. He rushed over to hug his grandfather. "You...you look great."

"Ach." Papa Shadi waved it off. "I just needed some good sleep for a change." He looked around the room. "Where is Shaila?"

Anger welled up anew in Darius, his skin taking on a slight glittery sheen. He looked at his own arms in confusion. "What is going on with me? You know what it is, don't you?"

Papa Shadi pushed Darius backwards until he was sitting in a chair. "My boy, I have raised you all these years as my grandson. But my grandson, you are not."

"I know that. Shaila told me that much last night. I am the son of Nefertiti."

"Yes. Her only son, whom she gave birth to not long before she was murdered."

Darius finally figured out what had been bothering him. Information he hadn't been given yet. "Who's my father?"

Marcus whistled. "So *you're* the deliverer?"

Papa Shadi nodded.

A big smile spread across Bakari's face, and he knelt down before Darius. "You are the prince of our people, Darius. You are the son of the Lord of

Command."

"Who the hell is that?"

"Seth." Both Papa Shadi and Bakari answered emphatically, and with great pride.

Marcus looked confused. "I thought Seth was the God of Chaos."

"Well, he is very dark and dangerous-looking, but he was not in the habit of fostering chaos," Bakari answered. "Although the Egyptians did peg his personality pretty well. You have definitely inherited some of his...irritability."

"And his cunning." Papa Shadi added quickly.

"So is that why he stumbled in here with glowing skin and a set of mini fangs?" Marcus asked.

"What?" Darius felt his jaws, and looked for a place to catch his reflection.

"You are half-human because of Nefertiti, but you are also half Anunnaki because of Seth." Papa Shadi looked square into Darius' eyes. "I am sorry. I should have told you long before this who your real parents were. When I brought you home from Egypt, I did not know anything about how to take care of a child. My daughter fell in love with you. She had lost a child, and you filled that hole for a while until the drugs destroyed her. And when I took you in, you would not believe any of the ancient prophecies. You thought me to be a nutty old man, and I let you go on without the truth. I did not see this coming so quickly. I am sorry, Darius. Can you forgive this old man?"

"Answer me one question. Did Seth and Nefertiti..." He let the question hang unfinished.

"Yes. They loved each other very much. As much as you and Shaila love each other."

Darius didn't try to hide his surprise.

"For you to have received your astral spirit, Shaila must have received hers. That would only have happened if the two of you combined your energies."

"Damn it, Dare. You mean I slaved over this computer all night, while you got lucky?" Marcus looked tweaked at first, but then he smirked. "I am wicked impressed."

"Okay. I'm okay with this." Darius massaged the back of his head and neck. "I've grown up my whole life thinking I was a normal human being. As normal as the next guy."

"And it turns out you're half alien."

"Shut up, Marcus." Darius sent a glare towards his best friend.

"You guys were right. He did inherit some very cranky genes." Marcus swiveled to his attention back on ALICE. "I study dinosaurs for a living and my best buddy is an alien. They couldn't write this stuff any better."

"Yeah, just don't piss me off or I might try out these new mini fangs on you."

"They won't stay mini for long, my boy. It just takes a while for them to break in the first time."

"Great, at thirty-five years old I'm teething again." Darius looked at Papa Shadi and Bakari. "Shaila and I got separated by a large crowd of protesters marching towards the Commons. I was angry for losing control of the situation and for losing Shaila. By the time I found her, Therion was shoving her into a big black van."

"Is that when the fury overtook you?"

"Yes. A powerful surge of angry energy just ripped through me. My face felt like it was exploding. All I could think about was to get back here." He hung his head over his knees, fighting off a new surge of energy just from thinking about Shaila being taken away from him.

"Don't worry, Darius." Bakari's baritone voice

held a purposefully soothing note. "We know where he's taking her."

"We have some time to make our plans." Papa Shadi began pacing.

"How much time do we have?"

Papa Shadi looked around anxiously. "Where's my pipe? I think better with my pipe."

"Time, Papa, time?"

"We will need to be ready," he said flatly, "when the red hunter's moon rises."

# CHAPTER EIGHTEEN

Shaila emerged from a dark, painful sleep. At first, she wondered if she was dreaming, or if everything before this moment had been a dream. She could almost think that she was back in ancient Egypt, waiting for her priest to preserve her in the statue.

She wrinkled her nose at the intense smell of the torches, which jutted from the walls like soldiers saluting. The limestone walls kept the room cool, and the only warmth came from the many torches. The paint in the hieroglyphs seemed darker than she remembered. She tried to sit up on the table, wondering where her priest had gone.

Pain seared her wrists and knifed through her body. The agony brought all of her memories to her in a rush. Her eyes darted frantically around the room, taking in all of the details she had missed a moment ago. The prophecy on the wall was much different. All of it honored the *Age of Awakening* in bloody detail.

The humorless laughter echoing across the bare floors was not her priest. Bracing against the pain, she twisted her shackled body around to see Therion sitting regally upon a black throne and grinning with a victorious smile. She bit her tongue to keep quiet as she watched him toy absently with her dagger in its sheath.

She tried to flash out of the room, but convulsed as the effort brought a renewed wave of piercing torture to every nerve in her body. A tear slid down her cheek as her pain and frustration grew. She felt

Therion's approach.

"Welcome to my temple, Shaila. We have some very important things to discuss."

"Where is Lilith?" She gave him her best dismissive shrug. "I will only speak with her."

She felt his fingertips trail across her legs and stomach, pausing just below her breasts.

"Do you realize how seductive leather can be?" His liquored breath felt hot along her cheek. She jerked her face away when he licked at the tears. "Mmm. Tasty. I wonder how you truly taste?" He grabbed her chin forcefully. "Don't struggle so much, my dear. It only makes the pain worse, or so I'm told. I had to test the cuffs to be certain of their ability to incapacitate you."

"On whom did you test them?" Shaila had visions of her sister broken down with fear and pain. Bessie had told her that she had been in and out of the Troy Estate many times undetected. Had her luck run out?

He rubbed her arm just above the cuff. "Nobody of consequence, as it turns out. A very disappointing experiment, except to learn the value of these little babies." Instantly, Therion seemed to go from enjoying his little games to intense anger. "Where is the amulet, Shaila?" He roared into her face and slammed his palm into her ribs.

She gritted her teeth, preventing her fangs from descending. She held silent.

"Foolish woman." His demeanor snapped back to the confident conqueror. "You have always known where it is. Now, stop your silence and tell me."

She ignored him and looked around the room, taking note of any possible weapons or escape routes.

"Shaila? You are not paying attention to me. I have never allowed anyone to brush me off." He leaned in again, whispering in her ear. "Especially your little lover. Even as a boy I could kick his ass. He tried to ignore me. I had to teach him a lesson. He just didn't give a shit about anything...until I took this from him."

She looked up and saw the necklace he had hung around his neck. At the end of it dangled a small blue bead, one of many from Nefertiti's favorite throat collar. It must have been the one gift from his true mother that had survived the wickedness of time. She snarled, revealing her fangs. She could not wait to sink them into Therion's throat.

"There's my little hellcat."

"I am not yours."

"You will be, or I will be forced to kill you."

"You are forbidden to kill one of your own kind."

His laugh turned feral, and his black eyes blazed red for a moment. "The son of Apophis answers to none but himself." He slapped her ribs again, laughing at her pain. "I am stronger than you think, Shaila. I am so much stronger than anyone thought. My father understands my true potential. I am a god. Imagine that. I'm a god on Earth, and I deserve my full power."

Something in his words haunted her. "Therion, where is your mother? What have you done with Lilith?"

* * *

Darius closed the living room blinds, shutting out the final glow of the setting sun. Bakari shimmered into the room carrying a wicked-looking pistol crossbow. It was a perfect weapon for close combat: self-loading and self-cocking. Demons would be no match for the steel bolts that would detonate on impact.

Bakari approached him with the gold box he'd seen at the man's house that day with Shaila. "This belongs to you."

Darius lifted the ruby ring that once sat on the finger of the pharaoh Ahkenaten. The ring winked at him, as if daring him to accept his destiny.

"You might not have a kingdom to rule, Darius, but you have us." Bakari bent down on one knee to show his allegiance. Darius felt decidedly awkward. He didn't want to be the leader. He worked alone.

"Thank you, but I'm not cut out to lead a group." He dragged his hand across his brow. "There are too many variables that I can't plan for. Shaila's my responsibility. I promise I will get her and bring her back here. I can't be responsible for all of you."

Before anyone could object, Papa Shadi's pet cat sauntered into the room. Leaping onto an empty chair, she flashed into her human form.

"Did I miss the swearing-in ceremony?" She seemed to notice Papa Shadi sitting on the couch. "Papa!"

Rushing to Papa Shadi, she hugged him tight.

"Bessie, my girl. You look well." He pinched her cheeks.

She purred with child-like delight.

His grandfather approached, again looking apologetic for keeping the truth from him. "Darius, this is Bessie. She is Shaila's younger sister, and she is the one who helped me and Artie find the statue at Lilith's estate."

"We've already been introduced. She helped us find you."

Darius retrieved Papa Shadi's wooden walking stick from the closet and brought it over. His grandfather smiled as he welcomed it like an old friend. Then, pain flickered across his wrinkled face.

Everyone jerked when the front door and windows rattled violently. Darius could hear the muffled sounds of hissing and screeching. Something was desperately trying to get in. He cringed at the high-pitched wails of frustration. Peeking through the blinds, he saw nothing but darkness. The sun had finally dropped below the horizon.

"What is it, Papa? What's out there?"

"They are *shadow walkers*."

"Shaila said they're indestructible." Marcus shuddered.

The old man held up his walking stick. A bright glow emanated briefly from the top of it. "Bright light is their weakness. It temporarily blinds them. It also clears away the black fog that cloaks them and protects them from attacks on their bodies."

The attack on the house seemed to increase with renewed energy, but still the spell thankfully held them at bay. Darius did not like being a sitting duck. He needed to get out of here and over to the Troy Estate. Shaila might be strong, but she would still need him. He felt it.

"I have to go." Darius double-checked his belt buckle. Both throwing knives were safely snapped in place. He knew he would need more than throwing knives and a set of mini fangs, but he couldn't risk the lives of any other but himself.

Marcus stepped close to Bakari, pointing to the wicked-looking weapon. "You don't happen to have a spare one of those, do you?"

Darius had to intervene before this got out of hand. "No, Marcus. You're not coming with me. I've appreciated all of your help, but this isn't a superhero movie. Sidekicks can get hurt. Or killed."

"Thanks for the pep talk, Dare. I assure you that I can handle myself, and you sure as hell need someone to watch your back."

Bakari handed Marcus the crossbow, and then flashed out of the room momentarily. He returned with two more of the weapons, one of which he tossed at Darius.

Catching it, Darius inspected thoroughly. He was adept with most weapons, but he preferred hand combat. Weapons were good for picking off opponents from a distance, but too many variables hindered control of a situation. He appreciated the control he felt in using martial arts.

"Where is Shaila?" Bessie's eyes darted around the room suspiciously.

"That's who we're going to get." Marcus answered for everyone, moving in close to hold her hand. "Therion captured her this morning."

She looked stricken. "Oh, goddess. So that's who the gold cuffs were for. Last night I was there...in the basement. I saw Therion with Queen Tia's golden handcuffs, like the ones she used to capture Apophis." She approached Darius until she stood toe to toe with him. "Those cuffs will burn Shaila every time she tries to use any powers at all."

Darius felt the blood drain from his face. His soul was shaken to the core by the thought of Shaila in Therion's control, powerless to defend herself. For once in his life, he'd found something he wanted to keep. He swore to whatever god was listening that before this night was over he would have his goddess back...and that Therion would burn in hell.

"So I'm coming too." Bessie nodded, eyeing Marcus curiously. "But there's something you all need to know before we get there."

Now his palm itched. It wasn't Bessie; it was what he feared she was going to say. There's more...and he wasn't going to like it one bit.

"Lilith is not in charge any more. She doesn't lead the demon army or command the *shadow walkers*." She approached Darius slowly. Her eyes were a deep yellow and as lustrous as gold. There was no deception in their depths. "Therion has imprisoned his mother, and I think he means to sacrifice her tonight."

"How can he, when he doesn't have his full power?"

Papa Shadi answered. "The blood of Apophis has many secrets. It has given his son great powers, even without his Anunnaki spirit. He has become the *necrotherion*, the Death Beast. Even without the powers from the amulet, he is strong. Please, Darius, do not underestimate him."

"Come. We must go now." Bessie hurried toward the staircase.

"No." Darius would not allow his grandfather to be in harm's way again. "You can't go over there, and--"

Papa Shadi swiveled around and pointed the knob of his walking stick at him. Light blazed from it. "I may be old, but I am not without strength."

Bakari put a hand on Darius' shoulder, warmth spreading from the touch. "It will take all of us to succeed tonight. Both light and dark energies are fully powerful during the hunter's moon."

Resigned to his fate, Darius put the ruby ring on his finger. He thought it would feel heavy with the weight of responsibility. Instead, his blood pulsed faster and stronger as a new sense of determination swelled in his heart. "Okay then. Bakari, you can get there much more quickly. Can you flash into the basement of the Troy Estate undetected and scout it out for us?"

Bakari nodded and disappeared.

"I'll lead the way." Bessie turned to speak to

Papa Shadi. "With those things out there, we'll need to take them through the tunnels."

Papa Shadi lowered the walking stick, his blue eyes now shining with enthusiasm. "Darius, there is a reason that I bought this particular brownstone. Come along and see."

Marcus flashed him a nervous smile.

In the basement, Bessie lifted a square metal sheet, engraved with an old bootleggers seal. She dropped down into the darkness with the grace and confidence of someone who was acutely familiar with the place. Except when she knocked her head on the low ceiling. Apparently, she usually traveled this path in her cat form.

It took about ten minutes for them to wind along the narrow dusty tunnel and emerge through a drainage grate next to the Charles River. They made their way easily by the light of the full moon, its glow eerily enhanced by an orange red haze.

The smell of diesel fuel assaulted Darius, flaring his nostrils. He recognized the lagoon where he'd fished as a kid. Bessie led them to an above-ground entrance to the drainage system. Here the tunnel was high enough for them to walk upright, but not far in, it narrowed suddenly.

Bessie twirled a round metal pin and slid open a heavy door about the size of a small window. Crawling through it, Darius sighed with relief to discover that he could stand on the other side.

Papa Shadi smiled as he stretched his back. "Maybe I am getting too old for this kind of adventure."

Bessie smirked. "Come on, we're almost there. These tunnels run along Beacon Street, and the Troy Estate is about two blocks just ahead."

Darius felt his blood pulse more rapidly. A snarl

sprang from his lips and reverberated through the stone tunnel. He hadn't meant to startle everyone, but he couldn't wait to get his hands around Therion's throat. He felt his fangs descend, but the pain was tolerable now. He sprinted until he came to a door that must lead to the Troy Estate. He felt the vibrations of dark energy behind it.

As the others caught up with him, Papa Shadi approached, looking like a teacher about to scold his student. "Darius, control yourself." Softening, he continued, "Your powers are new to you. You've yet to learn how to use them. Stay focused. Raw emotions will weaken you, especially the dark ones. Control your anger, or Therion will exploit it."

A hollow click from the door interrupted them, and a friendly voice rang inside his head.

*It's about time! You might want to come and join the party, like...right now.* Bakari was waiting just inside.

Darius wondered how he'd heard Bakari inside his head, but that topic could wait. It was time to take down an evil bully...once and for all.

\* \* \*

Before Therion could answer Shaila's question about what he'd done with Lilith, energy vibrated throughout the room with increasing intensity. A black void opened up on the far wall, and Shaila watched demons file into the room. She was saddened to see so many young men and women who had lost their souls to the cult of Apophis. They would never again feel the blood of life coursing through their veins.

Pity, however, would not hinder her from doing her job -- destroying every one of them. "Your faithful subjects?"

He smiled wickedly at her. "Of course. Did you

think we'd be alone when you become my bride?"

"I will not be your mate, Therion." She struggled to avoid his lips.

"It really is not your choice, anymore." He veered towards her neck. Hot kisses abused her, trailing along the artery pulsing angrily just under her skin. Then, she felt them. She stiffened reflexively, waiting for his fangs to plunge into her flesh. She gulped down a sigh of relief as he stood up again. He had just been warning her.

"Listen well, Shaila. You belong to me, whether you are in the statue or not. It's my destiny to rule more than just the Underworld. With my father's blood, I already inherit that domain. But with your blood under my control, I rule it all. It's a full moon, and you'll get to witness the real strength of darkness."

A growl began deep in her throat and continued until it reverberated loudly throughout the stone room. She let her fangs descend to their full length, and she sat up as far as the chains would allow her.

He just laughed wickedly at her. "My wedding gift to you will be a choice. Which ritual would you like to enjoy first, a sex rite or a blood rite?"

She strained against her bonds again as he walked away, the chains clanked against the granite altar. "Go to hell, Therion. I will never allow you to enter me. Not while I have a breath in my body."

His aura changed again, and he roared furiously at her. Indeed, his fangs were every bit as long as hers, but his were black as an onyx stone. Apophis' blood flowed through this man's veins, and it somehow offered powers to Therion even without his astral spirit.

"You've made a choice then. Let's begin with a blood sacrifice." He moved over to the end of the tapestry on the far side of the dais. "This is your lucky night, Shaila. We have not one but two worthy souls to offer."

Her anger brought a new wave of pain from the golden cuffs. The torment nearly blinded her this time. Taking shallow breaths, she rolled over to see whom Therion expected to sacrifice. He had rolled back a portion of the tapestry to reveal his own mother hanging on the wall. She could not have been more shocked.

Pure hatred emanated from Lilith's motionless form. Therion must have poisoned her body with the venom that he, his father, and all their demon spawn carried. Thus immobilized, the blonde goddess had not been able to heal her wounds. Her golden dress was now torn and covered in her blood.

Shaila listened as the group of demons shifted nervously and mumbled with confusion. She wanted to know what that meant, but her attention was diverted by Therion's bloodthirsty howl.

"Mother, you look divine tonight." He leaned in and kissed her full on the mouth. "Did you get a chance to see who our guest is? It's your beloved Inanna's daughter. You see? I'm going to use her like you've been using me. For blood power."

Therion rushed over to sit on the black throne. "This is where I belong. Therion, son of the most powerful god to ever rule the Underworld. But I will do what he could not. I will rule the living world too. When Shaila tells me where the amulet is, I will have my full powers as a god."

He paused, resting his chin in his hand. "Ah, but that solves only half of my problem. The other half is the bloodline of succession. That fucking idea that only a female will rule, and that she passes that royal cell down to only her female offspring."

Shaila noticed there was no sign of submission in

Lilith's tawny eyes. Indeed, she looked as if her mind was as sharp as ever, calculating her revenge on her own son.

"Look at her, mother. She is the key. When I take her as my mate tonight, the bloodlines of light and dark will be united...both under my control. I will control her, and the line of succession will pass to me. I will rule both worlds, and she will give me sons to carry on *my* bloodline."

He rushed over to pat her head, tucking a stray golden curl behind her ear. "Oh, don't look so sad, Mother Dearest. I told you this wasn't going to be a Greek tragedy. I *am* going to kill you, I'm just not going to marry you first."

Spinning around, he smirked maliciously. "Shaila, my divine prisoner. Here is our first offering for the evening." He indicated his mother. "Or, we could start with this adorable baby."

He motioned for something, and within seconds a demon appeared with a basket. Inside, a naked human baby girl wriggled and cried. Her little feet were waving desperately about the rim of the carrier. With lion-like accuracy, Shaila's ears picked up new sound. Seeking the source, she spotted a female demon off to the side of the room. The soulless young woman rocked on her feet and whimpered. She seemed fixated on the babe in the basket. Shaila wondered if somehow maternal instincts survived even death.

Therion unsheathed Shaila's dagger and pointed the deadly tip down toward the baby. She couldn't tune out the sobbing demon. The connection was unmistakable. There was nothing she could do to save the mother, but gods be damned, she had to think of something to save the innocent human babe.

"Here's your choice, Shaila." He twirled the wicked blade closer to the child's body. "Tell me where the amulet is! Or I will spill the blood of every child in this city tonight, beginning with this baby, and it will all be your fault."

# CHAPTER NINETEEN

*Oh, Goddess, how do I choose?* Shaila deeply believed that all human life was sacred, and especially the life of an innocent babe.

Therion nicked the infant's foot, his expression showed blissful enjoyment of inflicting torture. His black eyes nearly scorched hers as his temper began to blacken again. She felt pressure tightening around her heart as the babe's cries pitched higher from the pain. Blood dripped from her tiny foot.

She could see Lilith's aura burn even brighter with rage. Therion carried the basket to the altar, placing it just beyond Shaila's grasp. He held the dagger between her and the child, continuing the threat. Her eyes pinned on the hilt of the dagger. Every life was precious, but how could she sacrifice the life of the world for the life of one babe? Or more?

Therion had grown tired of waiting for her choice. As the babe screamed, Therion lifted the dagger and swung it down toward the reddened infant.

"Halt!" Shaila's chest heaved with the fear of being too late.

"What was that you said?" The tip of the blade hovered over the babe's heart.

"You win, Therion. Give me the babe, and I will give you the amulet." She could not lay there and watch him mutilate an innocent life. No matter how small.

He shoved the basket closer to Shaila's outstretched arms. She slowly lifted the tiny human into her arms, ignoring the pain knifing at her from the cuffs.

"Where is it?" His question thundered across the room.

She prayed that she would get the chance to fight Therion. Even with his full power, he would never have the strength of his father. That was the one thing she counted on.

"It is in the dagger that you already hold in your hands." She could not keep the irony from staining her voice.

Guilt assailed her over the hasty, foolish choice she made. In saving the one soul, she had condemned the entire race. A tear slid down her cheek as she hugged the child in a tight, protective embrace. There had to be something she could do to stop Therion's transformation.

He sat in awe on his throne, now holding the dagger reverently. She watched him twisting it all around, looking for a way to open it.

Looking out over the dark army of demons, she realized that they were shuffling around in confusion. She listened as they pointed to Lilith and questioned why their queen was hung on the wall. They looked nervously in Therion's direction as if they were not used to seeing him on the throne.

While Therion was distracted with the dagger, Shaila silently urged the demon woman to approach the altar. With halting steps, the woman complied.

"Here." Shaila tried to look into the empty yellow eyes with compassion. "Take your baby somewhere safe."

The woman whimpered with gratitude and scooped her daughter into her arms. Even though the woman was frightening in her demon form, the child calmed instantly. Shaila smiled at the instincts of the innocent. The woman and child silently disappeared into an alcove.

A metal door at the back of the room opened swiftly, slamming violently against the wall. Demons shrank away from the sudden noise.

"Darius." Shaila's body trembled with joy and relief to see him.

Evil laughter rose from the dais. Therion stood now, facing the new arrivals with a wicked gleam in his eyes, like he had been waiting for just this opportunity.

"Yes, Darius and guests." Therion spread his arms wide. "Welcome. You are just in time to witness the dawn of a new age with a new ruler...and a new queen. Then, I will kill you and absorb your soul myself."

"You and what army?" Darius' eyes searched the demon horde. "This army? This inexperienced mob of college kids? The Death Beast doesn't seem to have inherited much of a kingdom."

Therion's energies darkened. "You shouldn't insult me, Darius. I have everything I need to destroy you and your world." Flicking open the hilt of the dagger, he poured the black diamond into his hand. His shoulders shook with laughter again.

The bliss on Therion's face quickly turned to shock. Gripping the jewel tightly in his fist, he doubled over, hissing and convulsing. Dark energy curled out like smoke from between his fingers and twisted around his body like a slick ribbon. He writhed on the floor like a creature trapped within a black cocoon.

Darius motioned for his team to fan out around the room. They aimed their weapons into the crowd of demons, who turned to face the new threat to their lair. Some demons didn't wait for a command and sprang toward them.

Marcus seemed more than happy to see a few demon heads explode. The crossbows made short work of eliminating those who chose to attack. The rest of the demons wisely held back, but continued to posture and flex their dripping fangs.

Darius didn't know how much time he had before Therion recovered from whatever transformation he was enduring. He reached Shaila in seconds, holding her tight.

"I love you," he whispered into her ear. "Don't you ever leave me again."

He felt a surge of light energy coming from Shaila, and he used it with his own to break the chains from the altar. But the golden cuffs remained. From what he'd learned from Bessie there was nothing that could break them.

"Where's the key?"

"I do not know." Shaila hugged him tight again. "I am sorry. I had to give the amulet to him, to protect the baby."

He believed her. "I trust you, Shaila. Whatever choice you made was the right one." He cupped her face.

Deep laughter boomed across the room again. The malevolent sound carried an ancient dark energy with it. Darius felt her shiver against him, but it was fury that vibrated from her spirit, not fear.

"How cozy the two of you look. But she's mine!" Therion lifted his hands and rocketed a blast of pure darkness. Horrified, Darius felt Shaila move with immortal speed, blocking the blast with her own body. The force of the blast sent them both careening off the end of the platform. Finally rolling to a stop, Shaila's breathing hitched with pain. Blood dripped from her lips.

"No." Darius held her head in his lap gently. He

could barely feel her heart beat. Never in his life had he cried, but the thought of her dead sent hot tears streaming down his face. He left them there to sting his skin. He glared at Therion, letting his anger suffuse his body with power. Digging deep into whatever source he could find, he let the energy pump blood furiously through his veins.

Up on the platform, his rival stomped angrily, ordering his army to attack the intruders.

\* \* \*

Shadiki entered Lilith's vision with a man that seemed distantly familiar. A nearby demon lunged for them but the man quickly aimed a crossbow and fired. Within seconds, she felt the shackles release their painful grip on her wrists, and Shadiki carefully laid her on the ground.

"Bakari, please help me remove the poison from her body." She could see the hesitancy in the man's eyes. "Please, trust me, old friend. It is not her destiny to watch helplessly as her son destroys our world."

The man nodded and placed his palms on her chest. She felt a warm sensation spread through her body. His light energy conquered the dark venom that Therion had injected into it. She closed her eyes briefly, succumbing to a strange sensation of comfort.

Bakari. She dug deep into her past. If memory served, he was a healer. One of the few Anunnaki who could heal more than flesh wounds. But she didn't want to be healed in that way.

No, she wanted every bit of furious energy she could muster.

"Thank you, boys." She patted Shadiki's cheek and avoided Bakari's eyes. "I'll take it from here."

Standing, she watched her son grow agitated that

the demons were not fighting hard enough. His voice was filled with frustration, and she watched his skin glitter with intense new energy. Darius lay on the floor with Shaila in his arms. She could tell by the fading aura that Shaila's life was slipping away. Lilith cursed Bakari in her mind. He must have loosened up some compassion in her.

Darius had been right. How had she ever thought she would be able to control her son's evil nature? He was already more powerful than she had thought possible. She smiled wickedly, because she knew that a mother had other weapons than strength.

She turned back to Shadiki and the healer. "Shaila will need her sword. You cannot defeat him without her at full power. Quickly. You will find it in the gallery. Just follow that hallway behind the tapestry. I will distract my son as long as I can. He needs a lesson in family respect."

Waiting until she felt Shadiki's energy leave the room, she knew it was time. Stepping back up onto the dais, she focused all of her energy toward a defense of her astral spirit. The assault would be painful, but she was ready to draw some blood of her own now.

"Well, it looks like my disloyal, backstabbing son can't control his army." She smiled disdainfully into his astonished eyes. His gaze darted around her, trying to see who'd freed her. "You have lost your touch. No wonder you never made it to general."

She tossed a light orb above her palm a few times, and then sent it slamming into his head. He shook off the puny energy blast. She knew she'd never get in another hit. Time to build as much of a defense as possible around her spirit. Ironic that she now prayed that Shadiki would hurry and get the sword to Shaila.

As angry as she was with her son, she knew

instinctively that she would not be able to kill him. It had nothing to do with the Anunnaki code, and everything to do with maternal limits.

She realized that somehow she'd known this day would come, when he would spurn her for his father's power. In her mind, that just aligned with her belief that men were basically stupid. It wasn't their fault, really, but that's why nature intended for the blood of succession to be handed down maternally. Nature had entrusted women with the sacred task of giving birth to new life. That was a power men would never know.

"Mother." Therion's black eyes began burning with a red glow. "Don't get used to the freedom, witch, for my father expects your soul tonight."

"You poor thing." She looked at him with pity. "What will he do to you when you can't fulfill your promise? You stupid boy."

She'd scored an emotional hit. Therion roared at her, pacing back and forth with indecision. She had to keep the pressure on.

"Did you think you could actually accomplish something that the great god of the Underworld couldn't?" She glared at him in disbelief. "He is Apophis, the Forbidden One. He is the one dark god that you will never be."

"Because of your lowly bloodline, Mother." He sent a pulse of energy, which she deflected, but it still rocked her back on her feet. "You Anunnaki whore. You consorted with all manner of men, of both races. Apophis used your body to create me."

She cackled with laughter, as if she'd heard the best joke in the world. "You silly boy. You think Apophis will share his throne with you? He will never share. You are competition, my son. He will absorb all of the powers you've gained, and toss your useless body aside like trash."

In speaking the truth, she knew she scored more emotional hits. He paced like a caged beast, his eyes flicked across the confused demon army. He roared at her in fury, throwing a huge dark blast at her. This one sent her flying into the wall. Her head thumped loudly against the stone. Breathing heavily, she decided that she had one last opportunity to emotionally castrate him.

"Therion, I'm so sorry." She approached him slowly, putting herself dangerously close to him. She continued in a voice loud enough for all to hear. "I had no idea retirement has so affected your leadership skills. Look at your soldiers; they seem confused. Who commands them? You? Hardly. I don't think you have the balls to lead an army."

She could almost hear the ripping of his emotional flesh. In his fury, his body shifted into a mirror image of her own, except without the blood and torn clothing.

He turned to face the demons, and in a voice identical to hers, he addressed the restless horde. "Hail your Great Dragon Queen. Show loyalty to your leader. Kill the intruders."

Then, the supple skin faded and shriveled to grey. Red blazed from eyes set deep. He cackled gleefully. Turning, he licked a tongue across his lipless mouth, as if ready to taste her blood again.

Lilith stared at the four black fangs that had speared into her neck yesterday. Her own fury rose to new levels. Her golden hair flipped and twisted as pure energy swirled around her in a gale. The golden goddess stood fearless against the malevolent Death Beast.

The demon horde finally launched into a bloody battle.

# CHAPTER TWENTY

Shaila was still unconscious, but Darius could not remain a spectator to the fight. He kissed her cold trembling lips and placed her head gently on the floor. He stood in time to see Therion's bony finger toss a violent blast at Lilith.

Instead of a short pulse, the energy streamed continuously at the weakened goddess. Impressively, she held her ground, her hair flying wildly and her eyes blazing with anger. He knew enough about Lilith to know that she would battle to the end. Lilith would never submit.

Leaping across the dais, he tackled Therion. No matter how frightening the asshole looked, he was still Therion on the inside. The sudden interruption of the energy stream caused an implosion, sending Lilith flying into the wall again. She lay immobile, blood dripping from her nose.

Therion didn't escape the blast unscathed, but the wound on his head from hitting the corner of the throne healed rapidly. Waiting for the infamous Death Beast to rise and face him, Darius crouched low and smiled, revealing his sharp new fangs.

The grotesque beast sneered at him. "You're a mewling little animal compared to me, Darius. You dare to think you can challenge me by flashing a couple of new baby teeth?"

In that moment, Darius realized that he'd been waiting for this opportunity for over twenty years. His skin glittered with a surge of energy like he'd never known before. He felt like he could do anything…beat anybody. Papa Shadi's warning rang in his ear. No, he wouldn't underestimate Therion, but he had to try…for Shaila. *Let's kick some ass.*

"Are you afraid to fight me like a man?" Darius taunted.

Shaila opened her eyes when the pain from her wrists suddenly stopped. Above her, the demon mother had returned. She cradled Shaila's head gently.

Rubbing her burned, aching wrists, she noticed the golden cuffs lying on the floor, the key sticking out of the lock. She had saved the woman's child, and the woman had returned the favor. Not in all of her life had she known a demon to show any of the light energies. Their soulless bodies were incapable of compassion or any of the good emotions.

Shaila smiled at the unique woman before her. "Thank you."

"Isn't she adorable?" The demon pointed to the little bundle wriggling in the basket.

The question was softly spoken, without any of the usual demon curses or venom. It was as if she sought a connection from her human past. Destiny was changing the rules in this new age. Life always found a way to adapt on its own.

"Yes, she is."

"Thank you." The woman picked up the basket with her child, but she hesitated to leave. "I'm sorry."

"It is not your fault." Shaila stood and touched the woman's face, ignoring the cold scaly sensation. "I hope you find a way."

The woman nodded and disappeared behind the tapestry.

Her strength returned with aching slowness. Shaila stepped backward into the shadows, where she could survey the room and gather her strength. A bolt from a crossbow flew wildly in her direction, exploding a section of the hieroglyphs beside her head.

The young demons were no match for the well-armed group that came with Darius. Shaila smirked as she watched her sister smash a fist into the skull of one sorry beast. Marcus stayed right behind Bessie, protecting her back. Bakari had no trouble clearing his part of the room with his wicked-looking weapon.

On the dais, Darius battled admirably against Therion. They exchanged many blows and kicks, but Therion was tiring. She could see it in the short breaths he took and in the sag of his bony grey shoulders. His aura gathered dark energies. She was certain he prepared to blast pure energy at Darius, whom she knew had not yet learned how to build a defense.

Before she could move toward the battle, Therion threw a large pulse at Darius. Horrified, she expected to see him go flying in the tapestry. Instead, he flipped over Therion and the deadly vibrations. The force of the blast ripped the tapestry from the wall. As the heavy fabric fell forward, the edge of it draped across the beast. Darius took the opportunity to kick Therion in the head, sending the big man into the bloody altar.

"Relax, did you think he wouldn't know how to fight a bully?"

"Shadiki." She twirled around and hugged her priest. "You are awake!" She turned back to keep her focus on Darius.

"I have a gift for you, *nefer*." She felt the power surge from it even before he unwrapped the hilt.

"My sword." Reverently, she ran her fingertips along the flat side of the blade. Though it had dulled with age, she felt the strength inside it. The ancient power of the ruby strained for release. Oh, how she knew that very feeling. One of the most powerful stones in the universe, it enhanced her vitality as a

Protector and represented her royal bloodline. She gripped the hilt and reacquainted herself with its weight and feel.

"Maybe it is time to show Therion just how powerful you really are." His eyes held a strange twinkle of pride.

"Thank you, Shadiki."

"It is Lilith to whom you owe your thanks. She told me where it was, and she distracted Therion long enough for me to get it to you."

"Lilith?" Shaila searched until she spied the witch across the room. Bakari carried her limp body away from the battle on the stage.

"Yes. She knows you are the only hope we have of stopping her son, and not just because of the prophecy."

A war cry shrieked across the room. Therion's body transformed again. His grey skeletal body filled out, muscles rippling across his arms and chest. His legs turned as red as blood, and his toes lengthened to black talons.

Cold darkness seeped into the room. The few remaining demons cowered and scattered to the shadows. Amid the distraction of the new arrivals, Darius roared with pain. Therion had impaled him to the wall with Shaila's dagger.

"The *shadow walkers* are here. It is time to take your place in the prophecy. Fulfill destiny. Protect the deliverer...your mate...your lover."

* * *

Being underground, Shaila could not tell where the full moon was positioned, so she let her sword guide her instincts. As she aimed it skyward, she halted when the blade of the sword vibrated with energy. She flashed away the leather outfit and stood clothed in the pristine white robes of her people.

Holding the sword aloft, she raised her voice above the din. "I am Shaila a'k'Hemet, Lady of Flame. I am the daughter of Inanna a'k'Suen, Lady of Life. I am the granddaughter of Tia'Mat, the Great Dragon Queen. My soul is most powerful and it is given in service to slaughter the dark ones who threaten our world. My power is also blessed by the sword...my sword...*al'ak su far'vadin*. None shall hinder me. None shall slow my cause. Black souls, beware."

Shaila expected the rush of power. She had prepared her body for the sudden onslaught of pure blue energy the sword would awaken. Destiny surprised her once again. An immense pulse of clear white light, the light of divinity, blasted through the room and beyond...across the astral plane.

Lightning flashed across her sword, and it shone with renewed life. Sheer determination kept her upright. The white hot pain that knifed through her body momentarily blinded her. The sword grew heavy. She held it aloft as long as she could until it sagged toward the ground. But the ground seemed far away. She felt weightless, floating above the faces that all stared at her in amazement.

Her skin glowed until it illuminated the dark room. The wicked *shadow walkers* shrank back into any shadow they could find. She laughed at their feeble attempts as their cloaks of fog sizzled away.

Warmth spread through her body, and she clung to it, grateful for the respite from the pain. But the reprieve was brief. Her robes tightened against her skin. She heard and felt the flesh on her back tearing along the scars she had been born with. The warmth in her chest turned into intense pressure. She howled and stretched, trying to push the pressure out of her body.

Finally, she felt the crushing tension burst free.

Her body tingled from the release of adrenaline. Nerve endings fired up with static as she felt her body transforming, but she had not willed it to change. She felt skin tensing along her back, and tried to look behind her to see the cause.

Huge white wings stretched and flexed, testing the weight they would carry. Slowly, they brought her back down to the ground. She knew what this meant, but the knowledge was bittersweet.

"Holy hell, sister." Bessie stood off the side, fear and awe mingled in her eyes. "You're the new Dragon Queen."

Bakari's voice held such sadness. "That would mean that Queen Tia is dead, and Inanna must also be..." He choked, unable to finish the sentence. He must have held out hope for all of these ages of time that her mother was out there, somewhere.

Shaila would have shared that hope if she had lived all of those thousands of sun cycles too. Even now, she felt the bitter taste of despair in her mouth. Inanna had helped her start this journey to meet her destiny. *I love you, Mother.*

Evil laughter rang out strong and fierce. "Family trees can be so confusing. Such drama."

Shaila stepped up to the platform to face the Death Beast. "How do you talk to your father, Therion?"

He smirked at her and moved between her and Darius who was still impaled to the wall. He nodded his head toward the *shadow walkers*, who hovered as far from the light as they could get. "They are my link to Apophis. They were a gift to me, in exchange for an Anunnaki soul. And I don't want to disappoint my father."

"Indeed, it seems he has some power that reaches

beyond his prison. I would not want to fail him either. I am so sorry I will be the cause of your failure. You will not enjoy his torture once your soul goes to the Underworld."

Before he could stammer a response to her needling, Shaila launched at him, tackling his midsection and throwing him into the altar. Her eyes blazed with hot energy, which she glared at his head in two beams of pure light. He fell to the ground, covering his eyes to block it out.

The *shadow walkers* moved to attack her, but Shadiki stood in front of the platform and raised his walking stick toward them. The light that emanated from it held the beasts at bay for the moment.

Darius realized that he was still holding his breath. He was stuck to a wall, but he wasn't unconscious. Thankfully, because he would have hated to miss the transformation he'd just witnessed. Memories surfaced of the day he had watched Shaila meditate in her white robes. He'd thought her an angel then. That vision held nothing compared to one he beheld now.

Her robes had transformed to emulate the black leather outfit she'd been wearing. The white leather looked pure next to her tanned skin, which shimmered with power. Her dark brown hair spread about her in wild abandon, contrasting starkly with the clean whiteness of her wings. This goddess was indeed an angel from the heavens. He silently prayed that he could keep her in his life.

As he watched her battle with Therion, he could see that the dark beast was gaining in strength, drawing from all the negative energy in the room, from fear to anger. He was absorbing it all. He wondered if Shaila was weak from the transformation.

Seeking to buy her some time, he used his free

arm to toss the throwing knives into Therion's body whenever the opportunity presented itself. The last one sunk deep into his ribs, lodging between two of the protruding bones. Twisting and thrusting his body, Darius tried to dislodge the dagger from the wall.

Savagely, Therion retaliated by sending a powerful blast at Darius. Weakened from blood loss, he was unable to withstand the wave of dark energy. Nearly on fire, Darius felt his skin burning. He screamed from the madness.

Seeing Darius tortured by pain, Shaila flew into the air and lunged for Therion. Her nails turned to talons as she ripped his skin and tore at his flesh. Throwing her arm tight around the beast's neck, she willed her wings to carry the extra weight into the air.

In her glorious fury, the walls of the room disappeared as she dragged him into the astral plane. There was only herself and Therion in the ebony darkness. Here she would dominate the beast.

They battled for what seemed an eternity, neither submitting to the other. Both grew weary, their chests heaving from the effort of maintaining their full powers.

She realized her error too late. Sensing weakness, she had crawled onto his back, ready to pierce his body with her sword. She had no defenses up at the time, being so close to him.

He sent a pulse of energy backwards, aimed directly at her chin. As she spun away, he flew to her, wrapping large grey arms around her neck. He brought them both back to the underground temple. She felt his blood rushing with the taste of victory in his grasp.

Her skin sizzled as his fangs sank deep into her neck, his poisonous venom spreading quickly through her blood. Immobilized, she could only whimper as he ripped out a handful of feathers from her new wing.

She felt no pain as he tossed her limp body across the altar. He held her feathers in the air for all to see.

"Destiny is mine, and none shall challenge my power. I have defeated your so-called queen." He tossed the feathers into the air, and fingered the belt around his waist. "Now you can all witness the dawn of a new age, where kingship begins with me."

Darius held his anger in check this time, watching from the shadows of the alcove. When Shaila and Therion's battle seemed to draw the two of them into another dimension, Marcus and Bakari had used the opportunity to free Darius from the wall. For once, he'd smiled his thanks at Bakari, soaking in the warmth of the gifted healer's hands.

Grasping Shaila's dagger, he'd backed into the shadows when the pair emerged from the astral plane. He'd quickly noted the victorious look in Therion's face.

As Darius watched his enemy lording over them all, he willed his body to stay still for as long as it took. He focused on calming the fury that wanted to unleash in his heart. The time for action neared, as he watched Therion's aura build a wall of defense around him and his victim.

Darius readied his own body to withstand the assault of Therion's power. Years of studying martial arts had taught him to read his opponent quickly. He'd seen one thing tonight that might give him the opening he'd need. He had no idea if it would work, but it was worth a shot.

*Lilith? If you can hear me, I need you to insult your son again.* He hoped his mental message would reach her, just as Bakari's had reached him earlier. *Please, will you help me?*

As Therion climbed on top of the altar,

positioning himself between Shaila's legs, Lilith laughed, in between coughing fits.

"My son has balls after all! Shouldn't I be the proudest mother on this day?" She shook her fists at her son. "Yet, I am shamed that this vile beast pretends to have the strength to rule a woman. You're a stupid boy. You will never have the true power that nature has bestowed only on her female creatures. You will never have the power to truly pass on your bloodline."

*You owe me one, Darius.* Her voice sounded annoyed but clear in his head.

*If I survive this moment, I will honor that debt.* He meant it.

Just as Darius had hoped, Therion could not ignore the emotional emasculation from his mother. The energy wall that he had constructed came tumbling down as fast as his fury rose.

As the moment came, Darius launched noiselessly from his hiding spot in the shadows. As he neared Therion, the beast turned to counter the attack, but he was too late. Darius plunged Shaila's golden dagger deep into the heart of the Death Beast.

Therion fell from the altar, desperately gasping for breath. He crawled toward the edge of the dais, collapsed against it, and slowly pulled the dagger from his chest. He looked at it in confusion as his body flashed back to his human form.

Darius followed him and whistled. "Look at me." Darius grabbed a handful of Therion's hair and yanked upward, enjoying the pained expression in the dark eyes. "Your kingship has been revoked."

Using the momentum of Shaila's sword, he spun around and sliced it downward. Therion's head tumbled across the dusty stone floor.

Darius turned toward the *shadow walkers* still hovering in the dark corners of the room. He pointed to Therion's body. "You can fulfill your task. Here's an Anunnaki soul for your master. Let him know there's a new queen in town, and she'll kick his ass if he dares to interfere in her life again."

Stumbling with exhaustion, he climbed up to the altar and found Bakari working his magic again. Even he looked tired. Shaila's wings had disappeared, and her leather clothing had darkened to black. But her emerald eyes burned brighter than he'd ever seen.

Lifting her up, Darius carried her away from the bloody table. Sinking to the floor, he cradled her, rocking back and forth. A lullaby tumbled from his lips. He didn't know why, it just felt right, even though he had no idea what he was saying.

The familiar Egyptian song brought a stream of tears, which Shaila had no will to stop. "Darius, that was the song Nefertiti used to sing to you as she rocked you to sleep. How do you know it?"

He shrugged. "She sang it to me in a dream."

She smiled and memorized every detail of his commanding face. "I think this belongs to you."

As she opened her fist, Shaila watched Darius' eyes as he realized what she held. Bringing her palm up to his lips, he kissed the blue bead. His eyes, the color of dusk and sand, told her that all was now right with his world.

"Kiss me, goddess."

"As you wish, my pharaoh."

She purred as his lush lips claimed hers in a fierce, possessive kiss.

# CHAPTER TWENTY-ONE

Shaila a'k'Hemet stood at the railing in amazement, taking in the evolution of Egypt. The café where Shadiki brought them was on the third floor of the building. From the balcony, they drank in the sight of the whole Giza plateau: the pyramids, the sands, the date palms, and the hustle and bustle of a city, which had sprawled up to the very toes of the mighty Sphinx.

The pyramids proudly pointed to the heavens, but the luster of their outer layer was gone. Yet, even in their crumbled state, they were a majestic reminder for her of the heart and soul of humankind. As the sun set, within the span of a few moments, the colors of the brick shifted and evolved. When the sun shone unhindered, the pyramids were bright and yellow. Under the shadows of dusk, they were a warm orange-red.

"You are home, Shaila."

She loved the way Darius wrapped his arms around her from behind. She snuggled deeper into his embrace.

"No, Darius, this was just a part of my journey." She pointed to the stars. "My home is up there, many light cycles away."

"But you loved this land, didn't you?"

"With all of my eternal heart."

Above her, dusk was at war with the night sky. Half of the heavens still clung to light, bursting with vibrant shades of purple and blue. The other half rolled in the night sky like a dark wave. In Boston, the stars seemed fewer and fainter, but here they shone bright and strong. Here she could read the sky with more accuracy.

A man in white robes brought a tray of *cappuccinos* for everyone.

Shadiki sat at one small table with Bakari. Both of them hugged their shesha pipes with serene reverence. Sitting on the ground, the pipes gurgled with water and steam as the two men puffed clouds of apple-scented smoke into the air around them.

"Shadiki, do you know where Nefertiti is buried?" Shaila could barely pull her gaze from the splendor of the twilight. "I would like to pay my respects."

"As far as anyone knows, her body has yet to be discovered. The one who finds it will undoubtedly receive much praise and reward." He smirked at Darius. "Are you up for the challenge?"

"Someday." Darius sat down and took a short sip of the hot drink, watching the changes dusk brought to the plateau. He always enjoyed watching the evening lights flicker on around the pyramids. In some way, the small lights in the great darkness brought the huge wonders to life. "I would like to find my father."

Papa Shadi leaned forward. "Darius, please understand that Shaila and her mother did what they believed was right."

"He speaks the truth." He heard Shaila move to stand behind him. Closing his eyes, he enjoyed the feel of her palms on the back of his head. He loved her touching his skin…as often as possible.

"My mother and I knew how desperate the human priests had become. Under Ahkenaten's rule, they received no funds to maintain the temples of their gods, and they blamed Nefertiti. They attempted to kill her on several occasions. After the king's death, Seth was sent to help Nefertiti negotiate with the priests. They fell in love."

"That was a romance that was absolutely inspirational." Bakari nodded and puffed a larger smoke ring than Shadiki had. "It is a shame that humans do not know their story. They were like the Romeo and Juliet of ancient Egypt."

"When we told Seth of Nefertiti's murder, we led him to believe that you had died as well. Unborn." Shaila's voice lowered to a whisper, filled with shame. "I am sorry that we lied to Seth, but we knew the odds of you surviving that moon cycle were almost non-existent."

"They hid your birth from him, a miraculous feat to begin with. Seth was incredibly attuned to his mate." Shadiki calmly demolished Bakari's smoke ring with a smoke bolt. "After Nefertiti was murdered, Shaila came up with the plan to sleep through time. My visions told me that your soul was destined to live far in the future."

"How did my father handle the news?" Darius was still too numb to evoke any emotion other than curiosity.

"Furious would be too light a word to describe his anger." Bakari looked squeamish at the memory. "He despaired over your loss."

Shaila finally moved to sit and face him. "If Seth had known of your birth and our true plans, he would have moved heaven and earth to find you. That would have doomed the humans of this age. The prophecy would have begun regardless of your place in this time."

Darius watched her aura burn with intensity. He still marveled about this woman's conviction. Her emotive nature was going to keep him very busy and very entertained.

Marcus and Bessie burst onto the patio like desert dust devils. "Howdy, folks. Sorry we kept you guys waiting."

"Nice to see you finally made it." Darius grabbed his friend's hand, but Marcus pulled him in for a big hug.

"We've been through too much for a simple macho handshake." Marcus smiled. "You're family."

Bessie was still dressed in true steam punk fashion, but she'd toned down the make-up. Between gum bubbles, she was bursting with excitement. "Hey, Shaila, check out my new raptor tattoo. I told you I liked the scientific types."

Darius chuckled as he watched his best friend tap his toe impatiently.

"So, Papa Shadi, what's next?" Darius brought his full attention back to his grandfather. He knew there was a reason the old man wanted all of them to come to Egypt together. "I know you have something up your sleeve. What I don't know is whether I'm gonna like it or not."

The shesha pipe burbled again as Papa Shadi drew in a deep breath. As he exhaled, the smoke curled around his head. "Shaila, this is your dynasty now. The *medjai* are needed once again."

"But who is left here?"

"They are out there, *nefer*. The moment you inherited your queenship, you sent a great pulse through the astral plane."

"So they will know that a new queen is alive, and will be calling on them to gather?" Darius pulled Shaila away from her own chair to sit on his lap.

Papa Shadi nodded. As he grinned at Darius, smoke fanned out from between his teeth.

"What about Lilith?" Shaila asked.

Darius noted how Bakari shifted uncomfortably.

Papa Shadi patted her knee in a comforting gesture. "Do not judge her so harshly now. She is no longer a threat. Lilith has gone away for a while to search for her true soul. We will cross paths again."

Clearing his throat, he motioned for all to pay attention.

"Therion's defeat does not prevent the prophecy. The *Age of Awakening* is coming. From his prison in the Underworld, Apophis has had thousands of years to plot his revenge on the Anunnaki. We have recently witnessed for ourselves that his evil is not completely restrained by his imprisonment."

"Great. That puts us way behind on the planning part." Marcus saluted him. "That's gonna send Darius into a frenzy."

Darius glared at Marcus to *shut up*. "Go on, Papa. How do we assemble this team?"

"Seven *medjai* warriors will be trained and led by Shaila."

"Okay, so my task is to find and bring in six more Anunnaki warriors?"

"I did not say that they would all be Anunnaki, but they will each be bound to a special sword. Like Shaila's, the swords carry unique powers which only their true owner can wield."

"Oh, this just gets better by the minute." Darius scoffed. "So, now we're up to six individuals who happen to be warriors and who each need a special sword?"

"What's so special about the swords?" Marcus sat at the edge of his chair.

"They were each forged more than ten thousand years ago and they are made of a metal only found on Shaila's home planet."

"Good luck with that, Dare."

"Marcus." A mischievous grin spread the

wrinkles across Papa Shadi's face. "You are a part of this team now."

After a moment of stunned silence, Marcus brightened. "Do I get one of those cool swords?"

"No." The old mage laughed. "You have many skills that will be valuable in aiding the team. Wouldn't it be more exciting to research dragons instead of dinosaurs and dirt?"

"Dragons! Don't mess with me, old man. I'll be wicked torched if you're pulling my leg."

Darius had had enough of the prophecy for one night. He pulled Shaila back across to the railing. For now, he just wanted to soak in the cool Egyptian evening, and watch the glory of the moon passing above the Great Pyramid of Khufu.

"So, my goddess. What would you like to do tomorrow?"

"Well." She shifted her body against his, and his blood pulsed rapidly in response. "Since I see no chariots about, I would love to go for a motorcycle ride again."

"An excellent idea, and I know exactly where we can rent one." He snuggled his lips behind her ear and felt her tremble. "And what would my goddess want to do right now?"

A purr vibrated in her chest. She turned her lips to his ear and whispered until he felt his face flush.

"Okay." He loved the way the moonlight set her green eyes aflame. "But you can keep the boots on. Just...the boots."

# EPILOGUE

Apophis wanted to hit something, but there was nothing left in his prison to destroy. Instead, he tapped a long black talon against the arm of the stone chair. The puny carving was an insult. He deserved a real throne. He, the most powerful god in the universe, sat on a fucking cold chair.

His white eyes shifted to fiery red, blazing with irritation. A beetle had the audacity to crawl across his limp black kilt. The insults would not stop coming. He squashed the impudent bug between his fingers.

A pair of golden wrist cuffs chaffed at his skin. He'd long ago tuned out the occasional shot of pain the bracelets sent him. They would be child's play to destroy, if he'd had his full powers.

Therion had failed, but that wasn't what incensed Apophis. He'd been expecting his son to find a way to screw it up. It wasn't the boy's fault that he had a lot of his mother's blood in him. *A few hundred years in the Underworld will toughen up the boy.*

What infuriated him most was the sudden blast of pure light that had assailed his mind. Shaila a'k'Hemet was now the Great Dragon Queen. That meant her mother was dead.

His eyes became obsidian orbs, so black was his rage. His beautiful Inanna had been taken from him forever. He raged at Destiny for denying him the right to make her his mate.

Fury, however, quickly dissolved into deep malevolent laughter. The prophecy had begun, and once started it would continue until the great gathering. The *Age of Awakening* would soon arrive, and with it would come his freedom.

Hell on earth. Sinister laughter boomed across the Underworld.

*** The End ***

# ABOUT THE AUTHOR

**Lynda Haviland** is a USA Today Bestselling Author of paranormal fantasy romance. She is addicted to coffee, caramel, and ancient alien conspiracy theories.
*Immortal Dynasty* is the first novel in her debut series, *Age of Awakening*.

Visit her anytime online at **LyndaHaviland.com**

*Photo courtesy of Kevin Kolczynski*

*A sample scene from the next installment in the Age of Awakening series…*

# IMMORTAL DOMINION

## By
## Lynda Haviland

Seth blinked a few times, adjusting his eyes to the pitch darkness of the cave. Something had jarred him out of the deep sleep of hibernation. The oracle in the pool pulsed with excitement. Its light blue glow illuminated the cave. He would have ignored its unusual display, but he spied a small pile of sand on the floor. The pile seemed to grow as more sand trickled down from the airshaft in the ceiling.

After a ritual stretch of each limb, he circled twice on his pallet and settled in to rejoin his slumber. Drawing in a deep breath, he inhaled the unmistakable scent of blood. He snuffed the air more deeply. Human blood. His senses thirsted for more information.

He didn't have time to think any more about it. A low hum reached his ears, quickly followed by a loud clatter that drew closer by the second. His skin flinched with each irritating bang.

Then, more sand tumbled onto the pile, followed by a metal box with a spinning blade. On impact with the floor, the machine smashed apart. He tucked his head under a wing to muffle the explosive sound, which was amplified by the granite walls. Ropes still dangled from the hole until a large mass of fabric landed on the floor with a strange thump. The smell of fresh human blood flooded his nose.

He tried to force the scent out of his nostrils in a huff, blowing a trail of white fire upward. Too late. His lungs were so filled with the smell that he could taste it. He shook his head and gave in. He uncoiled his long body and crawled over to investigate.

He resented the intrusion into his peace, but deeper instincts compelled him to investigate the human's condition. He nuzzled along the body and felt the curves of a female. His whiskers followed trickles of blood down the side of her face to the floor. He watched her aura fade as her life force ebbed with each shallow breath.

Heedless of good sense, he drew his tongue across the warm pool. Her blood tasted so sweet and tingled all the way down his parched throat. Hunger rumbled loudly in his stomach. Luckily for the woman, he did not eat humans.

But death seemed certain for her without medical attention. Quickly, he shifted to his human form. A blue glow emanated from his palms and illuminated her body. Calling upon an ancient skill, he assessed the damage inside of her.

Slamming into the granite floor of the cave had left a large crack along the back of her skull. He sensed swelling and tension in her brain, a fatal combination. Her internal injuries seemed to be equally traumatic. Three ribs had speared into both of her lungs. Collapsed, they had no way to drain the fluids. She would drown slowly in her own blood.

As if in response to his assessment, her body stilled at the end of one last gurgle.

Quickly, he willed his fangs to descend from their sheaths. Finding a vein in her forearm, he bit down as gently as he could. His fangs slid easily through her skin and injected a toxin, which would temporarily paralyze her and give him time to heal her. If she started to move too soon, she could do more damage or hinder his efforts.

Even in the ebony darkness, he moved unerringly to a crevice in the wall behind his pallet. Removing his sword, he brushed away dust and sand from its blade. He held it horizontally over the dying woman and whispered a spell. It had been too long since he'd spoken the language of his kind, yet it flowed easily from his lips.

The sword glowed with pure white energy as he summoned the healing powers from within the diamond in its hilt. Slowly, Seth's mind moved through the woman's body, mending fractures, repairing lungs, and resealing ripped skin.

As the glow from the sword faded, he set it aside. Leaning over her face, he pressed his lips against hers and blew. Her chest rose as air refilled her lungs. He waited patiently until finally she coughed and drew in a long breath all on her own.

He returned his sword to the crevice and collapsed on his pallet. The effort to heal another had drained his energies.

New sounds travelled down through the hole. Human men gathered far above on the surface. Humans occasionally grew curious enough about what was underneath the Sphinx that they would dig tunnels and pits in search of treasure. Seth had tapped into one of those old tunnels to allow some fresh air to find its way down to the low-lying cavern.

Grimacing at the unconscious woman on the floor, he cursed his luck that more than just air had wound its way down into his solitude.

He listened as the men argued about where the fugitive had landed. Could they mean the woman? He evaluated her features: small, petite, blonde. Definitely foreign.

Fortunately, no more sounds came from above. The men likely backed away in search of her in other areas. It wouldn't be long before someone decided to descend into the hole, but he hoped he had time for now. He needed rest and time for his energies to replenish enough for him to close up the airshaft.

The distinct clack of teeth drew his attention back to the woman. Fever. Her body racked with it. She needed warmth in this damp place. In this empty cavern, he would be the only source of that.

Resigned, he moved to lay his own body next to hers and willed his temperature to rise. Instinctively, her body rolled toward the source of heat. His skin flinched at the cool touch of her palm on his stomach and the warmth of her breath on his chest. How long had it really been since he'd felt the touch of a woman?

Memories of another woman and another time flicked through his mind. Memories that he'd purposely buried thousands of years ago. Teased by fantasy and flesh, parts of his body thrummed to life.

Instead of enjoying the sensation, it irritated him.

Soon, his muscles shivered from the effort to control his body heat and his lunatic erection. But the woman still shuddered feverishly. Stretching his limbs, he shifted back to his beastly form and curled his body in a circle around hers. At least in this form, he could warm her unconscious body while it fought through the chills…without doing anything stupid.

He stayed wrapped around her through the many hours until he felt her body still. The fever had finally broken.

Slowly, he backed off into the shadows to wait for her to awaken. Circling his pallet twice, he settled in a good spot. Sleep eluded him. Too many thoughts needed attention.

When could he take her back up to the surface? Through the airshaft, he heard the activity of tourists. He couldn't take her back up that way until nightfall.

He shouldn't have licked her blood. He remembered the sweet taste of it and how it tingled on his tongue. He prayed the Rage would not return. Exile was supposed to ensure that it didn't happen again. He growled his frustration.

Why did he save her? He'd successfully avoided humans for a long time. Then, when one practically landed in his lap, he even used old magic to save her. He'd lapped up her blood and tasted her life force. He'd healed her. What had possessed him to do this? And now what the hell was he going to do with her when she woke up?